NEMESIS

AXEL BLAZE THRILLER
(BOOK TWELVE)

BILL RUNNER

RUNNER HOUSE BOOKS, LONDON
www.bill-runner.com

This is a work of fiction. Names, characters, places, and incidents either are the product of the author's imagination or are used fictitiously. Any resemblance to actual persons, living or dead, events, or locales is entirely coincidental.

First eBook edition November 2025

978-1-917652-06-3

www.bill-runner.com

PROLOGUE

It was cold.

The kind of cold that slid into your bones and stayed there. I stood next to my brother Ryan at the edge of the cemetery, the wind slicing through us like razor wire. Dry leaves scraped against marble like whispers.

Mom was down by Dad's headstone—wrapped in that old denim jacket like it was body armor. She didn't move. Just stood there with her hands clenched into fists, like she was holding herself together by sheer force.

Ryan's arm was around my shoulders, steady and strong like always. I was eleven. Too young to know what real loss was. Old enough to carry it anyway.

"We'll get through it, Ax," Ryan said. "You, me, and Mom. No one else is gonna do it for us. So we hold the line."

That was Ryan—thirteen going on thirty. Carrying the weight like he was born to. His voice had that edge—the one that said he already knew what the world could take from you.

Then he leaned in, voice low.

"But if something ever happens to me... don't believe what they tell you. You hear me?"

My pulse kicked. "Ryan, what—"

He nudged me forward. "Go stand with Mom. She needs you. I'll be right behind you."

I walked. The grass felt slick, soft. I reached Mom's side.

When I looked back, I couldn't see anyone there.

Ryan was gone. No sound. No footsteps. Just gone.

I spun around, heart pounding, breath catching. Scanned the trees, the hill, the sky.

Nothing. The whole place suddenly felt wrong.

The wind howled louder. And underneath it—an aircraft. Distant, steady.

My breath hitched.

I started running back toward where he stood—where he should have stood.

"Ryan!" I shouted.

Nothing but swaying trees and dead silence. The plane's rumble faded into the sky.

My chest clenched. My voice cracked. "Don't do this, man. Don't leave me again."

And then the world yanked sideways.

I woke up choking on air, the sheets tangled, my fists clenched like I had been fighting ghosts.

My brother kept leaving me. Even in my goddamn dreams.

That's the thing about grief. It's not polite. It doesn't knock. It kicks the door in, drags you to the floor, and leaves you bleeding in the dark. Then it keeps coming back for whatever's left. Over and over.

My brother didn't just die once. He died every time I remembered. Every time the silence got too loud. Every time I caught myself breathing and wondered why he wasn't.

Every man's got a breaking point. Mine came with a flag-draped coffin and a pile of questions no one wanted to answer. A fearless Marine burned down in a drone strike they called a "regrettable error". Regrettable? That's the kind of word people use when they have never had to pick bone fragments out of the dirt. I had heard that word before, from officers who never left the green zone.

They buried Ryan under a flag, under silence, and under lies. And I had been carrying the weight ever since. While Ryan was just a name carved in stone, the people responsible sat breathing free air. I had been told to let it go. I wasn't built for that.

Grief tends to change shape if you let it live with you long enough. At first, it eats you alive. It's all teeth and claws, tearing you apart. I had been there, knew how that felt. But if you hold still, if you feed it purpose, it becomes a different animal—cold, patient, and surgical.

I wasn't angry anymore. Anger burns fast. This was colder—quieter. The kind of fire that smolders under stone, waiting for the wind. The kind of rage that waits, plans, and dismantles an enemy piece by piece.

Some men pray for justice. Some men wait for it. I had waited long enough. Long enough to know that justice wasn't coming my way unless I grabbed it by the throat and pulled it out of the shadows.

People say revenge makes you lose yourself. They are right. That's the point. You burn away what's left of the man you were until only the blade remains.

It had taken a long time, but finally, I was on the trail of the men who buried the truth—and almost got away with it. Their nemesis was coming.

CHAPTER 1

I didn't usually go looking for trouble. In my line of work, trouble had a way of finding me—usually with a weapon in hand and bad intentions in its eyes. My job had been to make sure those intentions died before they reached anyone else.

But that night wasn't business as usual. I wasn't waiting for trouble to find me. I was already in the dark—watching, hunting.

The time: 2000 hours. The place: Ashwood, New York State. Population: two thousand on a good day. A one-stoplight speck of a town where everybody knew everybody, gossip moved faster than the mail truck, and nobody locked their doors because they thought evil lived somewhere else. A town that rolled its sidewalks up early and left the night to crickets and the occasional truck rumbling down Route 9 toward New York City. The kind of place that had once fed on factory whistles and shift changes, but now sat hollowed out like a dozen other dying mill towns scattered across upstate New York.

Main Street ran right through the middle of the town like a spine. At 2000 hours in small-town America, the Street was already a corpse—shuttered windows, dead neon, the diner closed, the hardware store dark, pawnshop padlocked. Only the bar on the far edge of town still had a heartbeat, neon flickering as drunks staggered under the glow.

The police station sat on the other end of Main, a squat two-story brick box with five empty parking spaces and a flagpole out front that looked forgotten. In the day, five small-town cops went about maintaining law and order. At that hour, they had all clocked out. They didn't have the faintest idea of the storm about to come rolling right through their backyard.

But none of that mattered to me.

I wasn't watching the station or Main Street. I was buried in the shadows of a residential side street where the houses leaned close together, porches sagged, and curtains stayed drawn. My eyes were locked on a beat-up Ford pickup parked halfway down the block. Two men inside, silhouettes in the dull glow of their dash lights. Local muscle with city connections. Predators, but not smart ones. The kind who confuse intimidation with intelligence. They were babysitting a house—making sure the woman inside didn't move, didn't talk, didn't breathe in a way that rattled the gang's plans.

The woman they were watching was Dana Kincaid—someone I hadn't even known existed until that morning. Widow of Staff Sergeant Mark Kincaid. That was a name I knew, and not in the casual way you know somebody from a roster. Mark had been the JTAC—Joint Terminal Attack Controller— the guy on the ground who called in the Reaper drone strike that erased Ryan's position in Helmand Province. The strike that ended four good Marines, including Ryan.

Mark had lived with that mistake—if it was actually his mistake—until it chewed him hollow. He had left the Army, gone through the shrink's obstacle course, and even sent me and my mom personal letters of apology. Along with the letter, he had sent a transcript of the radio call that led to the strike. It read wrong. All of it. But I always believed somebody had set him up. I just wasn't able to figure out who, or why.

So when Dana called me out of the blue that morning, I thought maybe the trail had finally stirred. But she wasn't calling with answers—she was calling with a gut punch. Mark was dead. A week gone. "Road accident," she said, like she was just reading it off a police blotter. My gut didn't buy it.

Then she told me Mark had been trying to work up the nerve to contact me before he died. Couldn't seem to make himself do it. But he had told her that if anything happened to him, she should hand me a flash drive. She had asked what was going on. He told her not to worry. Which is exactly the kind of thing men say when they know damn well the worry is already inside the house.

It took her two weeks to call me. I understood that—grief has its own timetable—but my instincts were already tapping me on the shoulder, whispering that this smelled wrong. I told her I would come see her that same afternoon.

Ashwood looked like most dying mill towns upstate—small, gray, too many ghosts. Dana opened the door like she was afraid to open it all the way. Pleasant face, but the kind of pleasant that looks like it used to smile more before life started landing body blows. She was pale, jittery, eyes darting over my shoulder like she expected shadows to follow me inside.

"Come in," she said, but it didn't really sound like she wanted me to. Inside, the place smelled faintly of brewed coffee and dust. She led me to a small living room, didn't bother offering me a seat, and pressed a flash drive into my palm like it was burning her fingers.

"This is what Mark left," she said, voice tight.

I didn't waste time. Slipped it into my laptop, screen lighting up with two files—an obituary for Ryan, and a short note that read: *I was responsible for Captain Ryan Blaze's death. —Mark.*

That was it. No details. No truth. Just a line designed to twist the knife.

I looked up at her. "This all he gave you?"

"Yes. I—" Her voice cracked, and she shook her head. "He didn't tell me anything else. I didn't even read it. I couldn't."

I believed her. But I also didn't buy for one second that this was what Mark had intended me to get. No way he would sit on something for weeks, risk telling his wife to pass it along after his death, and then hand me nothing but a barebones apology.

Someone had swapped the payload before it got to me. This was the decoy, the thing you feed someone to shut them up. Somebody got to Mark. Maybe before the accident. Maybe because of it.

Dana stood there like she had forgotten how to breathe. Shoulders tight. Eyes darting to the door and then back to me. The flash drive felt like a piece of ice in my palm.

"Got kids, Dana?" I asked, like we were just two strangers filling dead air.

Her answer had a shake in it, the kind you hear in a voice when someone's balancing on the edge. "One. My son... Jesse."

I nodded, like it was just small talk. Meanwhile, my laptop was already open, screen angled toward me. My fingers moved on the laptop, opening a blank doc.

I typed: *Is someone threatening you?*

I turned the screen toward her, just enough for her to read without breaking eye contact.

Her eyes told me more than her mouth ever could. Something sharp flickered there—fear wrapped in anger—but she kept her lips shut. She just looked at me, then at the door again, then back.

I typed again, this time letting the words carry the weight they needed to: *I'm special forces. I take apart lethal threats for a living. If someone's got you cornered, I can end it.*

Her eyes brimmed. She didn't speak. Instead, she tapped her right ear with two fingers—small, quick, like a nervous scratch. Somebody was listening.

I didn't break eye contact as I typed: *Is Jesse OK?*

She swiped at a tear, gave the slightest shake of her head.

I typed: *Did someone take him to keep you in line?*

Her nod was almost imperceptible. But it landed like a brick in my chest.

I reached into my jacket pocket, took out a small pencil and folded sheet of paper, and slid them across the table toward her.

I typed: *Write details. I'll rescue Jesse. Trust me.*

I kept talking over it, voice steady. "Looks like it's going to be a hell of a winter. These old towns do get quiet in the cold, don't they?"

While I spoke, she hesitated for a second before writing in sharp, clipped sentences: *Men came after I called you. Took Jesse. I don't know where.*

Said no cops. Said I get him back if I give you fake drive and you leave.

The moment I read it, something inside me clicked into place. That deep, cold switch flipping over. I had been chasing shadows since I got here. Now I had the scent—warm, human, and exactly the kind of prey I knew how to run down.

Then she scribbled another line under it: *Think my phone's tapped. Don't call.*

I gave a slow, deliberate nod. Message received.

My fingers moved again on the keys: *Don't worry. I'll get Jesse. I'll make them think their plan worked—leave town—then come back and get him.*

She swallowed hard and nodded. This time, her expression shifted—still nervous, but with a trace of relief working its way through.

I wrote again: *Keep acting scared. I'll get him back to you tonight. That's a promise. Be ready to leave town when I do.*

She nodded again, blinking hard. Then she straightened in her chair, getting her game face on.

I leaned back, shifting my voice into that lazy, nothing-to-hear-here tone that people stop paying attention to after a minute. "I get it. Losing someone... it's like they take a piece of you. I've been there."

Dana's voice was steady enough for whoever was listening. "Yeah. Some days it still doesn't feel real."

"Yeah," I said, sounding like I was halfway to the door already. "Anyway, I better get moving. It'll be dark soon, and I've still got some road ahead of me."

"That's probably for the best," she replied.

I gave her a faint smile. “No sense hanging around when there’s nothing left worth hanging around for.”

“Right,” she answered right on cue. “Nothing left here anyway.”

Good. She was learning.

I closed the laptop with a clean, final click, pocketed the folded paper without looking at it again. “Alright, Dana. Sorry for your loss. And thanks for this—Mark’s words matter. I won’t keep you any longer.”

She gave me a small nod. “Safe travels.”

I offered her a quick, reassuring squeeze of the hand before I stepped outside into the cool evening air, my jaw clenched so tight it hurt. Somewhere in this town, a scared kid was waiting for a mother who couldn’t help him. Being used as leverage against me.

They thought that would work. They were wrong.

But that made one thing certain. I was on the trail now, and I wouldn’t stop until I ran it all the way to the kill.

CHAPTER 2

They had taken the kid to keep me off the scent. That cut deeper than I let Dana see.

She didn't have to spell it out—I saw it in the way her eyes wouldn't stay on mine. This happened because she reached out to me. Because her husband left a breadcrumb they didn't want followed. Somewhere out there, Jesse was in a dark room, too scared to cry. That was the cost of me getting too close to the truth.

Which meant I owed him.

His safety, his life—they were on me now. And God help whoever stood in the way when I came to collect.

When I stepped out of Dana's place, I already had the thought: if they had gone to the trouble of planting ears in her house, they might have eyes on it too. The anger was still there, coiled and hot, but I forced it down and walked out like nothing was wrong—hands loose, eyes soft. Just a man heading for his truck.

Halfway down the block, I saw it: a rust-scabbed Ford pickup parked at an angle it didn't need to be. Two shapes inside. One behind the wheel, one riding shotgun.

I didn't give them anything to work with—no extra glance, no hitch in my step. Just climbed into my pickup, turned the key, and rolled away easy toward Main Street.

In the mirror, I caught them pull out, keeping their distance. When I hit Main, they swung wide into a U-turn, rumbling back toward Dana's street.

That's when a second truck came from the opposite direction, slowed, turned, and picked me up like we had rehearsed it together.

I kept my speed lazy until the last building in town was in the rearview. Then I let the engine breathe. They followed for ten miles before easing off, flipping a U-turn, and heading back. They thought I was gone.

I pulled over on a gravel turnout, got out, and ran a slow hand under the wheel well, along the bumpers, behind the plates. Nothing. No trackers. Clean.

An hour later, I looped around and came back in from the far side of town, left my truck in a half-lit lot, and took the rest on foot. By the time I was back on Dana's street, the light was dying and the shadows were long. That Ford was still there.

I watched them from across the way. I was sure now—they were part of the crew that put Dana's husband in the ground and stamped "accident" on the stone. Mark had been a piece of the puzzle that pointed to Ryan's killers. And now the same hands that killed him had taken Dana's boy. The ones sitting thirty feet from me in that truck.

Snatching the kid would have been enough reason for me to break both their skulls. But them being tied to Ryan's death? That was gasoline on a fire already burning. That made it personal. Blood-deep.

I didn't look at the two men in that truck as a problem. I looked at them like the door I needed to kick open. An opportunity.

They didn't look worried. The driver smoked, the cigarette tip breathing red in the dark. The passenger stared at his phone, thumb scrolling. Complacent. Comfortable.

Good.

Because when trouble showed up, it was going to be wearing my face.

I waited for the street to die completely. No movement behind the windows, no porch lights, no kids on bikes, no voices. Just the kind of silence that meant no one would see what was about to happen. Then I moved.

I crossed the blacktop fast, a shadow breaking loose. Driver never even had time to say "what the—" before my fist smashed through his half-turned face. The punch cracked jawbone, split lip, sent blood spraying across the inside of the windshield. His head snapped sideways, and I bounced it hard off the door frame. His cigarette dropped to the floorboard. His lights were out before the smoke hit the mat.

Before the second man's brain even had time to process what happened to his partner, I had ripped open the driver's door and leaned in hard. No time to circle around—the passenger might have gone for a gun, or worse, bolted. So I went through the driver.

My hand shot past the limp body, clamped around the passenger's collar, and yanked him across the seat with enough force to rattle his spine. His phone clattered to the floor as I ripped him out through the driver's door, his skull smacking the steering column as well as the metal pillar on the way out. Hard enough to spray a mist of blood onto the windshield.

The scream that was about to escape his mouth got cut off as I slammed him down onto the pavement headfirst. The crack echoed down the quiet street. But he still wasn't knocked out.

He twitched, tried to reach for something at his waist. I brought my boot down on his knee, stomping down hard enough to make bone crunch. I bent down and clamped my hand over his mouth, stifling the scream before it tore loose. It turned into a choking sob. I crouched over him, watching the pain roll through his body, watching the realization in his eyes that he was prey now—and I was the wolf.

The first one lay slumped against the wheel, blood leaking from his mouth, unconscious. The second was still squirming under me, trying to catch his breath, fear written large across his face.

And I let myself linger there a beat longer than I should have. I wanted him to know what was coming. I wanted him to feel that the night itself had closed around him and mercy wasn't on the menu. Those two had chosen the wrong family to terrorize, the wrong town to rot in, the wrong war to step into.

And me—I was testing the edge of the blade I had become. A final blow to the side of his neck knocked out the man.

Ten seconds. That's all it took. From when I stepped out of the shadows to when I was sliding behind the wheel of their truck.

I threw the broken one into the bed like trash. The unconscious one, I shoved across into the passenger seat. Then I climbed in, started the engine, and rolled out onto Main Street.

The hunt had officially begun.

CHAPTER 3

I rolled the truck through Main, quiet as a ghost, past the neon glow bleeding out of the open bar at the far end of town. Some drunks were staggering into the night, none of them paying a damn bit of attention.

I drove straight through, headlights low, and put the town behind me. The road out was empty, dark as the inside of a coffin. After a few miles I veered off onto a dirt track that rattled the truck's frame and ended near a ravine that cut through the woods. Nobody came out there unless they wanted to disappear. Perfect.

I hauled both bodies out, dead weight in my hands, and dumped them near the edge. They still hadn't stirred. The one with the broken leg—my personal project from earlier—looked like hell. His face was purple and swollen, lips split, skull tender where I had bounced him off the pavement. I had made sure he remembered every second of that before I shut the lights out on him.

I uncapped a bottle and splashed water across his face. He jolted awake with a wet sputter, coughing, sucking in air like a drowning man. Then it hit him. Recognition. His eyes went wide and wild, darting from me to the darkness around him, then to the ravine just behind, like there was somewhere to run. He soon realized something—there wasn't.

His breath quickened, ragged, panic setting in hard. He remembered. He remembered me ripping him across the driver's seat like he was nothing, his leg snapping like dry wood, his face bouncing off the concrete while I held him down and let him taste the street until he blacked out. That memory was painted on his face now—fear etched into every twitch of muscle.

"There's a ravine behind you," I said, matter-of-fact, like I was giving directions to the gas station. "That's where you're headed if you waste my time. That's why I hauled you two out here. Saves me trouble when I have to dump the bodies. Clean, simple."

He whimpered.

"Here's how this works," I went on, squatting down so he couldn't escape my stare. "You're gonna talk. I've got no doubt about that. But every time you don't answer, or every time you lie, I break another bone. Human body can only take so much before it shuts down. Your choice how fast we get there."

"Please," he gasped, voice breaking. "Please don't kill me—"

I slapped him hard. His head whipped sideways, spit and blood flying. The sound cracked across the night air.

"Shut up. You want to live? That depends on one thing. The kid. If he's alive and breathing, maybe I let you crawl back to your sorry life. If he's not, I throw you in that ravine, and your buddy follows. Then I walk away and sleep just fine."

His lip trembled. "What kid?"

I didn't bother answering. I just took his hand, grabbed his middle finger, and snapped it back until the bone cracked like a dry twig. His scream tore through the night, echoing across the trees.

I let him thrash a couple of seconds, then leaned in again, voice cold and steady. "That's what I meant. Every lie costs you a bone. Now—do you remember the kid?"

"Yes!" he panted, eyes wide, wet with tears. "Yes! I remember. The kid's fine, he's alive!"

"Where?" My voice was flat. No bark, no raised volume—just dead weight in the air.

The guy was already pale and sweating from the first few minutes we had had together, and from the way his eyes jumped between me and the ravine's edge, he finally understood I wasn't bluffing. The fear in his eyes had burned past doubt and landed square in the truth-telling zone. He coughed, winced from the pain in his ribs, then blurted it.

"Abandoned textile mill... outskirts of town... half mile off the main highway. Red brick place, all the windows busted out. Roof's leakin' so bad you can smell the mildew from outside. Place's been dead since the layoffs years ago. Big rusted sign still hangin' on one side, half the letters gone."

I knew there were plenty of towns like this in upstate New York, just north of New York City—old industrial dots scattered across the map like bullet holes. Mills, foundries, machine shops... all gutted and left to rot as the jobs dried up. And in their place came the meth, the heroin, the gangs that made a living off a dying economy.

"Why that building?" I asked.

He shifted, hissing when the movement jarred his shoulder. "It's outta the way. Nobody goes there 'cept us. We keep it quiet—real quiet. That's where we stash the dope. Heroin, mostly... cook meth there sometimes if we can't do it elsewhere. The guys runnin' the show got a cop in their pocket—not the whole department, just one. He gives a heads-up if there's ever heat comin' our way. We clear out fast, let the place sit cold till it's safe again."

"Who's the dirty cop?"

"Uh, Lyle Denton."

I made a mental note of the name.

"What's the layout of the mill?"

He licked his lips, eyes darting like he was trying to remember every inch before the pain came again. "Big open space in the middle, where the looms used to be. Along the west wall, you got a row of old offices—manager's office, storage room, that sorta thing. Some rooms upstairs but they're all stripped bare. Back side's got a loading dock, two side doors. Front entrance still works if you got the key, but we mostly use the dock."

"Where's the kid in all that?"

His head jerked side to side. "Dunno for sure. I been parked outside his ma's place all damn evening, watchin' her like I was told. Last time I saw him, he was in one of them side offices, crashin' on a cot. Looked like he was sleepin' it off. That's all I know."

I had what I needed to save the kid, but there were many more questions burning in my head. The first one was about Mark Kincaid—the kid's father. Dead in what the cops declared a "road accident". I was sure it was more than that. Too clean, too convenient. I wanted the truth.

I stared at him for a long beat. "Mark Kincaid. Was it you who killed him?"

He blinked fast, caught off guard. "That... that was just an accident. Road accident. Nothin' to do with us."

"Wrong answer," I said as I bent, hand reaching for his, ready to make another one of his fingers sound like popcorn.

But just then, the other guy groaned and rolled onto his side. I took a step toward him and slammed my right heel into his ankle. The wet snap was swallowed by his scream before he again slipped back into merciful unconsciousness.

When I turned back, the first guy's face had changed. The little horror show had worked even better than cracking his finger. Terror had eaten whatever scraps of defiance he had left. His eyes were too wide, his breathing too shallow, his skin pale enough to pass for moonlight.

Before I could even touch him, the words came out in a rush, pitched high with panic.

"Alright! Alright! It wasn't me! It was Deke and Randy! They're the ones! Had the bartender—Marty—slip somethin' in Kincaid's drink, then hauled him out to his car, parked him right smack in the middle of Route 9. Then they got a truck... and they just drove it right into him. He never had a chance."

Deke and Randy. I rolled the names around in my head.

"Who are Deke and Randy?"

"Deke's my boss," he said, voice breaking hard. "Randy's his main muscle. And they're gonna kill me for tellin' you this, I swear to God they will..." His voice cracked into something close to a sob. "You—you ain't gonna kill me now, right? I told you everything..."

I let the silence sit between us, heavy as a loaded mag.

"Why'd they kill Mark?" I asked finally.

He shook his head frantically. "Hell, man... Deke gets gigs like that now and then. All I know is... some fellas from D.C. gave the word. There's this tough crew from Baltimore working for them.

Some big deal drug runners down there. Don't know their names. Don't wanna know, neither."

"How do I know you're telling the truth?" I asked, my voice flat.

"Cause I don't want no more busted bones. I'm bein' straighter with you than I ever was with my own ma. You can ask Marty. He's a sly one, keeps a security cam behind the counter—might even still have the footage of Deke and Randy with Mark that night."

Wind came up out of the ravine, cold and smelling of wet rock. The cold and the pain from his broken bones made him shiver harder.

"Why were you watching that house?" I asked, low and steady.

He glanced over his shoulder at the drop like it might answer for him.

"We were supposed to make sure she don't do nothin' stupid, like... I dunno... slippin' off in the night to talk to the cops. Deke said the woman had somethin' on her the Baltimore boys didn't want her handin' off to some fella comin' to see her."

Up until then, he hadn't gotten a real good look at me. When I dropped him earlier, it was dark and I had moved fast. And out in the wilds by the ravine, it was pitch black, no moonlight. Even though he had seen me in daylight at Dana's place, he hadn't connected the dots. But I could see the gears grinding now, the picture starting to form.

His brow pinched. I took a slow step closer until my boots were almost touching his, cutting him off before he could get there.

"Who planted the bugs in her house?"

That stopped him dead. Eyes went wide, like I had just pulled a rattler from my coat pocket.

"Bug? How the hell you know about that? You... you the guy she was meetin'?"

"Stick to answering questions." My tone left no room for discussion.

He stammered it out, words tripping over each other. "Five guys from that Baltimore crew showed up this mornin'. Real tough-lookin'—had that soldier look about 'em, y'know? Square shoulders, short hair, the kind of gait that says they've kicked in doors for a livin'."

"Where are they now?"

He hesitated just long enough for me to lean in, and then it spilled. "Motel. The Pine Hollow Motor Lodge. Out on Route 6, by the old feed store. They're probably still there."

That was all I needed to get moving. I had already stripped both of them of phones and weapons—one Glock, two cheap burners—and tossed the lot in the truck.

He licked his lips. "You ain't... you ain't gonna kill me now, right? I told you everythin'."

I looked him in the eye. "I'll give you a chance. But only if what you told me holds up."

From the bed of the pickup, I pulled a gallon jug of water and a couple of old Army surplus poncho liners. Tossed them next to him. "Stay put till somebody comes by. An hour or two, maybe. You and your buddy better be here when they do."

"We ain't goin' nowhere with our legs busted," he muttered.

I believed him. Out there, miles from the nearest paved road, with nothing but cold dirt and dark trees for company, they weren't crawling anywhere on broken legs.

"Good. The others you run with?" I started back toward the truck. "They're about to get a more painful education."

His eyes followed me all the way into the cab. I fired up the engine and rolled out, gravel popping under the tires. The Pine Hollow Motor Lodge lead could wait. Right now, there was an abandoned mill on the edge of town, and inside it, a scared kid named Jesse.

Time to give the rest of the gang a lesson they would never forget.

CHAPTER 4

The road back from the ravine wound through the kind of black that swallows headlights whole. Pine shadows pressed in from both sides, their branches clawing at the night sky like they wanted to drag it down on top of me. The gravel under the tires sounded too loud in the stillness, every crunch a reminder of how far off the grid we were.

When I hit pavement again, I pulled over under a crooked road sign and killed the lights. Dug the map out, spread it on the dash. My finger traced the thin line of county road to where it hooked south. The mill sat right there—a place nobody sane would go unless they were looking for trouble. Ten miles of asphalt, then a dirt spur even locals forgot about.

I sat there a beat longer, listening to the tick of the cooling engine. Then I folded the map, put the truck in gear, and let the road unspool ahead of me.

The miles slid by slow, nothing but the hum of tires and the soft thud of my pulse in my ears. No moon that night. Just the faint glow of my dash lights and the occasional flicker of a reflector post catching my high beams.

When I saw the dirt track, I slowed to a crawl and turned in. The forest closed in tighter, a tunnel of black pines and cold air that smelled of damp soil and dead leaves. And then, through the trees, the silhouette of the old textile mill rose up—big, boxy, and dead-looking.

It had been left to the weather and the woods for years. Rusted sheet metal siding sagged in places, the roofline sagged in others. Vines and saplings had claimed the loading dock, roots prying at the concrete. A place like that should have been nothing but raccoons and mold. Instead, the wrong kind of people had moved in, turning it into a clubhouse for whatever filth they were cooking, selling, or breaking.

I killed the engine and sat there for a beat. I already knew the score: I couldn't start stacking bodies from upstate New York to wherever the trail led me. Not yet. I would have to leave the men inside broken but breathing—for now. Once I had this figured out, once I had eyes on Ryan's killers, I wouldn't give a damn if the trail of bodies stacked all the way to hell and back.

I reached into the passenger seat and grabbed the baseball bat lying there—a thirty-three-inch Louisville Slugger with more than a few dings in it. I figured it was about to get some new ones. The Glock I had lifted from the ravine boys went into the back of my jeans, heavy and cold against my spine. My boot knives were snug in their sheaths, one in each boot, just in case this got personal.

I left the truck in the trees and closed the last hundred yards on foot, keeping low, letting the night swallow me. The mill loomed larger with every step, black walls blotting out the sky, the place breathing faint yellow light through boarded windows.

I worked the perimeter slow. Most of the windows were covered in warped plywood, but here and there the boards didn't quite meet. Where the cracks lined up, the light from inside spilled out in narrow yellow stripes, just enough to see through.

One side of the main floor was a half-assed meth lab—plastic tubs, chemical drums, glassware stacked on folding tables. A box fan in the wall rattled like it was the only thing keeping the stink from choking the place. Nothing was cooking at the moment, but the stink still bled into the night.

The rest was pure squatters' den. Four men sat hunched over a battered table, cards in their hands, smoke curling from their cigarettes. Another four were parked in front of an old flat-screen in the far corner, eyes fixed on a football game while empty beer cans littered the floor around them.

I couldn't make out which ones were Deke and Randy. Most of them were thick through the shoulders, hard around the eyes. The kind of men who looked like they had been living rough a long time.

Then I found the window I needed.

West wall. One of the side offices. Just a narrow slit to look through, but it was enough.

A kid sat in the corner, knees drawn up, arms wrapped around them like he was trying to make himself smaller. His head was down, his chin on his forearms. Even from here, I could see how he rocked just a little, back and forth. That's the kind of movement kids use when there's no safe place left, not even in their own heads.

My jaw locked so tight I heard my teeth grind. I felt the blood in my chest go hot, slow, heavy. They had scared him so bad, he was trying to disappear into himself. And these eight pathetic excuses for men thought that was just another night's work.

I stepped back from the crack in the boards, my hands loose at my sides, the bat warm in my grip. Those eight didn't know it yet, but their night was about to end very differently.

But rather than rushing in blind, I weighed my options.

Ripping those boards apart would have been like ringing a damn dinner bell. Too much racket, too much light. And halfway through, those eight bastards inside would come crashing in to see what the hell was going on. That wasn't the way this played. The only way this worked was going through the main hall, dropping the trash first, then coming for the kid.

I leaned close to the slats. "Jesse," I whispered.

Soft at first, just to test it. Nothing.

I tried again, just a touch louder. "Jesse."

The gentle rocking stopped. The boy froze mid-motion, head cocked like he wasn't sure he had really heard it. In a place like that, hearing your own name whispered softly was probably the last thing you expected—you surely wouldn't expect it coming from one of the animals holding you.

"I'm outside the window, buddy," I said, keeping my voice low and even. "Your mom sent me. I'm here to take you home."

He didn't move, didn't blink. Just kept staring toward the sound like the darkness outside might lie to him.

"Your mom told me what a brave little boy you are," I went on. "Said you took care of her when she needed it most. That's big stuff, Jesse. Now I need you to do something for me—get up and come over to the window."

It took him a second, but then he uncoiled himself from the corner and stood. Small steps, hesitant, slow, like every step had to be weighed and measured. Then he came closer, small sneakers scuffing the floor, until I could finally see his face in the faint spill of light—ten years old, baby-faced innocence hanging on by a thread. Dirt and tear streaks carved pale rivers down his cheeks, and his light brown hair stuck out in tufts like it had been slept on a hundred different ways without a pillow.

"It's dark out here," I told him. "So you can't see me. But don't worry, I'm here to take you home."

"OK," he said. His voice was so small I almost didn't hear it.

"My name's Axel."

He blinked. "Hello, Axel. I'm Jesse."

"Hello, Jesse. Good to meet you." I slid my fingertip through one of the cracks in the boards, and his tiny finger pressed against it from the other side. Just like that, a bond was made. Might have been the only pure thing in a building full of poison.

"That's a brave boy," I said. "Now I need you to listen real close."

The truth was, once I started making noise in there, there was a chance a few bullets might fly wild. I wasn't letting one find its way through that door and into him.

"I need you to move over to that corner where the walls meet," I told him. "Crouch down real low and stay put until I come in through that door. No matter what you hear, you stay right there. OK?"

"OK," he confirmed.

"There's gonna be a lot of noise and yelling outside that door," I went on, "but don't worry about any of it. Just keep your head down in that corner and don't move."

“I won’t be scared,” he said, voice steady.

I believed him.

“Good. Now go take your position. It’ll all be over in ten minutes.”

“OK,” he said—and for the first time, his mouth twitched into a tiny, almost shy smile. Something pure, floating in all this filth.

I let go of the slat and melted back into the dark, circling wide toward the loading dock at the back.

The eight men inside were the kind of guys who broke people for a living. There wasn’t a doubt that there would be guns inside. It didn’t really matter. I had walked into plenty of rooms like that—in worse places, against worse odds. The difference was, this time, the op wasn’t sanctioned. This was personal. And none of them was walking out.

I didn’t care if those men inside were running dope, guns, or any other poison. That was all background noise. What mattered were the good people they had stomped down like trash to make their living. Those men in that warehouse were overdue for judgment.

I wasn’t just going to stop them. I was going to hurt them. Make them feel real pain.

CHAPTER 5

The loading dock looked like it hadn't seen a delivery truck since the turn of the century. It was a mess of rust and rot—warped wood, peeling paint, and a busted roll-up door that had been hit so many times it looked like it owed money.

A single light fixture dangled by its wires over the bay, swaying just enough to make the shadows shift across the cracked concrete. A couple of old pallets leaned against the wall, warped from rain and stacked with trash bags that probably had more wildlife than the local woods. The smell coming from inside was the usual cocktail for a place like this—old oil, stale smoke, and the faint chemical tang of meth cooking somewhere down the line.

I was a step from going in when I caught the faint scrape of a boot on concrete. I slid back into the shadows beside the dock, hugging the wall where the night swallowed me.

A man shuffled out a few seconds later, half-buttoned shirt, cigarette bouncing from his lip, and a lazy walk that told me he had already had one too many beers. Big guy—broad across the shoulders, gut hanging over his belt, the kind of guy who thought size alone made him dangerous. He had a knife scar running from his cheekbone to his jaw, the kind you earn in a fight where nobody wins clean. He headed toward a tree at the edge of the lot, clearly looking to water it.

Given the pile of empty beer cans I had clocked inside, I figured the others would be making that same walk soon enough. No way that wreck had running toilets—and even scum had a breaking point when it came to breathing in their own stink.

Problem was, I didn't have time to sit around waiting for them to wander out like ducks at a carnival game. But one less man inside was still one less problem.

I stepped in behind him, silent, the aluminum bat already cocked. The first swing caught him clean on the side of the head—a solid, bone-on-metal crack—and he dropped like a puppet with the strings cut, face-first into the dirt. Out cold.

That's when I went to work.

I knelt beside him, grabbed his leg, and brought the bat down across his knee. Once. Twice. Bone gave both times, sharp and ugly. I moved to the other leg and did the same. Then I shifted, raised his arm, and brought the bat down hard until I felt the joint pop and the bone splinter.

It wasn't rage swinging the bat—not the kind that blinds you and makes you sloppy. I had learned to put that fire in a cage and use it like a tool. My fury wasn't gone; it was just cold, aimed, and efficient. This was about control. About making sure he would wake up in a world of hurt, months of rehab ahead of him... if he ever walked right again.

I frisked him quick, running hands over his pockets and waistband. Pulled a 9mm from his hip, dropped the mag, and chucked it into the weeds. The empty frame went sailing in the opposite direction. Found a folding knife in his back pocket, flipped it open just long enough to check the edge, then tossed it deep into the dark where it wouldn't be found anytime soon. Dug deeper and came up with a phone. I slid it into the sling bag riding across my back.

Then I straightened up, eyes on the dock. Seven men left in there. And before the night was done, I was going to break every last one of them.

I knew damn well the guys inside were strapped. Not just pistols either—there would be shotguns, maybe an AR or two tucked in some corner. And the last thing I wanted was lead flying in every direction, ricocheting off walls with Jesse locked in one of those side rooms. That kid had been through enough without catching a stray because I decided to go loud.

Besides, a full-on gunfight inside a meth lab was a bad idea on principle—too much flammable crap, too many unknowns. I also didn't need the headache of explaining why there were seven corpses cooling on the floor. Not yet. Not until I had Ryan's killers in my sights. For now, I would leave them breathing... just broken.

That meant cutting them down before they even knew they were under attack. Reduce their numbers fast. Shock, overwhelm, and finish—the holy trinity of Close Quarters Battle. Surprise, speed, and controlled violent action. I had been eating, sleeping, and breathing CQB for years in Delta. It was second nature now—muscle memory so ingrained it was practically part of my DNA.

And these idiots inside? They didn't even know what a real fight looked like. They were drowning in their own smug, half-assed confidence, thinking no one would ever walk through that door.

I slipped in through the shadowed corner of the dock, keeping my steps light, letting the racket of the TV and the mumble of card-game trash talk cover my approach. The flicker of the TV lit the room in pulses, masking the edges of my shadow as I closed the gap.

The four at the card table were too locked in on their game to even notice me. Cigarettes dangled from lips, beer bottles sweated onto the table, and their hands twitched over bent playing cards. No situational awareness, no security, no plan. They thought they owned the night.

I stepped in close enough to feel their body heat.

The bat came around in a blur, catching the first guy on the side of the skull. The hit landed with a deep, meaty *thunk*. The man folded in his chair before the others even registered movement.

I pivoted, driving the bat straight down onto the second guy's collarbone. The bone gave instantly, a sharp *pop* under the aluminum, and he let out a scream that was cut short when I reversed grip and slammed the end of the bat up into his chin.

The third man barely got his hands up before I backhanded the bat across his jaw. His head snapped sideways so hard I half-expected it to spin all the way around. He dropped, chair tipping with him.

The fourth guy was quicker. He shot out of his chair and lunged for the shotgun propped against the wall. I lunged faster, chopping the bat down on his extended arm just above the elbow. The snap of bone was clean and loud—cut right through the TV noise. He howled and doubled over, clutching the arm.

I shut him up by grabbing a fistful of his greasy hair, yanked his head back, and drove his face straight into the wall. The plaster gave way with a crunch, showering us both in dust. His body went slack, dropping to the floor like laundry.

Out of the corner of my eye, I caught the couch crew moving—the three in front of the TV starting to get to their feet. The game was about to get loud.

I knew the second their eyes locked on me, the stealth game was over. My advantage was gone, and in a place like this, hesitation was just another word for suicide. Time to let the gun talk.

One of them dove for a side table, scrambling for a pistol lying there. I didn't hesitate. My hands let the bat go, and it flew like it had a score to settle. It spun through the air end over end, the wood whistling like it was pissed off.

The bat smashed into his face dead-center. The sound was part *crunch*, part wet *pop*—the kind you only hear when bone and cartilage decide they are not in that fight anymore. His nose flattened into a bloody smear, spraying blood like someone shook up a soda can, his upper teeth clattering onto the floor like poker chips. His head snapped back so violently that a tendon in his neck probably popped. His knees gave out before his brain even caught up, and he went down like a dropped sack of laundry.

By the time he was eating carpet, my Glock was already up and barking. The second man—a wiry guy with bad tattoos crawling up his neck—had managed to get a gun into his hands and was just starting to bring it in line. I double-tapped his right shoulder. The first round punched through meat and bone, making his whole arm jerk sideways, the second chewing a crater into his deltoid and spraying the couch behind him with blood. The revolver spun out of his hand and skittered across the floor, leaving him clutching at himself and shrieking.

Then the third one stepped up. Big boy. Easily six-four, maybe pushing 275, and not all of that donuts. Still, he moved fast—too fast for a man that size. Fear will do that. He yanked wounded-guy into a headlock, using him like a slab of meat armor, and started bull-rushing while scanning for something to throw. He settled on a table. Lifted it like it was cardboard and flung it straight at me.

The table came in high and fast, but I slipped sideways, feeling the air stir past my cheek as it smashed against the wall and split into kindling. I could have just dropped rounds through wounded-guy's torso, angled low so every round punched through and found Mr. Mountain behind him. Clean, efficient. But dead bodies meant cops, and cops meant my plans went straight to hell.

Big boy must have sensed I wasn't going to shoot through his shield. He shoved his human shield straight at me, hard, like a linebacker clearing a lane, and came in with a knife he had conjured from nowhere. The blade was ugly—serrated, with enough grime to tell me it hadn't just been used on food.

I pivoted left, leaning back and twisting my torso so the blade only cut air. My left hand clamped his knife wrist in a steel grip before he could recover. I wrenched it outward and down, hard enough to feel the bone in his forearm snap like a dry stick. The bone went with a sharp *snap*, followed by a deep, grinding crunch as his forearm bent in a direction nature never intended. The sound came with a jolt in my grip, familiar and ugly.

Before his brain could process that new reality, my right foot slammed into both his shins just above the ankles—hard, low, and fast. The shock ripped through his legs, buckling them in opposite directions. His momentum carried his upper body forward while his legs quit, dumping him face-first onto the floor with a dull *whump* that rattled the boards.

I didn't let go of that broken wrist. Instead, I stepped up, planting my boot between his shoulder blades and wrenching his arm back. His elbow was already ruined. Now the shoulder gave with a sickening, wet *pop*, like tearing the wing off a cooked chicken. The roar he let out was primal, spittle flying as his face pressed into the dirty floor.

I stepped off his back, shifted my weight, and planted my right boot on the back of his thigh. Yanked his ankle up toward me, then twisted hard and fast with every bit of torque I had. Another *crack*, sharper this time, another scream that turned into a wet gasp. And he was done—breathing heavy, eyes swimming, too busy drowning in pain to think about moving.

Blood was pooling under his cheek from a split lip he had picked up in the fall. His size, his role here—it clicked. This had to be Randy, Deke's pet gorilla. And if Randy was here, Deke wasn't far. I just didn't know which of the bodies or cripples in the room was him.

I turned to look at the only other guy still conscious—the meat shield Randy had been hiding behind earlier, the one in whose shoulder I had already punched two nine-mil holes. He was doing his best impression of a garden snake, trying to ooze toward a table leg like he could disappear behind it.

Nice try.

I spotted the bat where it had landed earlier, stepped over a body, and scooped it up. Felt good in my grip—solid, familiar. I closed the distance in two steps, brought it up over my shoulder, and brought it down on the back of his skull. The *thock* was clean, almost surgical. His arms went slack, and his face hit the floor like someone pulled the plug.

The other five were already sprawled across the floor in various states of unconsciousness.

I moved through the room, scooping up every gun in sight—three 9mms, a battered twelve-gauge pump, and an old AR-15 that had seen better years. I carried the lot into a side room, dumped them in a corner, and shut the door behind me. No reason to make it easy for anyone to rearm.

Then I went back to Randy, gave him a quick pat-down, and came up with nothing but a phone, which I pocketed. He glared at me, but it was the kind of glare a man gives when he's in too much pain to stand.

I gave him one last glance. He was down for the count—ankle bent sideways at an angle God never intended, howling through clenched teeth. That man wasn't going anywhere. He would be lucky to crawl even a month later. That was good enough for now. The kid came first.

Time to let him know he was about to get out of this shithole.

CHAPTER 6

The door to the side room was latched, cheap metal bolt wedged into a splintered frame. I flicked it open, slow and quiet. No sense in making the kid think the bad guys were coming in again.

Jesse was exactly where I had told him to be—corner of the room, knees pulled tight to his chest, arms wrapped around them like he was trying to hold himself together. Head down, eyes shut. The picture of small and scared, but still following orders.

"Hey, buddy," I said, keeping my voice low and steady. "How you holding up?"

His head snapped up, eyes wide for a split second, then softening.

"Axel?" It was halfway between a question and a prayer.

"Yeah, Jesse. It's me. Bad guys are done. They're not going to touch you again. We're heading home to your mom real soon."

It was like a shadow slid right off his face, but his body stayed locked up. Fear's funny like that—it doesn't let go just because the danger's gone.

I crouched in front of him, looking him dead in the eyes. "You hurt anywhere?"

He shook his head. "No."

"Good." I kept my voice even, like we were talking about the weather. "Before we roll, I've got to ask those bad men a few questions. Make sure they don't run before the cops get here. Think I should do that? So they never bother you or your mom again?"

His answer came fast, no hesitation. "Yes."

"Alright," I said, giving him a small nod. "We both agree, then. I'll take care of it. You hang tight just a couple more minutes, I'll be back before you know it."

Jesse hesitated, then reached out and clutched my hand for just a second, like he was making sure I was real. "OK... but come back soon."

"I will." I reached over, mussed his hair just enough to let him know he wasn't alone, then stood up.

I stepped out and pulled the door close behind me. The latch clicked shut, and the little warmth I had found in that room with Jesse went cold in my chest.

My eyes went straight to Randy. He was still right where I had left him—sprawled out on his stomach like a beached whale, chest heaving, one good arm braced against the floor like he might push himself up, but not actually moving. He had tried to roll himself over, but with only one arm and leg working right, he wasn't going anywhere except deeper into his own misery. Every twitch sent jagged bolts of pain through him, and I could see the effort in the way his breath came shallow and quick.

I crossed the room, stepped past an overturned chair, and headed for the TV. Some half-lit football game was playing—grainy, low volume, muffled crowd noise. I grabbed the remote off the table, cranked it until the crowd's roar filled the warehouse. I didn't need Jesse hearing what might come next.

Then I turned back to Randy. His head shifted just enough to catch me in his periphery, but mostly he was stuck staring at the concrete. He tensed when I closed the distance, like a man bracing for the next hit before it landed.

I came around to his good side—the left. The right side was a disaster zone: shoulder dislocated, forearm busted, ankle shot. I set my boot against his ribs, got a good wedge, and grabbed a fistful of his jacket at the back. He was a heavy son of a bitch, and it took a little muscle, but I rolled him over. His body fought me all the way, and the moment his busted limbs shifted, he screamed—raw, deep, and loud enough to cut through the football commentary.

I let him get it out for a second, then leaned over him. "You'd better knock that screaming off," I said, voice low and even. "I'm not planning on breaking any more bones. Not yet, anyway."

His eyes were glassy, his breath hitching through clenched teeth. I studied his face—sweat, blood, and something else under all that: pride that didn't know when to shut up.

"You're Randy, right? Tough big guy. Likes breaking people?"

He stared at me like he was trying to size me up through a fog of pain. "I don't know who the hell you are," he rasped, then his lip curled just enough to make it a warning. "But you don't know who you're fuckin' with."

I gave him a small, humorless smile. "That's adorable." I crouched so he could see the dead calm in my eyes. "Here's how this is gonna work. I'm gonna ask questions. You're gonna answer. And I'm not gonna break you any more. But don't even try lying to me because believe me..." I leaned in just a fraction closer. "... you don't want me getting unhappy."

He didn't say a word, just glared—trying to put a dent in me with his eyes.

"See, Randy, that's not the right answer." I nudged the side of his broken forearm with the toe of my boot. Not enough to shatter anything else—just enough to make his nerve endings light up like a Christmas tree.

His scream tore loose again, and this time it came with a quick gasp: "I understand!"

"That's better," I said, almost conversational. "Now let's start talking. Which one of these sleeping beauties is your boss Deke?" I asked looking over at the six sprawled out men, all of them still knocked out.

He tilted his head just enough to scan the room, though lying flat on his back didn't give him much of a panoramic view. I saw the flicker in his eyes—the quick mental shuffle to line up a lie—but then something clicked behind them, and he scrapped the idea.

"Deke's not in here," he said finally, voice rough. "Walked out to take a leak a couple minutes before you came crashing in."

That's when it hit him—Deke wasn't coming through that door to save him. His jaw clenched, like the thought had some weight to it.

"You take out Deke before you came in?" he asked, trying to sound curious, but there was a thin edge of hope in it.

I crouched down just far enough so my shadow fell across his face. "Take a guess, genius."

That shut him up.

I remembered Deke's phone—the one I had slipped into my sling bag when I frisked him outside. One of those fingerprint-unlock jobs. Convenient.

"Hang on," I told Randy. It came out half a joke, because the guy couldn't have slithered away if his life depended on it. Which it probably did.

I stepped out into the cool night air. Deke was still exactly where I had dropped him earlier, slumped against the side of the building like a rag doll, breathing shallow but steady.

I grabbed his hand, turned it palm-up, and pressed his index finger to the phone's scanner. A chime, a flash—unlocked. I went into settings, killed the fingerprint requirement, and set it to stay open. Whatever was in there, I wanted it ready without playing digital hide-and-seek.

I headed inside again with Deke's phone lit up in my hand, scrolling through his life like flipping a deck of cards. The guy had no idea how sloppy he was. Messages, photos, videos.

One name made me stop. Lyle Denton—the crooked cop that guy on the ravine had just told me about. Right there on Deke's speed dial. The texts between him and Deke were damning. Deke would drop a location and a time, and Denton would answer back, promising no patrols, no heat, no eyes. Bought and paid for. My jaw tightened. Good thing I had this in hand—evidence that would burn Denton down when the time came.

One other message thread caught my eye—saved under the name *Shade.*

Halfway through the exchange, Deke had sent him: *"Bird's plucked. Won't be flying again. Feathers everywhere."* Street talk for "job done—target dead". Attached was a photo of a car crumpled in a ravine, metal twisted like tinfoil, glass scattered like ice. The kind of wreck you don't crawl away from.

Right under that was Deke's follow-up: *"Want the vid?"*

Shade's reply came back fast: *"No. Delete everything. Pics, vids, all of it. Leave nothing behind."* The tone was sharp enough to cut glass.

Deke had typed *"Sure, boss"*—but I knew guys like him. They don't follow rules unless there's someone breathing down their necks. "Delete" was optional, and curiosity was a hell of a drug.

I backed out of the message thread and opened the phone's photo gallery. Most of it was the usual crap—cheap beer in plastic cups, piles of greasy food, the occasional set of bare breasts somebody thought was art. But I kept digging.

There it was—the wreck photo from the text. And right next to it—a video file. I opened it.

The footage was shaky, somebody holding the phone in one hand while the other hand gripped the wheel of a big transport truck. Diesel engine howling, the truck swerved, lined up on a small sedan parked on the shoulder. No warning, no hesitation—the truck rammed it dead-on. Steel shrieked, glass exploded, and the car launched into the air, twisted midair, and vanished out of sight, tumbling into the ravine. The camera stayed steady on the road like nothing had happened.

I didn't know all the details of how Mark Kincaid died, and I couldn't say for certain that the sedan in the clip was the one he had been in when it happened. But I was willing to bet anything this was the murder—right here, caught in greasy, pixelated glory. And now that I had the proof, I would see to it that Mark's wife got the justice she deserved... no matter how many bodies I had to step over to make it happen.

CHAPTER 7

I walked back into the room, phone in my hand, my mind locked on one thing—wrangling the truth out of the killer lying busted up on the floor. Randy's eyes tracked me the whole way, trying to read my face like he could get ahead of the storm coming for him.

I clicked the screen off and let my gaze bore into him. "Who gave you and Deke the order to kill Mark Kincaid?"

The reaction was instant. His eyes widened—shock first, then a hard swallow like his throat had just turned to sandpaper. He opened his mouth, probably to feed me some line of bull, but I cut that short by nudging his busted forearm with my boot. Not a hard kick—just enough to remind him what pain was.

"Think real carefully," I said, my voice steady. "Remember our talk about not getting me mad?"

"Yeah, I—" He sucked in a sharp breath. "Look... I say the name, I'm a dead man. They'll come for me."

"Newsflash, Randy—you're not exactly in fighting shape. And I already know it was Shade who gave the order. I'm just filling in the blanks. But if you're dead set on being useless to me, we can skip ahead."

I lifted the bat from where it leaned against the wall and let it hang over his head like I was measuring my swing. "You won't like how that plays out. And I'm not wasting a bullet on you."

"Whoa—wait!" His good arm shot up, shaking. "What do you need to know, since you already know it was Shade?"

"His real name."

"You let me live if I tell you?"

I tilted my head toward the six men still sprawled around us. "Everybody in here's broken but breathing. Deke's breathing too. I don't have a personal score with you, Randy. That's the way I intend to leave it."

He let out a bitter laugh that turned into a grimace. "I sure as hell don't wanna know what you do to the guys you *do* have a score with."

He paused, eyes flicking away for a heartbeat before locking back on me. "All I know is what Deke told me—Shade's an ex-army guy named Darius Wade. Don't know much else about him. But the guys he runs with? They're all killers. Ruthless. Seems like they've all worn a uniform at some point." He looked me up and down. "Same as you, I'm guessing."

I didn't bother to confirm or deny. I just stared at him long enough for the silence to get heavy.

"Go on," I said.

"They're dangerous men," Randy said, his voice low, like the walls might be listening. "They won't think twice about killing anyone. You cross 'em, they'll come after you and erase you."

"That's a bit rich," I said, "coming from a guy who kills people."

His eyes twitched. I held up Deke's phone, thumbed the screen, and let the video roll—grainy dash-footage of that big truck plowing into Mark's car and sending it into the ravine like a kicked can. The sound of steel tearing apart was jarring.

"You boys get a kick out of filming yourselves killing people?" I asked, voice cold enough to frost steel.

Randy's Adam's apple bobbed. "No... no, I swear. It wasn't like that. Deke—he's just as scared of Shade and his crew as I am. He wanted proof for them. That's all it was."

"That so?"

"We weren't in the business of offing people. This was a one-time thing." He licked his lips, eyes skittering to the door like he thought somebody might come through it. "We'd been running dope with Shade's guys. And when Shade 'asks'... it's not a request. You don't have the option of saying no."

I leaned closer. "What's the crew called? Who's Shade running with?"

He swallowed. "They go by the Black Dagger Syndicate."

He let that hang, then went on in a rush. "They ain't street punks, man. They're organized—money people, fighters, guys who used to wear uniforms. These guys run clean—muscle, paperwork, cash—everything. You cross 'em, they don't just whack you; they erase you. They rolled through and made the whole trade theirs. And you don't do that without stacking a lot of bodies."

I watched him for a beat, then asked: "What were you planning to do with the kid?"

His head shook, fast. "All I knew was we were supposed to wait until Shade told us what to do."

I leaned closer, boots creaking on the warped floor. "You weren't planning on letting him walk away."

"I swear that wasn't—"

"Bullshit," I snapped. "If Shade says it, you'll do it. And we both know damn well Shade's gonna give the word."

That shut him up. His mouth hung open for half a breath, but no sound came out. The game on the TV in the corner kept playing like none of this mattered, crowd noise and commentator chatter spilling over the silence.

I leaned in close. "Where's Shade?"

Randy licked his lips, eyes shifting toward the ceiling like answers might be written up there. "I... I can't say for sure. Shade could be anywhere. Probably back in Baltimore."

He was lying through his teeth. I could smell it on him. The other guy—the one I had worked over at the ravine—had already told me there was a Baltimore crew holed up at the Pine Hollow Motor Lodge, out on Route 6. Odds were Shade was in that mix.

"Funny," I said, voice low and steady. "Cause I heard different. So let me put this plain. Who's holed up at the motel?"

Randy's jaw flexed. He tried for the wide-eyed innocent routine, shaking his head. "I don't know what you're talking about."

I smiled, slow and cold. "Maybe I should use your phone. Call Shade. See if he picks up from the motel." I pulled his phone from my bag, thumbed the screen like I was lining up a call.

That did it. His eyes went big, and real fear leaked in. He shook his head fast, like a dog trying to shake off water. "No—don't do that. Look, he's there. Shade's there, alright? Him and four other guys... army type. I only caught the name of one. Calls himself Ironjack."

Ironjack. Figured. All these merc wannabes loved their tough-guy call signs.

That was all I needed. Shade and four other guys holed up at a roadside motel. Pieces slid into place in my head, and I didn't like the picture they made. Shade and Ironjack weren't here for a vacation. And they surely wouldn't leave a witness like Dana breathing.

I straightened, raised the edge of the bat like I was about to start round two, then swung it low and fast—caught Randy across the temple with just enough force. He slumped back, out cold.

I left him there, sprawled and broken, and crossed the hall.

The door creaked when I pushed it open. Jesse was perched on the edge of a chair, small hands clenched in his lap, eyes darting to me the second the door swung in.

I softened my tone, let the menace drain out. "Time to get you back to your mom, kid."

He blinked, almost disbelieving. "Really?"

"Really. But listen—once we step out that door, you walk quick with me, and don't look around. Eyes forward. Got it?"

He nodded, his head bobbing too fast. The kid had already been through hell—getting snatched by scum like Randy and his crew was trauma enough. No need for him to see them laid out broken on the floor.

I crouched, gave him the faintest grin, the kind that said *you're safe now*. "Let's go."

We moved fast, straight down the hall, my body between him and the carnage. Out the front, into the cool night air.

The pickup was where I left it. I got him inside, buckled, and slid in behind the wheel. Engine turned over with a rumble. Headlights washed over the cracked gravel lot.

I put it in gear, rolling us back toward town.

My eyes stayed on the road, but my head was already working ahead—Shade, Ironjack and their crew. Time was running out.

CHAPTER 8

I rolled the pickup to a stop on the same patch of curb where I had dropped the two watchers into the dirt not two hours ago. It had a clean line of sight to Dana's place and enough shadow to keep the truck from drawing attention. My gut told me not to roll straight into the driveway. I have learned to listen when my gut talks.

The street was deserted. Nothing moved. Not a sound. But the night still felt heavy—one of those still moments when the air's just waiting for trouble.

Before we moved, I shifted in my seat and turned to Jesse. "Alright, kid… here's the deal. I've taken care of most of the bad guys, but I can't promise we're in the clear. There's always a chance one or two are still sniffing around. So until we get your mom out, I need you to be solid. Think you can handle that?"

His chin came up a notch, eyes steady. "I'm not scared if you're here. Just tell me what you need me to do."

That hit me harder than I expected, but I kept my voice even. "Good. When we see your mom, you don't say a word. Not one word, not even a whisper. Bad guys planted bugs in the house—they can hear everything. We don't want them knowing you're safe until we're long gone. You with me?"

"I'm with you," he said, nodding once, looking all serious and focused.

"Good. First thing is figuring out where she is—front or back of the house. Once we know, we'll get her to open the door, and we're out. Simple as that."

We slipped out of the truck, moving quietly down the street toward the house. I kept him close, my hand brushing his shoulder every few steps so he knew I was right there. The blinds in the front windows were cracked just enough for me to get a read inside.

Didn't take long—Dana was right there in the front room, perched on the couch. TV on but muted, her eyes locked on it without seeing a damn thing. The kind of thousand-yard stare people get when they have been waiting too long with bad thoughts for company.

I tapped lightly on the windowpane, just enough to snap her out of it. She looked up, alarm sparking in her eyes. I leaned forward, gave her a clean look at me. Recognition hit, and the fear bled off, replaced by relief—and something else. She was searching my face, looking past me, hoping I had kept my word.

I tugged Jesse forward into the frame. The second she saw him, her shoulders sagged, and a wave of relief washed over her face so hard I thought she might collapse right there.

I pressed a finger to my lips, kept my eyes on hers. No words. She understood. I pointed toward the back of the house, made the twisting hand motion that meant "door". Her eyes flicked toward the kitchen, and she nodded once. I stepped back, turned to Jesse, and we started around the side, keeping low and quiet toward the rear entrance.

The back door eased open, and Dana stepped out. The instant she cleared the threshold, Jesse ran and threw himself into her arms. She caught him, clung to him like she wasn't ever going to let go. Tears welled, but neither of them made a sound. Jesse remembered my instruction. Smart kid.

I let them have it for a heartbeat, then guided them away from the door into deeper shadow. "We don't have long," I whispered, my voice low but firm. "You packed?"

Dana nodded, her eyes never leaving Jesse.

"Good," I said. "Grab your bag. We're moving now."

Dana slipped back inside to grab her bag, leaving Jesse planted right at my side. Kid stuck close, steady as a shadow. Brave for his size, but I could feel the tension in him, a coiled wire ready to snap.

I didn't know where I was going to take them yet—safehouse, motel, hell, maybe keep moving until I carved a hole in this mess. One thing I knew—Ashwood sure as hell wasn't safe. Not with the Black Dagger Syndicate sniffing around, tying off loose ends like they were cleaning house. I could smell it—the stink of bodies being buried. I didn't have the whole puzzle yet, but my gut told me they had Ryan's blood on their hands. That's why they were burning evidence, tying up loose ends before I ripped the mask off their operation.

That's when the headlights cut across the street—sharp, white beams sliding between the trees like knives. I pulled Jesse with me into the dark edge of the house, shadows swallowing us whole. We ghosted along the side of the house, boots crunching soft on gravel until we had an angle.

"Stick tight," I whispered as together we crouched low, eyes tracking.

A cop car rolled up, slow, deliberate. Not a sound but the idle tick of the engine. The cruiser pulled right beside the truck I had parked down the street. Not random. Targeted. Like it was following a map. Then the beams died. The headlights flicked off before the car stopped rolling.

That right there was a tell. Any cop checking out a suspicious vehicle would have lit it up like a Christmas tree—full red-and-blue strobes flashing, siren chirped once for show. That's procedure. This guy? He killed the light like a burglar slipping a key in the back door.

The door opened with that hollow metallic thud only a Crown Vic makes, and out stepped the cop. He strolled toward the truck, casual as Sunday morning, like he expected to find someone sitting there waiting. When he came up empty, he fished out his phone. Not the radio strapped to his belt, but his phone.

Big red flag. Any cop on the clock would hit dispatch, not speed dial. That meant only one thing: this wasn't business. This was a side hustle.

I felt Jesse shift next to me, nervous energy sparking. "You know him?" I whispered.

The kid nodded. "Yes. He came by our house... a few times. After my dad's accident." He swallowed, then added, "That's Officer Denton. Lyle Denton."

The name stuck in my head like a splinter. I had seen Denton's number in Deke's message thread on that phone. He was the dirty cop greasing the wheels for Deke's crew. The one making sure there were no eyes on their runs.

I breathed out slow, teeth tight. Something was rotten here. Not just shady—deep rot, down to the bone. Denton wasn't there by coincidence.

The way he had rolled up told me everything. He hadn't just stumbled on my truck. He was looking for it—expecting to find those two watchdogs I had dumped beside the ravine earlier. Somebody must have tried calling them, looking for a sitrep, and all they got was silence. So Denton came himself. Found an empty pickup. Cop uniform gave him the cover, but that phone in his hand told the real story. He was talking to the Black Dagger Syndicate.

That meant Shade's crew at the Pine Hollow Motel knew something was wrong. And if Denton was their eyes, then time was bleeding out fast.

Slipping Dana and Jesse past him wasn't happening with him planted in there. I could have gone full-on and knocked him out. Then dump him somewhere he would wake up with a hell of a hangover and a lousy memory. But I wanted to avoid that. Taking out a cop could bring complications. And I needed to keep things as simple as possible if I was going to keep these two alive.

Movement pulled my eyes back to the house. Dana stepped out, a big bag in each hand, her face pale in the dim glow from the kitchen light. She stopped when she saw me crouched with Jesse, eyes narrowing, reading my body language like a field medic reading a wound. Something was wrong, and she felt it.

I raised my hand, signaled her to stay quiet, and waved her over. She adjusted course and moved toward us, bags bumping against her legs.

When she got close enough, she leaned in, whisper sharp as a blade. "What's going on?"

I kept my voice low. "That cop out front—Denton—he's dirty."

Her eyes flicked toward the street, then back. "Are you sure?"

"Dead sure. Dug up plenty of proof in the last couple hours."

I saw her throat tighten, the question forming before it left her mouth. "Did you... did you find out anything about Mark?" She faltered, the name catching like barbed wire, and stopped when she remembered Jesse was standing right there.

I gave her the out. "Yeah," I said, keeping my tone calm, meant for her ears, but vague enough for the boy. "I found what I needed. The ones who did it aren't going anywhere. I'll lay it out for you later."

Her eyes watered, but she blinked it back, a hard nod sealing the message. She understood.

That's when Denton's phone lit up, screen glowing like a spotlight in the dark. He snapped it up fast, pressing it tight to his ear, shoulders stiff. His voice was low and urgent, like he was giving a field report. I watched the way his jaw worked, the way his eyes flicked toward the house—calculating, measuring.

He finished the call and tucked the phone away. Then he leaned into his cruiser and fumbled around. He pulled something out and slid it into his pocket with a practiced motion. Then he turned and started toward the house like he owned the block.

That was the pivot point. No more slipping past him. If Dana didn't open the door, Denton would hang around, sniffing, and work his way around to the back. Either way, he was going to be between us and the escape. I didn't want to be slugging a cop out on the street, even if it was a dirty cop. But

Denton was narrowing my options with every footstep.

I leaned in close to Dana. "We'll have to go inside. Let you show yourself," I whispered. "You open the door. Let him see you. I and Jesse'll hide in the bedroom. You make like everything's normal. If he starts to act funny, I'll take him down. Then we're gone. Don't panic."

She swallowed, the color draining from her face, but she nodded once—hard and decisive. Her hands shook around the bag straps but she squared her shoulders like someone who had learned how to do hard things without crying.

We slipped through the back door like shadows folding into a darker sleeve. Dana guided us down the hall into a bedroom at the side of the house. Jesse sat on the bed like he was expecting the world to explode; his little chest rose and fell so fast I thought it might stop. I crouched, gave him a quick look, the kind that said: "*I'm here. I'm not leaving you.*" He nodded once, all business.

A second later the doorbell rang—one sharp chime that sounded far too loud in the silence. Dana's hand trembled as she straightened. I heard her take a breath and walk toward the living room. I could see her silhouette moving through the thin curtains. Her back was a little tighter than before, but she was walking like she meant it.

She opened the front door. Denton stood there, shoulders broad in the dim porchlight, face arranged into a practiced concern.

"Evening, Dana," he said, all soft duty and practiced charm. "Heard reports of some disturbance—figured I'd check on things. You all right?"

She kept her face even. "We're fine. Thank you." Her voice wavered just a hair, the sound of someone measured enough to hide the tremor.

Denton smiled like a man who had already won half a wager. He didn't seem to want to leave. He stalled, looking past Dana into the living room, asking how she was holding up, how the boy was doing. My blood rose at that—the bastard knew very well the boy had been taken by the crew he was working for.

Then he surprised her with, "Mind if I have a glass of water?"

Dana hesitated, then turned toward the kitchen. "Sure—just... uh, in the kitchen." The way she moved was slow, like she was trying to stretch the seconds out, to let me read the whole room from where I sat.

He followed her, and that's when I saw it. As she headed for the sink, he reached into his coat where he had tucked that little thing from the cruiser. It wasn't a radio. It wasn't a badge. It was slick and black—a compact stun gun, one of those little devices that look like a toy but buzzed mean enough to knock you down without leaving visible holes.

In that breath, the plan became crystal clear. Denton wasn't there to check on the neighborhood. He was there to neutralize a witness. The Syndicate didn't want loose ends. Denton was the hand that tied them.

I could hear Dana's kitchen steps, soft and unaware. Jesse's breathing sounded too loud in the small space. When Denton began closing the gap, the world went slow.

There was no avoiding it now. The night was about to get uglier.

CHAPTER 9

I crouched, looked down at Jesse, and told him, "Get behind the bed. Stay put. Don't make a sound."

Jesse didn't hesitate. He scooted like a trained kid, small feet whispering across the floor, and vanished behind the mattress. I saw the way his back hit the wall and the way his fingers curled in a fist, eyes wide as a rabbit. Kid trusted me. That meant everything.

I slid my boot knife out slowly, the blade coming free with that soft whisper of steel, and palmed it. I felt the familiar weight settle in my hands.

Denton closed on Dana like a man who had practiced this little routine a hundred times—soft step behind, hand in the jacket for the weapon. When he reached for the stun device, my shoulders tightened and I moved.

The first he knew of my presence in the room was when my knife was at his throat—steel kissing skin with enough edge to cut clean through anything it encountered. I pressed the blade just enough to nick him. A thin bright bead welled, and he forgot how to breathe. Up close his pupils blew wide; the fear sucked the color out of his face.

I kept the blade pressed and leaned in so my breath was on his ear. "One twitch," I whispered, "and you're a dead man." Then I added, quieter, harder: "And get your finger off that trigger. Now."

He obeyed like a puppet whose strings had been cut—frozen, pulse hammering, sweat standing out on his brow. The world narrowed to him. He went stone-still, the way prey does when it finally understands there's a predator in the room.

My other hand flicked the signal to Dana: back door. She looked toward the bedroom, asking without words if Jesse was safe. I nodded, not speaking, because the bugs could be listening and every extra syllable was a risk. She nodded once, small and fierce, and slipped out the back like a ghost.

As soon as Dana turned, I snatched the stun device from Denton's hand like I meant to tear the thing from him. Fast, brutal, a move meant to hurt. I yanked with such a violent twist that the wrist snapped on the pull. A sharp crack cut through the quiet. He howled, a raw, sharp sound—one of those cries that makes your ears ring. It was music to my ears, but I didn't want Jesse getting unduly scared.

"Shut up," I hissed, pressing the blade closer so another hot bead of blood welled where the steel kissed skin. His cry cut off into a wet, broken sound. He wrapped his other hand uselessly around the broken wrist, eyes fluttering as shock rolled through him.

But I wasn't in the mood to waste any pity on him. I caught Denton by the collar and shoved him toward the back door, his feet struggling to keep up as I drove him forward. When we hit the yard I swept his legs out from under him in a clean arc. He hit the ground with a thud that rattled the quiet—back slamming into the dirt hard enough to flip the breath out of his lungs.

Denton lay there, wind knocked out, clutching the arm that no longer worked right. He knew exactly what broke and why he wouldn't be getting out of the night the easy way.

Dana stood on the stoop watching, face blank. No gasp, no tear, no little intake of breath—nothing. She must have already figured out Denton had a hand in Mark's death.

I showed her the device. "This is what he had on him. He was going to knock you out."

Denton made a feeble attempt to bullshit his way out, trying to spit authority like a shield: "I'm an officer of the law. You can't—" He stopped mid-sentence, his attempt faltering under the heat in my eyes.

I pressed the tip of the blade an inch under his right eye, let the metal rest there so he could taste it. My face said what my words didn't: I was ready to scoop that eye out if he breathed wrong. "One more word," I said, voice flat as a slab, "and you'll lose it." His whimper died and slid straight into terrified silence.

My gut told me Denton wasn't the end of it. The Syndicate wouldn't send him out alone. He was their scout—making sure the witness was still in place, marking the scene. That meant the real cleaners would be there soon: the professionals to finish the job and make the death look tidy, the tech to pull every wire and wipe every file until nothing tied them to the scene. Clean, efficient murder. That's how these boys rolled.

If Dana went down, Jesse was disposable to them—an orphaned loose end. Those guys don't leave loose ends. I didn't want to imagine what they planned for a kid. All I knew was they were about to find out just how badly that ended for them.

I couldn't risk stepping out into the street with Dana and Jesse. One wrong window of headlights and I would be trading bullets with men who had come prepared. A Glock against automatics and numbers was a bad bet. I would rather make the fight where I controlled the angles: inside, where surprise was mine.

And that meant it was time to call the cops. I hadn't killed anyone so far because I wanted a clean exit—drive out of Ashwood, chase the next lead. But these men were armed and ringing the block. If it came to killing to keep Dana and the kid safe, I couldn't just walk out of there and pretend it never happened. If there was blood on the lawn, I wanted it to read like self-defense, not a hit.

Getting the police on the record would do two things: it would frame whatever I did as a rescue, and it would bring official eyes to the scene. I wasn't sure how clean the rest of the local force was—Denton's name on Deke's phone told me not every blue shirt played straight—but a 911 call would also pull state troopers into the loop. That meant a federal-level responder could show up, fast, and the narrative would be locked before the Syndicate could spin it. Better the cops show up on a reported break-in and find the truth under the porch light than find me driving away with bodies left behind in my wake.

Denton was still curled on the grass like a beaten dog. I moved in and frisked him quickly, fingers running over pockets and belt until I pulled a Glock 17 free. Big, heavy, service-grade. I put the barrel under his nose, then leaned in close and said low and mean, "Don't you so much as blink." He didn't.

I flicked a look at Dana then, and signaled her—back door. I needed to talk to her where Denton couldn't hear. She followed like she had been ordered in formation. We huddled in the yard, shadows close, words clipped. I kept my voice low, careful; somewhere out there a tech had bugged the place.

"You have a basement or attic?" I asked.

"Basement," she breathed.

"Any gun in the house?"

She swallowed. "Mark kept his sidearm in the bedroom drawer—his old service piece. A Beretta."

Good. I didn't want her firing unless she absolutely had to, but a gun in her hands beat no gun at all. I told her straight: we couldn't outrun these guys if they rolled up in numbers. They would cut us off on the road or pin us at the truck. A Glock and a Beretta weren't enough if they had automatics and a plan. Best place to fight was inside where surprise was mine.

"Can you trust my word I won't let anything happen to you or Jesse?" I asked, the words small but sharp.

Dana looked me dead in the eye and I saw something harden. "Yes," she said. Not a tremor. "You kept your word. I'm not afraid anymore. If I get the chance, I'll put a bullet in the men who took my boy."

"We'll make them pay," I said. "But first we do this smart."

I remembered Dana had told me they were tapping her phone. So I handed her Randy's phone I had grabbed earlier and told her what to do, short and ordered.

"Use this to call 911 right now. Tell them there are armed intruders in the house, that you and your son are hiding in the basement, and that a friend is outside who came to help. Keep it short and urgent. OK?"

She nodded.

"After the call, go inside, and grab the gun. Kill the living-room lights but leave the kitchen lamp on. Take Jesse down into the basement and stay there until I tell you to come up. Got it?"

Dana nodded like she had been issued a rifle and a mission.

"I understand," she replied, her jaw set hard. She stepped into the shadow of the kitchen doorway, thumbed the phone, and made the 911 call in a voice so low it hardly left her lips.

CHAPTER 10

While Dana made the call, I went back to Denton. He lay on his side in the grass, face twisted, one eye already ballooning where I had hit him earlier. He hadn't moved since I told him to freeze—fear had glued him in place. No sympathy. I had questions for him. I needed him to talk. And time wasn't on my side.

I twisted his head, planted my knee into his cheekbone and ground his face into the dirt—not enough to crush, just enough to let him know I could. The pressure forced his face into the cold ground; grit pressed against his lips; his breathing shallow and focused—perfect for getting a scared man to sing.

"We're going to have a little talk," I told him.

I eased the pressure of my knee, just to let the pain roll like a wave through him. His eyes bulged.

He whimpered, high and thin. "What do you want?"

I pushed a little harder with my knee so his right eye watered and his breath hitched. "You were sent here to murder Dana in cold blood. And you helped bury her husband two weeks ago. I'll give you another sample of pain if you try denying it."

He cried out, muffled into the dirt. I eased my knee just a fraction and the sound cut off, replaced by the rasp of his breathing. "No. I'm... not denying... but I didn't kill myself... just let them do it," he confessed, too scared to lie anymore.

If he had lied, I would have crushed his skull. I was too mad at that weasel. I pressed on a little more until his eyeballs bulged and he clawed at the grass. "I'll ask questions; you'll answer. If you lie even once," I said, "I'll crack your face and I'll listen to the sound of your brains leaking out into the dirt. You understand?"

He made a tiny, terrified noise and said, "I understand," the syllables muffled against the grass.

While his head was turned and his eyes squeezed shut from the pressure, I pulled my phone and thumbed the recorder on. The little red dot blinked to life, then I set the phone down in the grass just far enough away that he didn't see the screen light up. The microphone picked up the soft scrape of the ground, the ragged pull of his breaths. Everything we said would be there. Evidence in a tiny glowing rectangle.

That's when Dana came back from the corner, phone in her hand. "I called," she said, breath small. She pressed the phone into my hand—her fingers trembled enough for me to feel it through the glass. "They said help's on the way."

"Good. Go get Jesse and head to the basement."

She nodded, but didn't move. "I need to talk to you first," she said.

I eased my knee off Denton's face and let him roll his head up so he could look at me. "Don't move a muscle," I warned.

Then I straightened and walked to the side of the back porch with Dana. She reached into her pocket and pressed a little flash drive into my palm like it was the last coin in the world.

"I wanted to hand this now," she said. "If anything happens to me when the killers come, you need to have this. This is the one Mark wanted you to have. Not the fake one. I kept this hidden."

Something cold and clean slid through me at that. For three months I had been poking at shadows, trying to find a face to aim at. This felt like a match struck in a dark room. "You still had it? The men who took Jesse— they didn't find this?"

She nodded, the motion small and fierce. "Mark made me two copies," she said, eyes already beginning to burn. "He told me to put them in different places. He was paranoid in the best way—said never keep your life in one box. The men took one of them—believed it was the only copy—and left me a fake to hand you."

Relief hit me like a punch—because surprises are good when you are looking for proof, and because it meant she had kept at least one line to the truth intact.

"It's got an easy password—one-one-two-eight. Jesse's birthday," Dana continued. "I played dumb. Said I didn't even know how to open the thing. They bought it—big men with guns, thinking a woman who cried and stammered was harmless. I told them all I knew was Mark wanted you to have it. They ate it up, asked me for my and Jesse's birthdays. I could see by the way they exchanged glances that they had opened it. Thought they had the only copy."

There was a flicker of something—admiration, grief—in my chest for the man who had thought of that. Making sure I got the flash drive—that was Mark's last move. He had left a breadcrumb that might blow the whole thing wide open.

I slid the drive into my pocket like a loaded pledge. "You saw what was on it?" I asked.

She nodded, small and terrible. "Mark made a video. He said Captain Ryan Blaze didn't die by accident. He said it was a conspiracy, that Ryan was murdered by dirty soldiers. He mentioned three names: Marcus Stahl, Darius Wade, Kyle Firth."

Darius Wade. The name landed with the force of a fist. The name Randy told me—Shade's real name. Things started snapping into place. The plan, the lies, the way men with brass and badges covered for each other. Fury uncoiled under my skin and snapped into a hard, bright focus. All those months of groping in the dark folded into one clean line of intent. I had a target.

"Thank you," I said, and meant it in a way that sounded like an oath. "I'll make sure Mark didn't die for nothing. And I'll make sure you and Jesse get out of this alive."

She looked like she might fall apart and then fold into something harder. "Did you... uh, were you able to find out about Mark? About why—" Her voice went thin.

"I did," I told her. "The ones who did it are lying broken and battered where I left them. I've got proof. When they can stand they'll walk into cuffs. I'll make sure they rot in a cell if they can walk at all." I let the promise sit there with a little steel in it.

She swallowed, nodded, and then finally moved. "I'll get Jesse." She started for the back door.

I watched her go and when the door clicked I let a slow breath out that tasted like iron. As I walked over to Denton, the urge to crush his skull was a live thing in my chest; it pulsed with every step. What he was helping them do—made my jaw ache.

I had to calm the animal down. I had to be the blade, not the tantrum.

I let the rage sit where it belonged—behind the teeth—and kept my movements clean. I crouched, tilted his face up, and slid the tip of the knife under his right eye until he tasted iron again. Enough to remind him. Enough to keep him honest.

Denton swallowed so hard his Adam's apple jumped. He blinked up at me through the smear of dirt and dried blood, trying to read what I was going to do next.

CHAPTER 11

Despite the rage flowing through my veins, I wasn't blind to what I was up against at that moment. The clock was loud in my head. The Syndicate boys would show up soon, and they wouldn't be half-assed hustlers like Denton. These Black Dagger types smelled ex-military—organized, efficient, dangerous. I needed answers, and I needed them fast.

"Who gave you the order to tase Dana?" I asked, voice flat and cold.

He went fishy, eyes sliding. To speed him up, I threw a couple of names in his face— let him know I knew stuff, made it real, made it easier to say. "Was it Shade or Ironjack?" I offered, like I was handing him a lifeline. Sometimes frightened men need a name to latch onto.

His mouth moved, slow as a wound opening. "Shade," he managed.

"How were you supposed to take her out?" I pressed. He tried to wiggle, hesitated, reached for a soft lie. I drove the blade a hair deeper under his eye and he let out a hiss that sounded like a match struck.

He gasped and then sputtered, "I was supposed to— I was gonna tase her, knock her out. Then the others would come in and... finish it. I don't know how they'd do it. I'm not a killer— I wouldn't put a bullet in a woman myself." He tacked that last bit on like a prayer.

"Save your breath." I cut him off cold. "Were you supposed to call when you were done? Confirm the job? Or do they just roll up?"

Heat crept into his cheeks like shame. "They—they'll call me. That's what they said. I can't say for sure. I swear it's the truth."

It made sense. If Denton was their scout, they wanted no fuss. They would avoid anything that looked messy—no loud headlights, no strangers on Main. In a town where everyone knew everyone and folks noticed everything, they would rather call in confirmation than risk being seen. That bought me a little time.

They could be idling a block over, waiting for Denton's signal. Making a run for it with Dana and the kid still seemed like a bad idea. Keeping them inside and surprising whoever showed up was the play. I asked about Mark while the scared cop was still under my boot.

"Who gave the order to kill Mark Kincaid?"

He swallowed like he had gulped gravel. "I— I didn't even know these guys then," he stammered. "There's this guy Deke, uh, runs a gang around these parts... he was the one who got me in it. Deke said Shade ordered it. Said he had no choice—said he'd get burned if he said no. I just... I was there. First responder. Filed it as an... an accident. I did what I was told." The last words came out thin as paper.

It was neat and efficient—Deke did the dirty work, Denton scrubbed the paper trail and the report called it an accident. Kill, then sanitize. Murder dressed as misfortune and a badge to rubber-stamp it. They had thought the whole thing through.

“Who’s coming to take out Dana?” I asked, and the yard seemed to lean in with me.

“Shade, I guess. Or Ironjack,” he croaked. “Or all of them. I can’t say for sure, I swear.” His eyes flicked to the porch light, calculating how long until headlights licked the trees.

And then, right on cue, his phone lit up against the grass—an incoming call cutting through the night. The screen flared—IRONJACK—big letters cutting the dark. I tipped the phone so Denton could see it. His face went white the moment he saw the name.

“You’re taking this,” I said. “Tell them everything’s gone to plan.” My voice was low and flat, the kind that didn’t invite arguing.

He gave me a look like I had just asked him to cut off his own finger.

“Get a grip,” I told him. “One of two things is going to happen right now. You take this call and sell them the story—everything went to plan—or I pick it up and tell Ironjack you told me he’s about to come over to finish Dana off and I’m waiting for him to make a move. Saves me the trouble of having to crush your skull with my knee. Want me to do that?”

He looked like he was ready to faint. “They’ll skin me alive if they know I talked,” he croaked.

“No, I won’t leave them able enough to do that. This is the only way you walk out of here breathing. You call them, tell them you did the job, and then you leave it to me to take them out.”

He swallowed like it hurt. “Look, I don’t mean no disrespect, but you don’t know what you’re up against. It’s five of those mob guys, and—Christ—there’s a dozen local muscle backing them. They’re heavy. You can’t—”

"You think Deke and his boys are heavy? Well, you don't need to worry. I left them all broken and bleeding at that textile mill out of town."

He opened his mouth but not a word came out—he just stared at me.

I added, sarcasm dripping in every syllable: "And I know you must be worried sick about the kid—Jesse. Well, you can relax. He's safe."

The call stopped ringing. The night fell quiet again. I wasn't worried—phones stop, they ring back. If they didn't, I could make Denton dial them.

"This is your last chance, Denton," I said. "When it rings again you answer. You tell them you knocked her out and you're waiting for them to come in. The front door's unlocked but you've turned off the living room lights so any nosy neighbors can't take a peek. Say it clear. Say it slow. Don't try any backflip bullshit."

The handset went off again like a gunshot. I shoved it into Denton's hand and barked, "Take it. Put it on speaker. Don't play cute."

Panic made Denton's fingers fumble with the phone. He was shaking so hard I had to clamp my hand on his wrist to steady him. His fingers fumbled like a man with frostbite, thumb slipping before he found the green. He hit speaker, the little tinny echo filling the yard.

The voice that came out was Ironjack's—flat, hard, the kind that could file a man down. "Where the hell you at?" Ironjack snapped. "You pick up or you wanna die with your phone glued to your ear?"

Denton babbled an apology that came out like a sob. Ironjack chewed him a new one, all contempt and menace. Then he barked about Deke not answering. "You idiots out there can't even pick up a goddamn phone? Deke's not answering either. What the hell's going on with you clowns?"

Denton didn't have a clue but I knew why Deke wasn't answering. That was because his phone was in my pocket and I had turned it off.

Denton sounded like a man reading from a script someone had stapled to his ribs. He stuttered the message I had told him to relay—Dana was knocked out in the kitchen; front door was open; everything was ready for them.

Ironjack wasn't the kind of sensitive soul who would pick up on the tremor in Denton's voice. He was too much in a rush to finish the job.

"Good. We'll be there. Shade's gone after those bozos at the mill to grab the kid. We'll finish the job here."

The line went dead and the yard went quiet. Shade was on his way to the mill. That meant the minute Shade rolled up, he would find Deke's crew in pieces and Jesse gone. He would realize their game was up. He would flip and warn Ironjack. That would blow whatever slim window I had straight to hell. I still had a small, hot window—maybe minutes, maybe less—to make this clean.

Part of me wanted to drop everything and sprint to the mill and gut Shade. Knowing he was one of Ryan's killers made it harder to think rationally. The impulse to rip Shade's throat out was almost overwhelming, but I couldn't abandon a kid and a woman in a house full of Syndicate men. Sanity returned within seconds.

I checked my watch. Four minutes since Dana's call. In a town with five cops, Denton was the single warm body on the night shift; the others were off the clock and probably in bed. That meant any local cruiser showing up was not a bet I could make. The fastest real help would be a state trooper, and that would still take time. I couldn't roll my fate on luck.

Time to get ready.

I stripped Denton's handcuffs from his belt, the cold metal clinking, and told him flat, "Turn over". He obeyed like a man who had already given up the right to breathe easy. I locked the cuffs on his wrists—his own cuffs—tight enough to bite into skin. Then I set the heel of my hand to the side of his neck with a hard, angled strike. It knocked him clean.

I dragged him into a corner and dumped him there. He would wake with a headache and a story to tell; I didn't much care which one he picked.

I pulled the two Glocks out—one from the guy at the mill, one from Denton. I racked each slide, thumbed the magazines out and looked at the rounds like a mechanic checks bolts. Both mags were full enough; I popped them back in, felt the click of metal that meant the guns would feed. I tapped the blades tucked in my boots just to make sure they were snug in their sheaths.

Satisfied, I rolled my shoulders, flexed my wrists until the joints sighed, let the anger turn into cold motion.

Then I picked the baseball bat and moved inside, quiet as a ghost and twice as hungry.

CHAPTER 12

I waited in the dark, pressed against the wall in the living room, one hand tightening and loosening on the grip of the bat. I had a perfect angle on the street through the window. Less than a minute later, headlights cut across the night, washing pale streaks through the blinds. Pickup truck. It rolled up, stopped near the cop car and the other truck on the opposite curb, lights cutting the yard into bright and black.

Three men climbed out. I guessed the other two of that five-man Syndicate crew were Shade and a fifth guy—those two must have made their way to the mill where Deke and his crew lay broken and battered. I pushed that thought to the back of my mind as I had an immediate threat to deal with.

The three guys who got out of the truck moved like soldiers—economy to their steps, shoulders set, hips used to carrying weight. Two of them were about six feet, lean and hard. The third was bigger, half a foot taller, thicker through the chest, shoulders like a doorframe. He stood back a step and watched the house the way a man sizes up a thing he's about to break. Ironjack, no question.

They started up the walk, boots crunching gravel. Then Ironjack paused, eyes scanning the street like he smelled a problem. He muttered something to his boys, then angled back to the pickup, pulling his phone out, thumbing it, and leaning against the truck to read something. That left the other two closing in. It gave me a little breathing room. Two problems at a time was better than three.

The two reached the porch, and just when I thought they would stack up and come in together, they split. They weren't amateurs. One of the two peeled off to the side, sweeping the flank, moving low toward the back. The other kept the front, easing up to the stoop.

That put a new shape on things: they were trained, disciplined, not some street-level hoods. I wasn't facing two thugs doing a smash-and-grab. That meant I couldn't afford any hesitation. I would have to take each of them out fast, clean, and quiet—one hard cut at a time.

The guy at the front eased the door, checked the hall with a slow, careful sweep. He eased himself in, gun hand low, scanning. The second he stepped inside and shut the door behind him, I stepped from the wall with the baseball bat already in motion—a long, hard arc that started on my shoulder and finished through his temple.

The wood met flesh with a sound like a branch snapping; his head turned on the hit and his knees forgot they were supposed to hold him up. His lights went out instantly—brain short-circuited, like someone pulled the plug.

After that blow to the head, the guy wouldn't be up for hours. Might also never wake up. I didn't care. Just to be sure, I hammered the bat down into his knee, felt the joint collapse with a crunch like snapping celery. He wasn't going anywhere, awake or not.

For half a breath, I let the silence sit on top of the place, listening for the world to catch up. It didn't. Ironjack out on the curb had no idea; the big man's back was to the house, his body leaning against the truck's cab. The other man moving around the side hadn't reached the back yet.

I didn't really pause to admire the mess I just made. No time for small pleasures. I moved toward the kitchen and stopped beside its entrance—quiet, precise, every step rehearsed from years of doing ugly things in dark places. The bat had done its work. It was over for things that needed reach and brute force. This was going to be clean and close.

I lay down the bat and pulled both boot-knives free in one smooth motion—cold steel sliding into my palms with the kind of intimacy I had learned to expect. One in each hand, balanced, deadly.

I couldn't use the gun—noise discipline was a must. I couldn't even risk the guy firing off a panic shot. One stray round and the whole op would unravel. Ironjack was standing cool outside on his phone, convinced his boys had it under control. I wanted him to stay that way—relaxed, confident—until both of the other men were quiet on the floor. One shot and Ironjack's head would pivot like a dog hearing a whistle.

So knives it had to be. Quiet, fast, brutal. The plan was simple: stop the guy before he ever knew the house had teeth. Disable him in seconds, take him out of the picture, and leave no noise for Ironjack to hear. If it got ugly and the man didn't shut down clean, then I would make it permanent. No hesitation. No misses. Close quarters, controlled violent action—the old rules of CQB, practiced until they sat in muscle and bone.

I could hear the other man moving—the soft thunk of boots on the side walk, the whisper of jeans against the siding—exactly the sound a man makes when he's coming in to find an empty house and an easy job. He was expecting Denton in the kitchen, a knocked-out woman on the couch, maybe a quick check and a clean job. He wasn't expecting me.

The door swung wide, and he stepped in, pistol up, scanning fast. I let the knife fly before his eyes could adjust. Steel punched into his chest with a meaty thunk. He staggered, shock plastered on his face as the gun slipped from his grip. Before he could even think about retrieving it, I was on him. My shoulder drove him back into the counter, rattling dishes. I slammed his skull into the wood. Once. Twice. Thrice. His body went limp and folded to the floor.

Two down. Silent, efficient. No alarms.

That left one man. The big one. Still out front.

But the night went wrong in a hurry. I heard the cruiser before I saw it—the thin, high wail of a cop siren cutting across the street like a hunting dog. State troopers, probably rolling down main, trying to work their way into the residential grid. I moved back to the front window because there was no way Ironjack was going to roll over and take cuffs.

I watched him through the glass. He was still half-turned toward the truck, phone gone, posture tight the way a coiled thing gets before it snaps. Then he pulled something out—an assault rifle—and shouldered it like a man who had spent winters making friends with recoil.

Even in the dark I could make out the familiar silhouette—an M4 carbine, short barrel, collapsible stock, and that ugly Magpul D-60 magazine hanging like a hungry heart under the receiver. Sixty rounds ready to tear down the street, putting down a wall of lead, spraying everything in front of it into silence and keep it that way until whatever was coming crawled back in a ditch.

Ironjack leveled it down the block toward the sound of the cruiser. It looked wrong in a civilized street: a rifle made to vomit rounds until whatever it hit stopped moving. This wasn't some robbery gone sideways. This was organized violence with muscle and a plan that could chew up a patrol car without leaving any survivors.

I pulled my Glock out because it was habit, because reflex is a muscle that never quits. Aim, one clean shot, problem solved. Two good men saved. Deal with the consequences later.

But the same second, Ironjack stepped out of sight. He moved fast and quiet to Denton's cruiser, flipped the strobe on like he owned the night. For a heartbeat I thought he was signaling the cops. But then he melted down behind the cruiser.

And I understood what was going on: he made the car look like a cop already on scene—an easy confidence trick to lull any incoming unit into thinking this was being handled. False sense of security. He had dressed the street in a uniform and a badge and a lie, and the lie would let him shoot them like fish in a barrel.

The cruiser turned off main and came down our block, headlights carving two bright knives through the dark. I still didn't have a clean shot at Ironjack. I did have a Glock and a very small window. If the cops rolled up closer before I figured him out, they wouldn't survived the surprise attack. I decided the first play was simple: keep the cops back. Then deal with Ironjack.

I moved before I thought it completely through. All I knew was I had to keep distance between the cops and that muzzle. Without losing a second, I shoved the door and ran into the night.

CHAPTER 13

I ran down the front steps and fired a few rounds at the cruiser's nose—short, loud snaps meant to unnerve, not to kill, not aimed for anatomy but for a command. Tires hissed as the driver stomped the brakes. The world shrank to brake smoke and a howl of rubber.

The troopers hit the dash like men who had remembered a nightmare. My bullets had done what I needed them to do: buy time.

Ironjack swore. The sound came raw, guttural. But he didn't look for me. In the dark, identity is a rumor. He assumed one of his boys had jumped the whistle and fired, and the plan had cracked. He stayed focused on the cruiser because that's what mattered: the bait, the trap, the move that let him vanish.

Then he let go.

The first burst flared from the muzzle with a punch—short, bright blooms, each muzzle flash like a tiny sun opening and snapping shut in the night. Each report was a hard bark, the 5.56's sting, quick and insistent. It sounded like someone snapping a thick rope over and over.

The D-60 magazine fed with a mechanical hunger: a soft, repetitive whining as the drum's internals indexed rounds, a tiny thunk when each cartridge seated, and then the bark again—feed-thunk-bark—an ugly, efficient rhythm.

Muzzle flashes painted the street in strobe—short, cruel daylight that washed and vanished. Rounds slammed into the cruiser like angry woodpeckers. The cruiser's hood dented like someone had punched it with a fist full of hammers. Metal pinged, a hollow ring that skittered across the asphalt. The windshield exploded inward in a spiderweb of glass; shards bit the air and winked like bad confetti in the headlight beams.

The engine coughed—a ragged, wet sound—as a round found its way under the hood and nicked something that made the whole car shudder. Paint peeled and blistered where hot brass kissed it. The first burst chewed a circle out of the rear door panel; the second opened a shower of sparks where it hit the chassis.

Inside the car, the troopers folded down. Shoulders hunched behind the dash, hands over heads, eyes trying to peek through shattered glass. Bodies bunched like men trying to be nothing at all.

Bullets chewed at metal and glass but didn't find meat. The good thing—if there was anything good about this night—was that the troopers were tucked behind the engine block. The mass of machinery served like an impenetrable shield. The coupling of steel and iron split the angle of the bullets enough that most of the rounds thudded into metal and bounced.

If Ironjack had been in a different position—leaning from the side, or on the cruiser's flank—the doors would have turned into sieves and the men inside would have been polite little pinpricks.

When the street lit up with each flash, I caught Ironjack's face for a second—eyes bright with the light, teeth set hard, the little torn grin of a man who liked the sound his work made. He was efficient. He was brutal. He was the kind of man who would empty a drum without blinking if it meant keeping his life's math in his favor.

The street belonged to Ironjack while his rifle sang. A mechanical, murderous voice—sharp bursts cracking in the night, brass spitting, that damn drum whirring as it fed his greed for blood. The staccato fire echoed off the houses like the devil hammering nails into the night.

Then silence.

The drum had run dry. I heard it click empty like a tired machine giving up a secret. The last bark died away and the night folded into a sudden, thick silence. A D-60 mag wasn't meant to be a quick swap. Ironjack had two bad options: throw the rifle and grab another, or climb in and drive. Both options needed crucial seconds he didn't have.

Because I wasn't about to give him a breather.

I was already crouched in the shadows of the porch, Glock steady in my hand, heartbeat slowing into that cold combat rhythm. I sprinted forward, my boots eating up the pavement. I fired as I ran—controlled pairs, chest high—forcing him to duck back behind the pickup. Ironjack had gone from hunter to cornered animal in a blink.

I closed the distance, ready to finish it.

Then the night ripped open again. Short, deliberate bursts from the far end of the street. Rounds chipped at the cruiser, glass fracturing further. Not the same fury as Ironjack, but enough to keep the troopers pinned, too scared to pop their heads up.

Another shooter.

My head numbed at the math of it; I had missed someone. That one detail was the difference between tidy and chaos.

The fifth man. The one I had written off as riding with Shade to the textile mill. My gut twisted—I had screwed that assumption. Shade couldn't have doubled back this fast, not with the clock we were running on. Which meant this bastard had been tucked away, waiting for exactly this.

That hesitation cost me.

Ironjack came off the truck like a freight train, launching into me with the full weight of a man who lived for fights like this. We slammed into the pavement, my Glock bouncing away into the dark.

Suddenly it was just me and him.

His hands were iron on my throat, squeezing, pushing my head back against the asphalt. His face was twisted, sweat and powder grime streaked across his cheekbones, teeth bared like an animal. His eyes—flat, cold, no hint of mercy. He wanted to crush the life out of me right there.

My training kicked in—elbows in, chin down. I rammed my palm into his wrist, breaking the lock enough to slide air. Then I jammed my forearm up under his jaw, levering against his windpipe, forcing space.

My other hand went low, hunting for my blade. Fingers found the hilt and ripped it free. I drove it upward, but he caught my wrist, muscles corded, veins standing out like cables. The edge bit into his palm, blood slicking both our hands. He grinned through it, that awful, broken grin of a man who didn't mind bleeding if he took you with him.

I twisted, slammed a knee into his ribs. Felt one crack. He grunted but didn't let go. His other hand fished at his belt—steel flashed in the dark. He had a knife of his own.

We were locked in a death knot, blades scraping, our breaths ragged, hot, too close. His knife kissed my ribs, carving a shallow line that burned like fire. I growled, shoved upward with everything I had, forehead smashing into his nose. Cartilage crunched. Blood sprayed warm across my face.

We wrestled to our feet, knives scraping, breaths ragged. He was a mountain of anger and I was the hammer. He got me with a short, savage uppercut that rocked my teeth together and left my mouth tasting like pennies. I tasted blood, felt stars, and used that blur like a mask. I planted my shoulder into his ribs and drove him against the truck. Metal screamed under our bodies.

He tried to headbutt me. I met it with my forehead, smashing his bloodied nose once again, making him see stars. He stumbled, and in that half-second I smashed my fist into his throat. My knuckles drove into him; he gagged, air cutting off. He clawed at my arms, fingers scrabbling for purchase. I yanked, twisted, and my boot found the side of his knee—hard. Something gritted and gave. He swore, a sound torn from the back of his guts.

He staggered back half a foot. That was all I needed.

I twisted my wrist hard, breaking his grip, and rammed my knife straight into his gut. He gasped, eyes wide, disbelief finally replacing that grin.

But he still fought.

His knife slashed my side, hot pain ripping through me, but I didn't stop. I drove my blade higher, found his chest, then his throat. Blood poured down his shirt, his strength collapsing, but his hands still clawed at me like he could drag me into hell with him.

I put my weight into the last drive, steel under his chin, forcing it up through flesh and into the base of his skull. His body jolted, twitched, then went limp. His face went slack, the hatred scrubbed away by whatever takes a man at the end.

Ironjack was dead weight. Heavy. Empty.

I shoved him off me, my chest heaving, lungs burning. My palms were slick with blood—mine and his. My side felt wet, throbbing where his blade had slashed me. The night stank of iron, gunpowder, and the copper tang of spilled life.

I wiped my cheek with the back of my hand and looked toward the far end of the block. There was no time to breathe. The other gunman was still out there.

CHAPTER 14

I figured the guy at the far end of the block had to be losing his damn mind. He kept stitching the air with little bursts—controlled, professional. He wasn't spraying, just reminding those troopers in the cruiser that they were mice in a trap and he was the cat with patience.

Problem was, his patience was fraying. I could feel it in the tempo of his bursts. He would be asking himself the same thing over and over—where the hell were his partners? Why wasn't Ironjack strutting back? Why wasn't anybody covering his flank?

The answer was simple. They were all face-down, broken, or bleeding inside this house of cards. He just hadn't gotten the memo yet.

Ironjack was dead on the pavement, two more were cooling inside the house, and the only one left alive to pull the trigger was him. He couldn't see me through the mess of Ironjack's truck and Denton's cruiser, so he probably thought his boys were still moving pieces on the board. Poor bastard didn't know the game had already ended.

I cracked open Ironjack's truck door, checked the cab, and peered inside. The backseat was a buffet of bad intentions—mag cases, a couple rifles, even a couple of shotguns tossed in like afterthoughts, and more ammo than a small unit would need for a weekend war. It was the kind of kit bag you only packed when you were planning to leave no survivors.

My hand closed around an M4 with a thirty-rounder already seated. I tapped the mag, racked the charging handle, and felt the bolt snap forward with that satisfying steel kiss. Hot. Ready. That solved one problem. Then I spotted the keys swinging from the ignition like a welcome-home sign. Perfect.

I slid in behind the wheel, smell of oil and cordite still fresh on the seats. My timing was about as lucky as it got: at the same second, the shooter at the far end finally got tired of waiting and started rolling toward the cruiser.

His headlights cut across the block as he rolled forward in his own truck, creeping, barrel still hanging out the driver's side like a shark's fin. He wanted a close kill. If he got beside that cruiser, the troopers were dead meat—engine block wouldn't save them from side shots through glass. That was his plan—hose down the cruiser, cops flailing, two more bodies on the scorecard.

Not on my watch.

I buckled up—because smashing headfirst into a windshield wasn't how I wanted to go—and stomped the gas. I was already thinking steel against steel. The truck roared, suspension screaming as it bolted forward. Tires bit blacktop, engine snarled like it was begging for blood.

The shooter was just a few yards from the cruiser when I caught him.

I dropped my shoulder, gripped the wheel, and slammed into his rig at an angle just behind the front wheel well. The guy was too confused by my actions to even think about swerving.

The world exploded in metal and sparks. Steel hit steel, momentum did the rest. His truck skidded sideways, then rolled like a toy kicked across asphalt, metal groaning, glass exploding, wheels spinning air. It came down hard, bouncing once before it settled upside down, hissing radiator steam into the night.

Silence again, except for the hiss and the distant chorus of sirens clawing closer.

I didn't need to check. Nobody crawled out of that in fighting shape. If the shooter wasn't dead, he was seeing stars at best. Either way, he wasn't pulling a trigger.

The troopers finally scrambled out of their cruiser, guns up, nerves raw, eyes wide like they had been dropped in the middle of Fallujah instead of their sleepy main street. Their eyes flicked from me to the wreck to the mess of trucks and rifles. I knew that look—everyone's the enemy until proven otherwise. I couldn't blame them. They didn't know who the hell was left standing, and from their point of view, I looked a lot like just another gunman.

I shoved the M4 onto the floorboard, got out slow, and kept Ironjack's truck between me and their muzzles. No sudden moves. Last thing I needed was a scared cop twitching a trigger and dropping me right there on the street.

"Easy, boys!" I called out, raising my hands. "I'm one of the good guys. Bad guys are all down. I'm unarmed. Coming out slow with hands high."

One of them barked back, voice sharp, nerves cutting through: "Step out! Don't do anything stupid!"

I stepped out, arms raised, blood drying tacky across my knuckles, face cut and bruised. I could see both their fingers tight on the triggers.

One of them yelled, "On the ground! Flat! Now!"

I shook my head and snapped back, voice cold: "How about you stop being stupid and secure that truck first? Gunman might still be breathing in there, and if he wakes up with his finger on the trigger, you're gonna have bigger problems than me."

That bought me a pause. They glanced at each other, then at the overturned rig belching smoke. The smarter of the two nodded, motioning the other to keep me covered. He went over, weapon ready, eyes flicking every shadow. He peered inside.

A second later he called back, "He's out cold! Banged up bad." Relief edged his tone.

That's when sirens started to stack up, overlapping. Four more cruisers came storming in, tires screeching, and red and blue slicing across the houses. Doors slammed. Uniforms spilled out, guns up.

And just like that, my quiet little fight turned into a circus. Residents crept out in robes and slippers, peeking from porches, eyes wide. Some had phones raised, already recording.

Small-town America had just gotten itself a front-row seat to a war they didn't know existed. And I was standing dead center of the stage, bloody, bruised, and unarmed, while a dozen cops tried to figure out whether I was hero, villain, or just another corpse waiting to happen. Some wondering how many more shadows this crew had waiting out there.

And nights like this? They kept giving surprises like a cheap deck of cards.

I was halfway through wiping blood off my knuckles when the night broke open again—not with gunfire, but with a distant boom. Sound rolled over the houses slow and heavy, then came back at us on the wind: a dull, throbbing explosion that made the panes rattle and set dog barks off down the block. A faint orange bloom climbed the horizon, a slow, hungry flare that lit the clouds like a bruise.

It didn't take much to guess what caused it. Shade had done his work. He burned the place down the way men burn bridges—no footprints left to follow, no fingerprints, no bodies that would talk when the cops came poking. He had taken to the business of removing loose ends the way a surgeon took out tumors—clean, efficient, cold.

The mill was gone from the map, unfolding into a small, perfect apocalypse—the flames painting the night orange for miles. I watched the light and felt a clean piece of the plan slide away.

But burning the mill didn't make the street any less Syndicate. The brown stains on the porch, the ripped curtains, the way the D-60 had hung under a rifle—they were signatures, a handwriting you couldn't scrub out with flame. A bomb ten miles away didn't change fingerprints on the scene or the names that lived on paper.

And it cost me.

I had wanted Shade in my sights. I had wanted to catch him before he tried to crawl away in that smoke. I wanted to put a round through the back of his head before he could blink. But I knew he was gone. There was no catching ghosts that decided to evaporate in a ring of fire.

As I watched the flames on the horizon, I knew Shade had heard the sirens and seen the strobes. He had realized the story: men down, trucks flipped, cops on the scene. He wasn't the kind to stick around to see what the law or I did next. He cut and run through the dark roads and disappeared.

The cops were busy cataloguing and questioning and circling the dead and the wounded. It would be days before the pattern clicked for them. Maybe weeks. Maybe never. Ironjack was dead. If any of the other three men woke up, they weren't the kind to sing to uniforms. That was a courtesy the Syndicate didn't afford its messengers.

I didn't care about the cops' timetable. I had something better than their subpoenas. Mark had given me a way in—names on a drive, a list that shone like a roadmap if you knew how to read it. Dana had lied to save one copy; she had tucked it away with a bravery that I respected and understood. She had put a map on my table and handed me a target.

The map sat heavy in my head like a promise. I had work to do.

Shade could scorch the mill and make his footprints vanish. He could cut roads and change plates. He could slip under every siren in the state. But he couldn't wipe Mark's whisper that cut through the gloom like a blade. Those were breadcrumbs, and I am terrible at leaving crumbs alone.

I would follow him anywhere. I would follow them until the road ended or they did. They would get what they deserved. That was a promise I didn't make with words—only with the cold, steady weight that settled in my gut.

CHAPTER 15

It all began three months ago, when my world cracked wide open and collapsed in on itself.

I was still wearing the dust of Iraq on my boots, Delta Sabre Squadron patch stitched tight on my shoulder, when the hammer dropped. We had just rolled back into Al Asad Airbase, sweat and cordite still clinging to my skin from a mission that cut the legs off a terrorist money pipeline. I was bone-tired, running on adrenaline and bitter coffee, expecting a hot chow, a cot, maybe a few hours of sleep before the next hit.

Instead I got a phone call that made my lungs forget how to work.

My brother, Captain Ryan Blaze, United States Marine Corps—killed in Afghanistan, Helmand Province. They said it quick, like ripping a Band-Aid. But the words didn't fit in my head. They felt foreign, wrong, like someone trying to jam the wrong caliber round into a chamber.

When you enlist, you carry that shadow somewhere deep in the back of your mind—that you might not make it home. You shove the thought into a corner, bury it under all the fire and patriotism that made you enlist in the first place.

Ryan carried that fire hotter than anyone I knew. He could have gone pro in football—hell, he had scouts watching him before 9/11. But those towers fell, and Ryan didn't just talk about serving, he did it. Because it was the right thing to do. Gave up crowds and bright lights, traded cleats for boots. Said America needed him more on the line than on the field. That was Ryan. And me? I was the kid brother who followed in his footprints, like I always had.

They told me it was friendly fire—that Ryan and three of his Marines got chewed up in a firefight, called in air support, and somehow, in that chaos, mislabeled coordinates and dropped hell on themselves. That's what the log claimed. That's what the Colonel's mouth said. Clear as day, they concluded. Paperwork that closed like a tomb.

But I knew my brother. Ryan wasn't the kind of man who panicked. He didn't fumble calls. He was steady the way mountains were steady—silent, unshowy, immovable when the weather got bad. The guy you wanted on the net when everything was burning down. And now they wanted me to swallow that he just... cracked? That explanation felt like ashes in my mouth.

But numbness has a way of drowning suspicion. I was too numb to push harder. Too busy trying to breathe through the weight crushing my chest. Too busy wondering how the hell I was going to tell Mom.

Questions screamed in my skull, but answers came back dull and dead. All I had were official lies typed on neat government paper.

I barely remember the flights before I got Ryan back on U.S. soil. Al-Asad to Bagram, Bagram to Ramstein, Ramstein to Dover. I do recall staring at walls, tarmac, anything but the flag-draped coffin. The words "Hellfire" and "targeted" mentioned in the report told me stuff I didn't want to know. I didn't need any euphemisms to know what they meant. I had seen burn patterns and craters before. I had seen what a missile could do to a man crouched on a ridge.

Pieces of my brother were in a box beside me. My best friend. My compass. My blood. I kept waiting to wake up, to feel the punch of his hand on my shoulder, hear him laugh and tell me to stop sulking. It never came.

When we touched down at Dover, the ramp dropped and I saw her.

Mom.

She stood out there on the tarmac, hair pulled back in a no-nonsense braid, upright and unshaken in that way only she could pull off. Her jaw was tight. She didn't break down. She didn't stumble. She just stood there, a pillar of strength, staring at that coffin like she could will her boy back out of it.

A cowgirl to the bone, skin lined by years of sun, hands calloused from rope and reins, and a backbone forged under Colorado sun. After Dad died, she had turned the Blaze place into a business and a cathedral all at once; the ranch ran because she willed it to.

She took the news the only way she knew how—quiet, chin up, eyes shimmering but steady. On the surface she was stone, but I saw it chewing her alive from the inside. And God help me, it was eating me too.

I walked down behind the honor guard carrying Ryan's coffin, boots heavy as lead. The flag rippled under the floodlights, the silence so heavy it pressed into my bones.

Mom's eyes found mine over the casket—blue like the Colorado sky on a winter morning, but clouded with something I had never seen before: a sorrow too deep to measure. She didn't break when I stepped close.

She reached for the coffin with fingers that didn't tremble much. She touched the flag at the head and I thought for a second she might say something fierce, something that could make a hole in the lies. Instead, she just reached out, touched my arm, and whispered, "Bring him home, Axel."

It was a command, and a plea, and more than I could answer in that moment. She didn't want him in Arlington; she wanted him back home at the ranch. Same ground Dad was in. Same sky over his head. I understood that.

It was only later I came to know the deeper cut—Mom already knew her own clock was running down. Pancreatic cancer. Fast, mean, no mercy. Four months, maybe. She had gotten the diagnosis just a week before. She had kept it from us, waiting for Ryan to come home from his deployment so she could break it to her boys under her roof. Ryan was supposed to come home a week later. Instead, he came home in a box.

That piece of truth burned hotter than anything else. She had been carrying her own fight while burying her firstborn.

I stayed. Compassionate leave at first, then I filed for temporary reassignment to Fort Carson, Colorado Springs. So I could stay close. Fort Carson put me in reach—close enough to help out at the ranch and sit with her when the light went thin. Time was something she didn't have spare, and I wasn't about to let her carry that grief alone.

Seven hundred head of cattle don't give a man much room to sit and brood. The ranch had a manager and plenty of hired hands to keep it running, but I wasn't there to oversee. I threw myself into the grind—saddling up to push cattle, hauling hay, patching busted water lines, pulling calves in the cold mud. Didn't matter what it was, as long as it kept my body moving. Pain in the muscles was easier than the kind that came when I stood still. Stillness was when the ghosts got loud.

At night, the noise quit and the dark took over. I sat on the back steps and thought of Ryan. The truth gnawed at me like a dog with a bone. I couldn't drop it. Mom saw it in the way I stared through walls like I was trying to punch a hole through whatever lie had swallowed him. She said nothing at first—just watched me.

One evening, we were out on the porch. The sun had dropped behind the mountains, leaving the sky that bruised purple you only see in Colorado. She was sipping coffee, her hands thinner now, but steady.

"Axel," she said, eyes cutting right through me, "you can patch fences and muck stalls till your hands bleed, but that won't fix what's eating you. You're wearing yourself out trying to hold me together."

I didn't answer. Just stared at the mountains, jaw clenched.

She leaned back, voice rough but steady. "Son, you can't rope the wind. My body's already making its peace. That's not something you can fix."

"Don't talk like that," I muttered.

"It's the truth," she cut in, soft but firm. "And I don't need my last months watching you tear yourself apart, trying to carry me and Ryan's ghost at the same time."

I looked at her, the porch light catching the lines in her face. Tough as rawhide, gentle as Sunday morning.

"You think I should just drop it? Let the official story stand?"

Her eyes narrowed, a spark under the weariness. "No. You'd never forgive yourself if you did. You're like your brother that way—stubborn as a mule when it comes to what's right. So am I—we're not all that different, the three of us. You go after the truth. Find out what happened to Ryan. Dig till your hands bleed. That's the work God left you."

I looked at her, not sure how to respond.

"Don't waste your fire worrying about me. I need the truth as much as you do. And I don't have the time to wait for it. Neither of us will sleep right till we find out what really happened to your brother. So quit fretting over me and go do it."

She always had a way of calling me out without raising her voice.

I let out a slow breath, nodded once. She had handed me marching orders, same as Ryan used to. And I knew damn well I would follow.

She reached out and rested her hand on mine. It was warm, steady. The sun dropped, and shadows swallowed her face. But her grip stayed firm. And I knew she meant every word.

Ryan was already gone. Mom was slipping. The world had handed me nothing but lies. The only thing left for me was the truth—and I would burn the earth down to get it.

CHAPTER 16

The first real clue that something rotten was hiding under the neat little story came at the funeral. I had been braced for grief—had been living in it like a second skin for many days—but I hadn't been ready for the smell of conspiracy to show up with the bugle and the flag. I got a glimpse of the sordid truth from a Marine who had stood next to my brother in countless firefights.

We lowered Ryan into the ground behind the house, where the cottonwoods made that soft, constant rustle in the wind, like somebody turning pages. The sky was hard and flat, the kind of blue that hurts when you are fighting to keep your emotions under control.

We carried the coffin, boots crunching on dry gravel, the ranch soil underfoot, the mountains standing watch like they had for generations. I had carried weight before, but nothing like this. My brother's coffin cut deeper than any ruck. Felt like I was carrying a piece of myself into the ground.

My Delta boys stood together—black silhouettes against the light—faces pinched but steady. Ryan's Marines filled the other side, dress blues stark and cruel in the country air. They stood tall, faces locked down, but their eyes told the story. Brotherhood hung thick enough to choke on; it was there in the way the men carried themselves and in the quiet that dropped like a blanket once the coffin went down.

Memories floated up in little, sharp ways—Ryan's laugh echoing on summer porches, the image of him throwing that old football, sun in his hair, him showing me how to square a rifle stock in the dark. Those pieces of him kept floating to the surface like wreckage—small, unavoidable things that made the absence feel stupid and mean.

The honor guard moved like a machine—precise, deliberate. Three volleys cracked out and hung in the valley, then the bugler cut Taps into the cold air. The flag—bright, perfect, too clean—lay on that wood like something stolen from daylight.

The Marine in charge of the detail—shirt ironed, rank sharp—stepped forward with the folded flag. He did it by the book: two hands, palms up, the tight triangle held like it was the last good thing on earth. He said the words—"On behalf of the President of the United States..."—and I felt every syllable like a verdict. He held the flag up with two hands and handed it to Mom.

She accepted the flag without flinching, her hands closing on the triangle. Her thumb moved once over the fabric like she was tracing a memory. Her eyes flicked to me, and there was a small, private fracture in them that I understood without words.

After the service, when the crowd thinned and the quiet settled in, a Marine in his dress blues came over. Staff Sergeant Logan Davis. Square jaw, that same tired look you see on guys who have been in too many fights. He looked like a man carrying his own grief in his ribs.

Logan and I weren't strangers. Our paths had crossed in Yemen—we had pushed together through an overrun embassy compound to get civilians out, watching each other's six until the job was done. We still used ranks, but there was a rough, easy thread between us that made the formalities feel thin.

"Captain Blaze... Axel," he said, voice low. "I'm sorry, man. For your mom, for you. Goddamn it." He reached out and clapped my shoulder, soldier to soldier.

"Thanks, Logan." I kept my face flat. Talking didn't help the weight. Carrying did. Delta had taught me that: move, don't marinate.

He lingered, eyes flicking toward the ridge where we had buried him. "Listen—the Captain... he was loved, respected. Everyone in the company... it's like losing family." He paused, chewing the words. "But I need to tell you something straight. I don't buy their story. Not for one second. It's bullshit."

I stiffened, my gut tightening. "You sure about that? 'Cause I'll be honest—my own gut's been chewing on it. None of it adds up. But with the official statement, the call logs... I don't know what to make of it. First thing I planned after this funeral was to listen to the audio files, line them up against the logs."

Logan shook his head. "That's the thing. There are no audio files. I had the same idea. Thought I'd line up the recordings against the call log, see if something didn't fit. Pulled strings, tried to get them. But apparently, there was a 'technical fault'. The files never got saved."

It hit me like cold water. "There were no audio files?" The world felt off-kilter, like some invisible scaffold had been yanked away.

"No. Nothing." He met my eyes hard. "The radio net's clean on paper, but nothing to back it up. That's not an accident. When I pushed, I was kind of told to drop it. They told me it was an administrative issue and the officers can deal with it."

This smelled like a cover up, not a doubt about that. You can hide paperwork, but you don't make the human sounds go away that easy. If someone wanted to cover their tracks—well, they would have to have enough influence to make it all vanish.

"And there's this. For a couple months before...we'd been picking up whispers. Rogue soldiers. Guys cutting deals with the Taliban, moving heroin back through routes that leave fingerprints in places you'd least expect. If there was one thing the Captain couldn't stand, it was these bad apples. He was investigating. Kept asking questions."

My blood went cold in a way grief hadn't yet touched. "You think they killed him for that?"

Logan's face was hard as flint. "That's what I think. Not just me—guys in our company are burning to get names. They're scraping sources, pulling threads. They think it's organized. People with reach. That's why they shut me down when I asked where the audio went."

We parted with the sort of look that didn't need words—an agreement inked in shared loss and fury. I watched him walk back toward his men, boots steady in the gravel.

I stood there a long time after Logan left, feeling the anger bloom hot and ugly under the grief. Logan's words sat in my gut like live coal. I couldn't spit it out, couldn't swallow it down. I had gotten my first whiff of the truth. Didn't matter how faint the trail was—I would dig until my nails bled.

But Fort Carson kept me tethered. Stateside, close to Mom, close to the ranch, but too far from the desert where the pieces lay buried. I felt a little impaired. Still, I had brothers who weren't about to let me carry it alone. Ninja Man, Raptor, Hawkeye, Echo. They kept digging out there. We had bled in the same dust. Men like that didn't just vanish from your corner.

I saw it in their faces as we stood outside the church after the funeral, black suits traded for the uniforms we would always wear in our bones. They wanted in. Pitch in any way they could so I could get my justice. They didn't have to say a word for me to know they were hurting too.

Deep down we all knew—this might have been the end of us as a unit. No one said it. No one had to. Their eyes said more than words could, but words came anyway.

Ninja Man broke the silence first, leaning against the stone wall, lean and wiry, eyes bright with that spark of mischief he never lost, even under fire.

"You sure you don't want me to stay behind and help run the ranch? Figure I could wrangle cows. Easier to deal with than Taliban, might be easier to herd."

I let the corner of my mouth twitch. "Hell, you wouldn't last a day. Cows don't take smart-ass backtalk."

Hawkeye chuckled, low and dry. "He's right, Ninja. You'd have the whole herd on strike before sundown."

Raptor—big man, quiet strength, hands like steel traps—shook his head. "Don't encourage him. We barely keep him in line overseas."

Ninja raised his chin, proud. "I bring the morale."

"Yeah," Echo quipped. "About as much morale as a toothache."

The banter was thin armor, but it held us together. For a few seconds, it almost felt like we were back on a rooftop in Iraq, waiting for exfil, the world boiling below us but still ours to fight.

Then the joking bled out, and we drew in close, shoulder to shoulder. Hands clasped, forearms locked tight, heads almost touching. A knot of men bound by more than blood. Men who would kill and die for each other.

"Any time. Any place. Just say the word."

That was it. No speeches, no drawn-out goodbyes. Just a promise, carved in stone between us.

I watched them walk away, boots heavy on the pavement. One by one, shadows peeling off into the world. Then it was just me. The ranch. Mom. Ryan's grave. And a truth buried so deep it would take blood, fire, and months of digging to exhume it.

I was ready for the hunt.

CHAPTER 17

The first real lesson I learned about digging into a conspiracy like this—it wasn't a sprint, it was a grind. Nothing came fast. Nothing came clean. Took me three months of pulling threads, following shadows, before I even started to see the faint outlines of the men who had buried Ryan and buried the truth with him.

Echo gave me the first crack in the wall.

Echo wasn't your average keyboard warrior. He was one of Delta's CNOS boys—Computer Network Operations Squadron. Tier-1 cyber muscle. One of JSOC's Digital Devils. If somebody so much as sneezed on a classified server, Echo could tell you what time it happened and what they had for breakfast that morning. I had seen him work magic before, pulling coordinates out of shredded metadata to put a drone on target. So if someone had messed with the strike records, he was the guy to find it.

He called me late one night. I picked up and heard his flat, controlled voice, the same one he used when he was talking drones onto a target, calling me by my handle—Cowboy.

"Cowboy. You were right. Those audio files? They didn't vanish. They were erased."

I went cold. "Talk to me."

"They weren't lost. They were replaced. Somebody swapped the original recordings with clean logistics chatter—fuel runs, supply requests. Same timestamps, same length. They even buried a fake error log to make it look like a technical glitch.

I almost missed it. Took hours of deep dive to spot the seams. This was sabotage, and it was fast—had to be within the first sixty minutes of the strike."

I gripped the phone so hard it creaked. "Can you find who did it?"

"Strong suspicion it was Technical Sergeant James Sloane. USAF intel tech. He was in the control room right after the strike. Mark Kincaid, the JTAC, was ordered out. He had to log off the net. Sloane was the guy still in the chair when the edits went down. I'm pretty sure it was him."

He paused.

"I hear a 'but' coming," I said.

"You're right. The thing is, Sloane's dead. Stateside. Got leave right after the strike. Next day he's killed in a car accident back home." Echo's tone was flat, but I knew the weight behind it. "You tell me if that smells like coincidence."

It didn't. It smelled like bleach poured over blood.

I stared at the wall, jaw tight. "And Kincaid?"

"He's not it. I dug deep. After the strike, he unraveled. Breakdown, discharge, locked into counseling. A man barely holding his shit together. Too messed up to orchestrate something like this. And that's probably why he's still alive. He's the patsy—no threat to the real players. If it were him, he'd be gone too."

I thought about the letter Kincaid had sent me—handwriting shaky, words bleeding with regret. He had included a transcript of the call, almost begging me to see he wasn't lying. He wasn't pleading innocence—he was drowning in guilt. But not the guilt of betrayal. The guilt of being in the wrong place, wrong time, with no way to stop it. I had earlier told Echo about it.

“He wasn’t pretending,” I said quietly.

“No,” Echo agreed. “He wasn’t. He’s no actor. But don’t mistake that for uselessness. He might be the only living witness. They picked him because he was convenient. Not because he was guilty.”

Two days later, I sat across from Mark Kincaid in a quiet room inside a military hospital. The man looked like he hadn’t slept in weeks. Shoulders caved in, eyes sunken, hands that wouldn’t stay still. He didn’t need to say a word—his body was screaming.

“Captain Blaze,” he started, his voice hoarse, “I don’t know how to live with this.”

“You don’t have to convince me,” I told him. “I’ve seen your letter.”

He swallowed hard, rubbed his hands over his knees. “Sir… audio files don’t just disappear from secure servers. It doesn’t happen. Somebody made them disappear. And whoever can do that… they’re not some tech sergeant pulling extra duty. This is higher.”

His eyes darted like he expected someone to kick in the door.

“Somebody with weight?” I asked.

He nodded quickly, like he was scared to even confirm it out loud. “Has to be a high-ranking officer. Someone who can bury evidence before it ever sees daylight. You don’t touch files like that without brass cover.”

He leaned in, dropped his voice. “You know what happened to Sloane. They’ll go to any lengths. That accident? It wasn’t an accident. He was the guy at the console after I was forced out. If they’ll do that to him, they’ll do it to me. To anyone who talks.”

“Then why tell me?” I asked.

"Because your brother was a soldier. A good soldier. He deserves the truth," he said without hesitation. "Sloane... he wasn't stupid. If he scrubbed it, he'd have kept a copy for insurance. A man like him wouldn't go blind into the dark. But now... he's gone. And whatever he kept went with him."

He sat back, rubbing his temples. "I wish I had proof. I wish I could hand you something. All I've got is what my gut tells me, and my gut says I was played. They set me up to take the fall."

I studied him. He looked terrified, but there was no lie in his eyes. Just a man living with the ghosts of what he had been told to do.

"You're not wrong," I said. "They're covering tracks. And I'm going to follow them. Doesn't matter how far up the ladder I have to climb."

He gave me a sad smile. "Then watch your back, Captain. They already killed one of their own. They'll kill again."

I walked out of that office with my blood running colder than the Colorado wind. If Kincaid was right—and everything in me said he was—then Ryan hadn't just died because of a bad call. He had died because somebody wanted him silenced.

Meanwhile, Raptor and the boys had been digging around in Afghanistan while pulling duty there. Our old interpreter heard talk in the villages. Americans killing their own. Afghan warlords tied up with crooked U.S. soldiers, smuggling heroin back home through military channels. Word was already on the street in Baltimore and D.C.—new supply, fresh fingerprints.

I pushed that angle. I pulled favors and made calls to a couple of DEA agents I trusted. They had heard whispers too. Afghan heroin, fresh channels, distribution on the East Coast. Baltimore was the hub. But no names, no faces. Just shadows.

Every lead was smoke. So it was just me, circling the same tracks, getting nowhere. Truth didn't come easy. Truth never did.

Three months. That's how long it took. Three months of piecing whispers together.

Then came the call from Dana Kincaid—Mark's wife. Her voice was wrecked, but she got the words out: Mark was dead. He had left something for me—a flash drive. Said I would know what to do with it.

For the first time in months, I felt the weight shift. Finally, something real.

I drove out to her place, thinking I was finally going to pull a thread that would unravel the whole rotten mess. I thought I was just going to pick up proof. What I walked into was fire—Deke's locals and the Black Dagger Syndicate waiting with teeth out.

That was the day the shadows turned solid. That was the day the hunt truly began.

CHAPTER 18

The place was crawling with uniforms by the time things settled. State troopers, county deputies, local cops trying to act like they weren't caught flat-footed—all tripping over each other with radios barking and flashers throwing red and blue across the street. Neighbors stood in clusters on their porches, whispering about how a quiet town had turned into a war zone in one night.

Dana and I laid it out clean. No exaggerations, no side routes—just what had happened. Took the cops all of ten minutes to piece it together. They had a crooked cop in cuffs, a kidnapping on the books, a house bugged, a murder that had been written off as an accident, and me dropping a phone in their lap with the video to prove it. Not to mention a major crime syndicate rolling heavy into their backyard.

Two troopers I had pulled out of a kill zone vouched for me, swore I had saved their lives. That carried more weight than any report.

Denton looked small in his own handcuffs. The tough-guy act was gone. He had thought he was untouchable, but now his own people wouldn't meet his eyes. I didn't feel a lot of love in the looks he shot me, but that was probably because his face was already swollen from where I had introduced it to the hard ground of Dana's back porch.

The police chief, though—he was drowning in his own embarrassment. Mark's death had been filed as an accident under his watch, neat and tidy. Now it was a full-blown homicide, tied to organized crime, and one of his own men was in on it. He tried to keep his chin high, but I could see it gnawing through him.

I almost felt bad for him. He wasn't like Denton—he wasn't rotten. Just a man who had been duped, played for a fool by someone he trusted. He carried the weight heavy, shoulders slumped, eyes avoiding mine when I handed him Deke's phone with the video of Mark's killing. Evidence doesn't lie, even when a few rotten cops do.

"Everything you need is on there," I told him. My voice had no bend in it.

He just nodded, jaw tight.

What I didn't hand over was the flash drive Dana had slipped me earlier. That was mine. I knew damn well what would happen if it went into evidence—it would vanish. Either it would rot in some evidence locker, forgotten, or more likely, disappear into the hands of the Syndicate before the ink dried on the paperwork. That drive carried a message from Mark. His voice. His words. It wasn't for the cops, wasn't for the courts. It was for me.

When the dust cleared, the troopers made the call to put Dana and Jesse into protective custody. No arguing. They had seen enough to know the mother and kid had targets on their backs. They understood what we all knew—the Syndicate wasn't finished. They would find another angle. A safe house was the only play. That was a big load off my chest—I no longer had to worry about their safety; I could focus on what I needed to do.

She came over before they loaded her into the cruiser. Her voice was steady, though her eyes showed the strain. "Thank you, Captain Blaze. For everything."

"Drop the Captain," I said. "Just Axel."

She nodded. "Alright. Axel."

She hugged me, quick and strong. Jesse clung to her side, staring at me with wide eyes like he didn't know whether I was real or just some force that had blown through their lives.

I leaned back, met her eyes. "Thank you, Dana. For trusting me. For risking everything to get that drive into my hands. I won't let Mark's bravery go to waste. The men who wrecked his career, his life—I'll make them pay. That's a promise. And you won't need more than a day or two in custody. I'll end this all very soon."

Her jaw tightened, but she nodded once. "I believe you, Axel. Good luck."

I didn't tell her luck wasn't my game. I played in blood and steel.

The troopers ushered them into the cruiser and rolled off. I stood there until the taillights vanished, the night folding quiet again. The stink of cordite still clung to the air. Engines clicked as they cooled. Porch lights flicked off one by one until it was just me, the truck, and the dark.

By the time I got back to my truck, it was past midnight. I climbed in and fired her up. Diesel grumble rolling steady under the hood, headlights cutting a pale tunnel through the night.

Route 9 ran due south. New York City lay a hundred miles south. I drove fifty miles, the road empty and the night pressing close. No music, no radio chatter. Just the road and the ghosts riding shotgun. Farms rolled by, then small towns asleep under sodium lamps.

By the time I spotted the neon vacancy sign buzzing weakly against the dark, I knew I had been looking for it all along. A place off the grid, out in the middle of nowhere.

The motel sat squat and tired, a single row of doors, paint peeling, buzzing light over the office. The kind of place truckers and drifters used when they didn't care what the sheets looked like.

I paid cash. The clerk was half-asleep, shuffling out from a back room in a faded T-shirt, hair sticking up, eyes squinting against the fluorescent glare. He didn't care who I was, didn't ask. Just took the bills, slid a key across the counter, and vanished again like he couldn't wake up enough to care.

The room smelled of bleach and old carpet. Luxury sure wasn't the defining feature of that joint. Didn't matter. I wasn't there on vacation.

I locked the door, dropped my bag, and pulled the laptop. Sat on the edge of the bed and slid the flash drive into the port.

Mark's voice was waiting for me.

CHAPTER 19

I opened the folder inside the flash drive. Two files sat there—one video, one audio. My gut tightened the second I saw them. I already knew what they were.

I moved the cursor and clicked on the video.

Mark Kincaid's face filled the screen. Not the broken shell I had seen in the psych ward a month ago, looking like a ghost of himself—eyes sunken, skin pale, nerves shot to hell. Now he looked... different. Still worn down, but steadier, almost hopeful, like a man who had clawed his way out of the dark and was holding on to something solid.

"Captain Axel Blaze," he said, looking straight into the camera, his voice steadier than I had ever heard it.

My jaw locked. He had made this for me.

"You remember what I told you at the hospital—that the audio files were erased. Deliberately erased. And I said a guy like Sloane would never wipe something clean without tucking away his own insurance policy. Well, I thought with Sloane gone, that proof was gone too."

My pulse kicked. I leaned in. On the screen, Mark's eyes sparked with something close to triumph.

"It wasn't lost. He kept it. He was paranoid, more than any of us knew. Paranoid about the kind of ruthless men he was dealing with. He gave a packet to a friend with instructions: if anything happened to him, send it to me. For whatever reason, it only showed up yesterday. Maybe the guy hesitated, maybe the post was too damn slow. But I got it."

Mark leaned forward, voice shaking with a raw kind of excitement. "Inside was the original audio file of the call for air support. I copied it onto this drive. You can listen for yourself and decide if it's Captain Ryan Blaze's voice. I've never heard him speak, so can't say for sure. But in a letter, Sloane wrote plain as day—the voice wasn't Captain Ryan Blaze. That's why the files were wiped."

I clenched my jaw, cold spreading in my chest as I leaned in, every muscle tight.

Mark's expression sobered. His hands trembled once before he clasped them together on the desk in front of him.

"According to the letter, the voice belonged to Sergeant First Class Marcus Stahl. Stahl and his buddy—Corporal Darius Wade. Those two killed the Marines. They murdered them while Ryan and three of his men were at an abandoned outpost with an Afghan source. That source was giving them intel on the smuggling op between a warlord and Stahl's crew. Stahl and Wade rolled up in a U.S. Army vehicle, wearing uniforms. Friendlies on the outside, murderers on the inside."

I could almost see it—the approach, the false smiles.

"They threw grenades into the enclosed room, then cut any survivors down with automatic fire. No warning. Killed Ryan, the three Marines, and the Afghan source. Everyone was already dead before the drone strike," Mark said, his voice low now.

My hands tightened into fists so hard my nails bit into my palms.

"Stahl called in the strike to cover it up. He needed the bodies burned. Otherwise, any investigator would've seen the frag shrapnel, the 5.56 rounds, and known that Americans pulled the trigger. And that trail could've led right back to him. So they burned it all with one call. Pretended it was Ryan who cracked under pressure."

I felt it then—that cold fury that starts in the gut and spreads like ice through the veins. My brother hadn't died because of bad luck, or enemy contact, or some tragic fog-of-war screwup. He had been executed. Executed by his own men.

Mark swallowed, gaze locked on the lens. "And the man who pulled the strings—the one who told Sloane to wipe the files—was Colonel Victor Harlan. Deputy Commander for Air Ops, Bagram. He had oversight on drone strikes, close air support, JTAC activity. Sloane said it was Harlan who must've come up with the plan. Said the panic call from Stahl's crew must've gone straight to Harlan. Harlan was the one who suggested the drone strike. He made sure it covered their tracks."

The name hit me like a hammer. Harlan. I remembered standing across from him at Bagram, his hand heavy on my shoulder as he fed me that line about Ryan freezing up, about him making a bad call under pressure. I remembered the way his eyes had slid off mine, just a little too quick, just a little too careful. He hadn't just lied—he had orchestrated the whole damn cover-up.

Mark swallowed, glanced down, then back at the camera. "Colonel Harlan called me a few times in the last couple months. Always real kind, real sympathetic. But each time, he asked if I'd learned anything more about that day. I didn't get it then. I get it now. He was checking—making sure his tracks were still covered. Making sure I hadn't pieced it together."

Mark paused, before continuing: "The fourth name in this gruesome affair is Staff Sergeant Kyle Firth. He's a Quartermaster. Handled logistics—the falsified manifests and the routing that made the whole thing run. He was the cog that made the machine work."

Mark leaned back, his expression grim. "I'll call you tomorrow, Captain. I'll explain everything I've pieced together. I'm making this video tonight just in case. Just in case something happens. You never know."

And the screen went black.

Silence.

I sat there, staring at my own reflection in the dark screen. My chest burned. My hands shook with the urge to put a bullet through the first wall I saw.

Tomorrow. That's what Mark said. But tomorrow never came. He was dead before morning.

I leaned back, staring at the ceiling, the pieces falling into place. Mark made this video the same night he was killed. My mind stitched it together in brutal clarity. Harlan had eyes on him. Maybe bugs in his house, maybe someone tailing him. The second Mark spoke those words into a camera, his fate was sealed. Harlan couldn't risk the truth reaching me.

Dana's voice echoed in my head. She told me Mark had carried the flash drive and Sloane's letter with him when he left that night. He had already given her two copies, just in case. And then he never came home.

Cops said accident. Dana knew better. She knew it was murder.

That's why she never told the cops about the drives. Kept them hidden. Called me a week later instead. Took the risk. She was gambling everything that I would take the shot at justice when the time came.

And now I had the truth. The names of the killers. The architect of the lie. The truth was ugly, but it was mine now.

I got further confirmation when I clicked the audio file next. The file opened with radio hiss. It started in the middle of comms, the kind of heat you get when everyone's busy and nothing can be wasted.

"—JTAC this is Hammer Two, authentication Alpha-Niner-Zero."

Mark's voice answered, calm and clipped, the cadence of a man who had done it a thousand times. "Hammer Two, this is Kincaid. Authentication Echo-Seven-Three confirmed. Say again your unit and clearance."

There was a breath, a rustle. A voice came back, low and steady, giving a unit call sign and a response code. A string of grid numbers followed—sixes and eights and nines that landed like a thrown knife on a map.

Kincaid read it back, slow, professional: "Grid confirmed. Weapons release approved. Clearance acknowledged."

My mouth went dry. I knew Mark's voice—I had just heard it in his video. Mark had confirmed the caller's credentials. That part was real, verifiable, honest. This was the actual call from that day.

But the other voice—calling in the coordinates, the man who had asked for the strike—that wasn't

Ryan. This voice was clipped, clinical. It had a hardness that made my teeth ache.

I listened to the grid numbers again, as if hearing them twice would change the shape of what I knew. It didn't. The strike call was signed off clean. The missile was on the way.

Silence spilled out after the last click, louder than the radio had been. I sat with the laptop breathing in the motel room, the blue light on the screen throwing my face into a hard half-shadow.

They had lied. They had dressed murder as a request for fire. They had made the kill look like a necessary, authorized op.

I stared down at the laptop again, rage boiling under my skin, but there was grief there too, heavy and raw. Ryan's death hadn't been about nerves or failure—it was betrayal. Cold, calculated betrayal. And Mark had died trying to drag that truth out into the light. All of it tied together by liars in uniform and cowards hiding behind rank.

They thought they buried it. Thought they could kill the story along with Mark.

They were dead wrong.

I shut the laptop, palms flat on the table, and let the promise settle in the dark: they would look me in the eye before I took them down. They would know who was coming.

CHAPTER 20

The room was silent except for the faint hum of the motel fridge. The laptop screen had gone black, leaving me staring at my own reflection, jaw set, eyes that didn't blink.

My phone buzzed on the desk, vibrating against the wood. I didn't flinch—I had been waiting for that call.

Echo.

I had set him on two trails. First was Shade—when Ironjack and his crew showed up at Dana's place without him, I knew I wasn't laying hands on him that night. Shade wasn't the kind to stick around once he saw his men broken at the mill and Jesse gone. He would vanish, go to ground. So I had pulled his number off Denton's phone and sent it to Echo, told him to track it, see where Shade ran.

The second task was heavier. The three names Dana had given me—Marcus Stahl, Darius Wade, Kyle Firth. I had sent those to Echo too, told him to dig. I wanted their careers, their stations, every detail that would tell me where they had been when Ryan was killed.

I thumbed the screen. "Talk to me, Echo."

His voice came through steady, low, with that dry edge he always carried. "Cowboy, you aren't gonna like this first part. Shade pulled a ghost on us."

My jaw tightened. "Go on."

"I ran his handset as soon as you fed me the number. I dumped the IMSI and IMEI identifiers, then threw a trace on it. Initial pings had him southbound on Route 9—looked like he was pushing toward New York. But then—midway—signal went dead. No tower handshake, no GPS drift. That means only one thing—he powered down and physically yanked the SIM. Old-school tradecraft."

I swore under my breath, leaning back in the chair. Dead end. "So we lost him."

Echo chuckled, that easy laugh of his cutting through the static. "Brother, you wound me. You really think I'd call just to hand you a goose egg?"

Despite the mood, a corner of my mouth twitched. "You got something?"

"Damn right I do. I geofenced the last active ping. See, when Shade killed his line, he was in the middle of nowhere. Woods, no traffic, no reason to stop unless he was swapping toys. I figured he'd light up a burner. So I parked myself on that sector's spectrum. Watched for any fresh IMEIs coming online. Sure enough, two minutes later, a new device ID lit up. Different IMEI, fresh SIM. Burner."

"You're saying you caught his burner?"

"Better. I didn't just catch it—I cracked it. Phone spun up, tried to handshake through a VoIP app. I backdoored the SIP protocol and ghost-patched into the live call. Took me a couple minutes to bypass the encryption, so I missed the open. But I caught the tail end of live audio, clean copy."

I straightened in my chair, pulse hammering. "What'd he say?"

Echo's tone flattened, businesslike now. "Shade was talking to a guy who goes by Reaper. Told him, quote: 'I blew the place, left no evidence. Had to skip town—cops and cruisers everywhere. Tried ringing Ironjack, but no answer. Dumped my phone. Can't be traced.' Then the call dropped."

Silence stretched for a beat, my mind racing through every angle.

Echo came back on, softer, almost grinning through the comms. "Shade thinks he's disappeared, killing handsets like that. He doesn't know he's got me riding shotgun on his ass. I've got persistent surveillance on the burner. Not just him, I've cast the net on this Reaper dude as well. They can't get rid of me unless they ditch their phones again."

I leaned back on the creaky motel chair. "Damn good work."

He brushed it off, quick. "Save the pats on the back, Cowboy. There's more you need to hear."

I straightened. "Hit me."

"Reaper," he said. "That's Stahl. Marcus Stahl. Profile: career NCO, combat-hardened. On paper, he should've been booted out last year—dishonorable discharge proceedings, language like *excessive violence* and *corruption* all over it. Somebody pulled the plug on it before it went anywhere. Paperwork vanished or stalled. Disappeared into the ether."

Stahl was the one who called for the air strike pretending to be Ryan. Echo just confirmed I was on the right track. I stayed quiet, letting Echo keep rolling.

"Second guy is Corporal Darius Wade. Callsign Shade. Demolitions and cleanup. Wired to blow anything with a fuse or circuit. His M.O. is to leave no trace. Explosives, burn patterns, that kind of cleanup."

I stayed quiet and let Echo roll.

"Third guy—Staff Sergeant Kyle Firth. Callsign's Torque. Quartermaster. His racket was shipping manifests. Moving gear around, cooking numbers, skimming off the top. He was under the scanner for rigging manifests, padding shipments, but somehow he walked. Never stuck. More pencil-pusher than grunt, but he's the nerve center of the logistics side. He makes the shipments disappear on paper."

I muttered, "Sounds like a real patriot."

"Yeah. Real flag-waver."

I could see them in my head already—Stahl, the predator hiding behind a soldier's patch; Shade the arsonist; and Torque the accountant who launders the whole mess. They weren't soldiers. They were rot.

"All three were based in Helmand province," Echo went on, voice flattening. "Same AO as Ryan's company. Same time window."

Silence sat heavy for a second. Helmand. The name tasted like iron.

Echo's voice went quiet, serious. "Were they involved in Ryan's hit?"

"Yeah." I didn't mince it. I told him everything Mark laid out—grenades, uniforms, American vehicles, the ambush, the drone called in to cover the crime. "Stahl called in the drone strike to bury it. Mark found the truth, and they murdered him for it."

Echo's voice wasn't calm anymore. It was edged steel. "Bastards." He let it hang, the quiet heavy on the line. "You're not carrying this alone, Cowboy. Anything you need—gear, data, eyes—I'm here. You just say the word. Ryan wasn't just your big brother. He was family."

I didn't answer right away. My chest burned, my fists tight enough to pop veins. I didn't have to say out loud what I was thinking—that I would never forget what Echo just offered.

"I know." I kept my voice flat. I didn't give him the theater of gratitude. But I said, "Thanks, Echo. Good work."

He didn't let me off easy. "Don't thank me. Use me." Then softer, like I had expected. "Look, Axel—Ryan wasn't just your brother. He was a Marine. He had a squad. We all feel it. If you want blood, say the word. Anything you need—SIGINT push, persistent geolocation, blind-side a tower, I'll get you the packet."

I heard the offer for what it was: full-spectrum CNOS support. That stung in the best way. I didn't say it out loud, but I registered it—my brothers weren't walking away. They were with me, even if I had to carry this alone.

"I've got my sights on the three," I told him. "But before I move, I need confirmation on one thing."

"Name it."

"Colonel Victor Harlan. Dig into him. I've just learnt he was the one pulling strings. Give me the lowdown on him."

I could hear keys rattling in the background already, Echo not wasting a second. "Copy that. I'll drop a deep pull on Harlan. Fifteen minutes, I'll be back with a sitrep."

"Roger. Cowboy out."

The line went dead. The motel room stayed quiet, the hum of the fridge the only sound. I stepped out of the room and into the night. Air was cool, clean, nothing like the rot inside my head. I let it hit me, strip everything down. Blank slate—

that's how I always got before a mission. No anger. No grief. Just the target, the path, the outcome.

Fifteen minutes slid by fast. My phone buzzed again. Echo was back.

"Cowboy, you were right to flag Harlan. He's not just tangled, there's a family tie in the mix. Shade—Darius Wade—is Harlan's nephew. Looks like Harlan's the de-facto godfather for these three. Keeps them useful and quiet."

"That family link's going to come handy," I replied.

I braced against the railing, let Echo's words roll in.

"Harlan was Deputy Commander for Air Ops at Bagram. Had control over drone strikes, CAS tasking, JTACs—the whole pipeline. Two months after Ryan's death, he rotates Stateside. Officially, it's a golden ticket. Director of Ops, J3 slot at Joint Base Andrews. Running planning for Air Combat Command. Looks squeaky clean on paper."

I stared into the dark, jaw tight. "Yeah. Mark and Sloane had it pegged. Harlan was the one who green-lit the cover job. Drone strike wasn't coincidence. It was cleanup."

The line went quiet. No typing, no background hum of servers, just Echo breathing. And I could feel it, that burn of fury he never let bleed into his tone.

When he spoke again, his voice was lower. "Tell me what you want me to do."

I dragged in air, slow, steady. "Not tonight. I'll rack out, come at it clean in the morning."

"Copy that. Whatever you need, just call it."

"Appreciate it, pal," I replied.

CHAPTER 21

After the call with Echo, the motel room was nothing but a humming fridge and the faint hiss of the highway. The night was cold and my head was clean—mission clean. I folded everything down tight, the way you do before you step out the door on a raid: feelings tucked away, only the job left to breathe.

Three months of punching air, chasing ghosts, and finally the fog had broken. I had names. I had a direction. That itch under my skin went from pained to hungry. I wanted blood.

They had executed the perfect crime on paper. Bodies buried, evidence burned, paperwork tidy enough to keep a jury asleep. Sloane was gone. Mark was gone. No witnesses left to point and say, "There."

The men who pulled the trigger had covered their tracks so clean the law would choke on them. The comms scrub, the bogus error logs, the staged accident. They had stacked the deck so a jury would shrug and call it bad luck.

I had watched Mark's face on that screen and heard the truth. But truth, legal truth, was a different animal. Mark's video proved a story to me, but in a court a prosecutor needs a chain you can drag across a table. The defense lawyers would paint Mark as a damaged man, the files as tampered, and the truth would be a rumor that dies in legalese. I knew the system's rules. I also knew their loopholes.

So the question sat heavy and simple: when the law fails, who cleans house?

The courthouse wasn't where Ryan would find justice. I had learned that in dusty FOBs and black ops rooms: law works when the right people pull the levers. When it didn't, somebody had to be the wrench. I didn't celebrate that. Somebody had to finish the job those men started.

Vigilantism sat heavy in my mouth like bad whiskey. On paper it read like sin. Up close it read like necessity. I thought about it hard—not as a free pass to play judge, jury, and executioner, but as a decision where the options were ugly and you picked the least awful one. I didn't have qualms about being the man who put his thumb on the scale if the alternative was walking away and letting murderers go home for dinner.

The men who had killed my brother hadn't left a venue where the system could touch them. If the system bent for cowards and brass, then somebody had to be the hand that straightened it. I didn't flinch at that. I didn't make speeches about it. I just knew the ledger needed balancing. In my book, you pay your dues. Period.

I came from a family of ranchers, and the old stories at the barn taught me something different about justice. Not the cowboy-in-the-movie shooting up the sunset, but the older code: keep your family safe, keep the gates locked, and answer threats before they become funerals. Those men defended land and life because nobody else could.

That was the kind of justice I knew. That was the justice I had signed up to enforce when I put on a uniform after the towers fell. I enlisted so the next time somebody tried to break a town, a son, a mother, there would be men who would go get them. I hadn't signed up to stand and clap while crooks called it a day.

The men who ran this Syndicate and their military puppets had ripped that code to shreds. They were the ones playing outside the law, so the protection the old men talked about—the hard, practical protection of people and land—fell to me by right of blood and oath. That wasn't an endorsement for murder for sport. It was a promise to defend the innocent when the institutions failed.

I didn't want revenge for revenge's sake. I wanted consequence. I didn't want to be a ghost in the night. I didn't want to ambush cowards and shoot them in the back like they shot Ryan. I wanted to see the guilt in Harlan's eyes. I wanted Stahl and Firth and Wade to know I was coming and feel the panic crawl under their skin. Make them run. Make them look over their shoulders until their legs were shaking. Then finish it. Let them taste fear before they died—make it personal, make it honest.

Still, I didn't kid myself about what I was stepping into. I understood the cost. Once I walked this road there was no clean return to the Army life I knew. Signing off the Army wasn't something I celebrated or mourned. Uniform or ranch shirt, I would still be a soldier. The uniform was a habit; the duty was something else. Whether I wore rank or ranch clothes, the calculus didn't change. I would keep the skills, the discipline, and the bitter pride—use them to do work the system refused. That was the deal I made with myself at the funeral as dirt fell on Ryan's flag.

Patience had sharpened me. Waiting had stripped the soft edges of grief until what remained was a knife honed by loss. I had become cold, patient, and surgical—not a raging bull, but a trap-maker. I planned like a mission: stack the intel, cut the comms, isolate the target, then take the shot that mattered. No bloodlust spectacle. No cheap glory. Only precise work that ended wolves.

I understood the moral cost. I understood that someone would call me villain and someone else would call me necessary. I didn't run from either label. I only ran the mission. The ledger had to be balanced. That was the only prayer I knew.

Tomorrow I would start shaping the kill chain. Tonight I let the air cut through me like a blade, felt the cold pull the edge keener. I walked inside, collapsed into the bed like I had spent a day on the line, and for the first time in a long time, I slept straight through—ready for the morning and the teeth of the work ahead.

CHAPTER 22

I rolled out at 0600 hours, coffee bitter and warm in my gut, truck engine low and steady under my hands. I had rented the rig out of JFK the day before, straight off the flight from Denver. Solid F-150, dark blue, clean lines—nothing flashy but nothing sloppy either. Perfect cover for a man just passing through.

I was headed for Joint Base Andrews, right outside Washington, D.C.—the little patch of asphalt where presidential birds get kissed by mechanics, and staff officers move heaven and hell without leaving fingerprints. Andrews had the 89th Airlift Wing, the 316th, billets for VIP lift and a lot of brass who liked papers tidier than people.

Andrews sits southeast of D.C. proper, a tight little base that looks small on a map but carries a lot of leverage. That's where Harlan had been living in his neat little world after getting my brother killed.

I wasn't going there because the mission was tidy in my head. I was there to rattle Victor Harlan until he did something stupid. Spook him into doing the one thing he had been careful not to do: let his dark side be seen in the light of day. A man like him, polished and political, didn't like shadows breathing down his neck. Push the right buttons and he would start calling the others—Stahl, Firth, and Wade. And when he did, Echo would be there in the wire.

Echo had already done the heavy lifting on the comms. He had already built the listening post, slipping a silent backdoor into Harlan's phone profile using a phantom tower overlay—basically, any call Harlan placed or took got rerouted through Echo's net first. Didn't matter if it was cell, VoIP, or Sat. If Harlan breathed a name or location, Echo would hear it in real time.

Until then, all I had was Sloane's word on Ryan's killers, and Mark's suspicion that Harlan was the puppet master. But suspicion wasn't proof. I wanted firsthand confirmation that Harlan was dirty. All I knew for certain was the voice on that call for air support hadn't been Ryan's.

I also needed a starting point on Stahl, Firth, and Wade, before I settled in on Harlan. Echo could ping towers all day, but in dense-ass cities like Baltimore or D.C., a tower ping doesn't pin a man to a mailbox. You lose granularity in concrete and glass. It would be like a needle in a haystack. I needed something sharper than a tower hit.

My plan was to let Harlan know I had figured him out. Not by spelling it out—but by circling him, talking low, reminding him that ghosts didn't stay buried. The idea was simple: get inside their heads, make them nervous, make them sloppy. Once they started twitching, I would bring them down, one by one.

Echo had sent me photos and dossiers before I flew in. Faces, ranks, scars, nicknames. Harlan, Stahl, Wade, Firth—all four faces imprinted like wanted posters on my mind.

Harlan—mid-fifties, solid-shouldered, slate hair, the kind of posture that made a uniform look like armor. Used to go by the callsign Preacher.

Reaper—Marcus Stahl—square jaw, a scar nicked along his cheek that pulled his mouth down when he smiled; eyes like split flint, the kind that never softened.

Shade—Darius Wade—older than his stripes, skin creased like dried leather, the quiet sort who watches how things burn and learns the best place to put explosives so nothing obvious remains.

Torque—Kyle Firth—thin as a ledger, knuckled fingers that always looked like they had been riffling paperwork and manifest slips; his face had the pale hardness of a man who lived by lists and lies.

The drive south was a long ribbon of asphalt and memory. I-95 was a vein I had ridden before—never pretty, never peaceful. Jersey barriers, warehouses, truck stops, gas stations with bulletproof glass. The road stretched ahead like an old scar—gray, cracked, familiar—each mile marker pulling me deeper into the hunt.

Philadelphia sat at the midpoint, skyline jagged and gray against a washed-out sky. I didn't stop. Didn't blink. Just kept my head down and kept moving.

Four hours in, I rolled past Baltimore—broken-backed skyline, cranes frozen mid-motion, piers rotting into the bay, alleys cut with shadow, glass towers trying too hard to look respectable. That city had its own pulse. The kind of place where men like the Black Dagger Syndicate thrived—moving dope and money through the ports, ghosts with ledgers. Those guys had dug in there—flooding the East Coast with their Afghan heroin. And somewhere above them, Harlan was pulling the strings from D.C. Clean uniform, dirty hands.

By 1030 hours, I was cutting around the eastern edge of D.C. on the Beltway, traffic stacked and crawling, horns chewing the morning air— a slow, honking river of commuters and government types heading in.

I slid off onto the access road for Andrews, badge and ID squared away, the base rising out of the morning haze, a city inside the city—order, precision, control.

By 1100 hours, my boots were crunching the gravel of the memorial courtyard outside the base chapel. The chapel itself was low and pale brick, a clean steeple climbing sharp against the sky, cross gleaming at its peak. The courtyard spread wide with a stone path running down the middle, flanked by a memorial wall etched with names. Benches sat under trees just starting to turn, their leaves flickering gold in the fall light. It was a place built to look peaceful, but the weight of loss hung heavy in the air.

I hadn't gambled on chance. Echo had slipped me Harlan's itinerary, right down to the service start time of 1100 hours at the base chapel. An AC-130 crew, gone on a recent rotation overseas. Harlan wasn't there out of grief—he was there because appearances demanded it.

I walked slow along the memorial wall, blending into the crowd, program in hand though I didn't read it, eyes scanning the military uniforms and dark suits, wives clutching programs, kids restless in Sunday clothes. People murmured, hands shook, NCOs stood with faces set.

Then I saw him.

Colonel Harlan. Mid-fifties, squared shoulders filling out the service blues, silver eagles gleaming on his collar, that practiced, public grief on his face. Clean shaved, hair gunmetal gray and tight against his scalp. His face was carved in that politician's mask—solemn, measured, every nod to the civilians rehearsed and flawless.

Up close, he looked every bit the senior officer who had been given a promotion and a post that kept his hands tidy. His eyes, though—they were sharp, restless under the surface, the kind of eyes that missed nothing and trusted no one.

He stood with a couple of civilians near the courtyard edge, listening with that official, practiced patience. I slowed my pace, locked him in my sights.

I had met Harlan before. In Bagram. The day I flew in to bring Ryan's body home. Most of that trip was a fog of noise and grief, formal condolences, and a coffin I couldn't stop staring at—but I remembered Harlan. Remembered the way he had looked at me, measured, polished—already building his version of the story. Smooth, precise, laying the groundwork to shift the blame.

He had been too eager to explain how the drone strike had gone bad because of Ryan's "tragic lapse of nerve". As if my brother's death was just a tactical failure instead of what it really was—a setup.

I had wanted to put him through the wall right then. But I was in the army. Ranks mattered. Protocol was set in stone. You don't put senior officers through walls, no matter how much they deserved it. But that was then. Now I was ice.

And here he was again. Same cool posture, same politician's mask. I made sure my face didn't show a damn thing—just polite curiosity, like I was watching a briefing I didn't care about. The kind of look that doesn't make people defensive—but makes them wonder what you know.

And that's when I saw him.

Standing a little behind Harlan, half in his shadow, clipboard in hand, waiting for instructions—Staff Sergeant Kyle Firth. Torque. Echo's photos had burned that face into my memory.

Narrow build, too wiry for his uniform, eyes twitching with that nervous precision of a man who liked control but didn't actually have it. I had seen that look in too many men who played both sides of the war. He wasn't exactly a combat vet—more a ledger man than a fighter, the kind who lived in supply rooms and spreadsheets.

The moment I recognized him, everything shifted. That quiet click in my mind—the kind you get when the last piece of a weapon locks into place.

I had just found my entry point. My thread into Harlan's operation.

I didn't look twice, didn't let it register on my face, but I was locked in on him like a scope finding zero. Twitchy eyes was the kind of prey you didn't chase. You watched him move, let him feel safe. Then you closed in when he wasn't looking.

The trip had just gone from recon to opportunity. Torque was part of it—the ring, the cover-ups, the dirty logistics. He would be my first breadcrumb.

I shifted my gaze back to Harlan, pretending to study the surroundings. And that's when his eyes found me.

He was mid-conversation with a couple of civilians in pressed suits, scanning the people around casually when his eyes swept past me—then came back and locked on. For a split second, the mask slipped. His expression froze, like he had just seen a ghost.

Only lasted a breath. Then the professional calm returned—shoulders squared, jaw firm, the officer back in full control. He straightened, gave me that crisp, diplomatic nod, the kind of gesture meant to reassert control.

I started walking toward him, slow and easy.

It was game on.

CHAPTER 23

I walked up slowly, the way you approach a rattlesnake—steady, deliberate, never blinking first. Harlan was mid-sentence with a couple of civilians in pressed suits and dead eyes, probably contractors.

He turned as I approached, that same politician's smile already fixed in place—polished, rehearsed, something he probably practiced in mirrors. His eyes flicked over me like he was scrolling through old files in his head.

"Captain Blaze, right?" he said, as if dredging it up from memory, while offering his hand like we had just bumped into each other at a damn golf club. "We met in Bagram."

"That's right, sir," I said evenly. "You spoke to me the day I came to take Captain Ryan Blaze home."

The words hung between us like cold iron. Harlan gave a slow, respectful nod—the kind people give when they are pretending to feel something.

"Yes, I remember," he said. "Tragic loss. Your brother was a fine Marine. I was just telling someone the other day—he was brave to the end."

He had no idea how false that sounded. The kind of line you deliver at a press conference, not over a coffin.

I ignored that. "Didn't expect to see you outside a tactical ops center."

"Memorial service for the AC-130 crew," he said smoothly. "You too?"

"Yeah. Thought I'd pay my respects."

He nodded, studying me. "That's a long way from Colorado."

That one slipped out before he could stop it. The pause after told me he knew it too. He had been keeping tabs. The flicker in his eyes confirmed it.

Then came the quick save: "We spoke about that in Bagram, didn't we? I never forget a detail."

I kept my voice mild. "Guess you've got a good memory."

He chuckled. "Hazard of command."

"I've been on the road since yesterday," I carried on. "Drove down from Upstate New York this morning."

"Ah." He tilted his head, feigning mild curiosity. "Old friends up there?"

The bastard knew full well I had been cracking his gangsters' skulls up there.

"Not exactly," I replied. "Met a few people. Interesting crowd."

That one landed. Harlan's eyes flickered just once—barely a twitch, but enough. From the corner of mine, I caught Torque stiffen—shoulders tightening, jaw working. Yeah, they had gotten the memo about the failed hit on Dana.

Harlan changed the subject fast. "So what brings you this far east, really?"

"Just tying loose ends," I replied. "Tell me, Colonel—do you remember the JTAC who coordinated that strike on Captain Ryan Blaze's unit?"

His expression barely shifted. "Kincaid, wasn't it? Yes. Damn shame. I heard he died in a road accident."

That told me everything. No way a flag-chasing colonel remembered a discharged sergeant's obituary. He didn't have a clue that I knew he was keeping regular tabs on Kincaid.

"Road accidents," I said softly. "Seems like they claim too many of our own. I heard about another one—Sloane. Worked Bagram, same wing."

Harlan's face was granite. "I remember the name. Don't recall the accident, though."

"Hmm," I said, pretending to think. "Guess memory fades. Happens to the best of us."

The silence between us got heavy. Just wind through the courtyard and the low scrape of boots. Harlan's aide hovered a few feet off—clipboard in hand, trying to look useful. Torque looked like he wanted to melt into the pavement. I decided to toss a line and see if he bit.

I said, almost casually, "Actually, that's part of why I'm here. I'm meeting someone in D.C. this evening. Claims to have information about Ryan's death. Hard evidence."

Harlan's shoulders tightened like a wire being pulled. He had taken the bite full-on. His eyes sharpened—full attention now. His tone stayed smooth, but the edge showed. "What kind of information?" he asked, polite and probing.

"Not sure yet. But apparently it involves a flash drive. Audio files that went missing after the strike."

Harlan gave a short laugh that didn't reach his eyes. "I heard about that. Rumor, nothing more. Those files never existed."

"Oh, they exist," I said quietly. "Kincaid made two copies. Left one with his wife. Another with a friend in D.C. I'm meeting that friend today."

That hit like a hammer. For a split second, everything behind Harlan's eyes went glassy. Behind him, Torque's jaw was working like he was chewing gravel. Harlan recovered with a tight smile. Then, almost casually, he asked, "Who's this source?"

He was fishing. I let him.

"Seems to be a common friend of Kincaid and Sloane—you know the one who died in an accident you don't recall."

Harlan wasn't sure if I was being sarcastic. But as long as he thought me dumb enough to share all my intel with him, he seemed to be fine with it.

He asked again, as casually as before: "What time are you meeting this source?"

This time I gave him more than he was hoping for.

"2000 hours. Lincoln Memorial," I said flat, watching the muscle in his throat move. I added, with a little edge of sarcasm, "If I turn anything up, I'll be sure to keep you in the loop—if you're interested."

Harlan blinked, then nodded. "Of course. But if I were you, I wouldn't hold my breath over it."

"Yeah, right." I checked my watch. "I better start making a move. Got to meet a few people before that meeting. I'll remember your advice about not holding my breath, but you know what, Colonel—truth has a funny way of crawling back into the light, doesn't like to stay buried."

He gave a small nod, jaw tight. "Good luck with that, Captain."

"Luck's never been my thing," I said, and extended my hand. "Good seeing you again, sir."

He took it, grip firm but cold. "Likewise."

I turned and walked off, boots crunching gravel. I caught Harlan's reflection in the memorial glass—his face darkening, his gaze cutting toward

Torque like a blade. Whatever was coming next, Torque was about to get hell.

My pulse stayed steady, but inside, gears were turning. Not once had I glanced at Torque. I didn't give them a hint I knew him from Adam.

Which was good.

Because my plan was simple: hang around the base, keep my eyes on the exits, wait until Torque rolled out. Then tail him, grab him somewhere quiet, and make him talk.

This was one hunt I had waited a long damn time for. And I wasn't leaving Maryland without blood on the hook.

CHAPTER 24

I drifted away from the memorial courtyard slow and casual, like a guy with nowhere urgent to be. My boots crunched the gravel, but my head was mapping lines of sight, exits, angles. From the corner of my eye, I scanned for spots that gave height and cover—an admin building on the far side with tinted windows, a maintenance annex with a service ladder that probably led to a flat roof, and the second-floor balcony of the chapel itself. Good spots to watch someone without being seen.

I didn't break stride or turn my head; just let the scene roll through my periphery, cataloguing everything in that slow, drifting walk. The trick was to look bored, not hunting. Harlan's people would already be moving—probably scrambling to figure out how to shadow me without being obvious. I figured I would give them a little time to organize. No fun spooking the fox before you know which way he's going to run.

That's when I saw her again.

She was standing behind a small check-in booth—a wooden desk under a canopy marked "Visitor Assistance". Chapel volunteer detail, from the look of it. Short-sleeved blues, dark hair pulled back in a regulation bun, light catching off green eyes that said she smiled a lot, even if duty didn't give her many reasons lately. She had that classic all-American smile—the kind that could make you forget the world was burning for a second.

We had locked eyes earlier when I first walked in. She held the look half a second too long. I had filed it away at the time, gave her a polite nod and kept moving, too focused on Harlan. But right now, I needed an excuse to linger.

I strolled over, hands in pockets. “Afternoon, Sergeant. You keeping the faith alive out here?”

Her eyes flicked up, the faintest smirk tugging her lips. “Someone’s got to, sir. You Army guys come around only when there’s free coffee.”

I chuckled. “That’s slander, ma’am. I came for the scenery.”

“Oh really?” she said, raising an eyebrow. “And what part of the scenery’s got your attention?”

“The architecture,” I said, straight-faced, then let a grin slip. “Mostly the part smiling back.”

She gave a soft laugh—real, unforced. “Smooth answer. You always this charming, Captain...?” She tilted her head, reading the name tape. “Blaze?”

“Only when I’m trying to make a good first impression.”

“Well, mission accomplished,” she said. Her tone was playful, but her eyes studied me like she was trying to read something deeper. “You stationed here?”

“Nope. Just passing through, paying my respects,” I replied. “I was trying to keep the mood light. You’re doing a decent job helping with that.”

Her smile widened. “Well, I’ll add it to my mission statement, Captain. Plan to stick around for a while?”

“Unfortunately, no. Long road, quick stop.”

“That’s a shame,” she said, pretending to pout. “We don’t get many like you hanging around.”

For a few seconds, the heaviness that had been sitting on my chest for months eased off. Just a woman, a smile, sunlight on her cheek—normal life bleeding in through the cracks. Another time, another place, maybe I would have let it go somewhere. But not today. Not with what was waiting out there.

"Next time I'm around, maybe I'll hang around a little longer."

She caught that, the warmth in her eyes softening just a notch. "Well, Captain Blaze, next time you're at Andrews, I expect at least a coffee. No excuses."

I smiled. "Deal. You got yourself a rain check."

As I stepped back, she flashed me that bright, killer smile. "See you around, Captain."

"Count on it."

I walked off, keeping my stride steady, letting the moment fade behind me like a quiet echo. As I passed the reflective glass of the admin building, I caught sight of Torque—trailing me, subtle as a marching band. Amateur hour. He was pretending to check his phone, but the body language was all wrong—stiff shoulders, head on a swivel.

I almost smiled. The guy I had planned to tail was now tailing me. That was convenient.

I kept walking toward the car park, posture loose, keys in hand. In another reflection—a chrome strip on a nearby doorframe—I saw Torque raise his phone to his ear. Calling Harlan, or maybe his ride.

I hit the remote key. My pickup chirped back. I opened the door, leaned in, and started rummaging through the back seat—gloves, map case, empty coffee cup—giving Torque all the time in the world to get his ride ready.

My burner buzzed at that moment. Echo. I answered on the little handset I had lit up that morning—no trace on my main line, no chance Harlan had tapped it.

"Cowboy," Echo breathed, flat and weirdly electric. "You got him to bite. Harlan popped Shade's head off good."

"Spill," I said, jumping on the back seat.

"He called Shade and chewed him out. Tore his head off. Said the flash drive was supposed to be destroyed and now the dead Marine's brother shows up on his lawn saying he's meeting a source in D.C. tonight. Shade was pissing himself. Cursing Kincaid's widow and promising to make it ugly. Sounded unhinged." Echo's tone tightened. "You got Kincaid's wife in custody, right?"

"Affirmative. Troopers have her. She's locked down." I didn't bother with theatrics. "And she won't need to worry about Shade after tonight anyway."

Echo caught my drift and kept rolling. "Harlan went nuclear on Shade. He's pissed—mostly about sloppy work. Said he's sent Torque to shadow you. Shade doesn't seem to think much of Torque's combat skills. Harlan said Torque's moving with a tough Baltimore crew with hardware. Torque and his guys will just tail you until you hit the Lincoln Memorial at 2000."

"Good. I already see Torque with that crew," I replied, looking through the back window at an SUV Torque had just climbed into.

"Then I take it that crew isn't going to make it to the rendezvous at 2000."

"Affirmative."

"I thought so. Well, those guys are well armed. Watch your six. Also, Harlan ordered Shade to be ready with a heavy team regardless. Finish the source at Lincoln Memorial at 2000." Echo hesitated. "Shade asked, 'And after that?' Harlan said, 'We'll cross that bridge later. Don't fuck with an active special forces operator unless you've got a plan. Don't improvise. Don't get cute.'"

"So they're worried. Good."

"Yeah, Harlan's no fool. Shade asked if you're special forces—Harlan told him, yeah, he's Delta, and asked Shade if he didn't get the memo when you took out his entire crew in that shit town upstate. Shade tried to laugh it off—said you got lucky as the cops came in. Harlan called him an idiot and told him to go heavy and not screw this up. Harlan's trying to control the burn—put muscle between you and that drive."

Echo paused, then asked: "So—Lincoln. That real, or bait?"

"Bait," I replied. "Sounds like they're falling for it. I'll be waiting."

"And the time? 2000?"

"Just random. It will be dark by then. Makes it easier to hunt."

"Copy," Echo said. "I'll keep tabs on comms. If Shade lights up a channel, I'll give you a shout. Stay frosty, Cowboy. Harlan's got resources—don't go playing hero theater."

"You ever heard me sing show tunes?" I asked, trying to lighten the mood. "I'll keep it quiet."

"Roger that. Keep me posted."

We signed off. The burner went dark. I stepped out of the back and climbed into the cab.

Torque's SUV was ready. He had slid in with four others—too many, too obvious, doing their best at subtlety and failing.

I slid into the cab, started the engine, eased out of the gravel, and let them fall in behind me like eager hounds.

I pointed the truck toward the riverfront and the old industrial strip by National Harbor—the forgotten yards and loading docks I had scouted on the feed. Empty lots with cracked asphalt, broken chain-link, and warehouses with boarded doors. Daytime, but dead—no security patrols on that shift, no cameras watching every footstep, no traffic to draw attention. Perfect for corralling a crew and taking them apart without curious neighbors.

Torque stayed glued to my tail like a bad habit. I drove them toward the lot, letting them follow me right where I wanted.

CHAPTER 25

I peeled off the Andrews access road and hit the Beltway like I was cutting loose a rope. Traffic choked slow, government SUVs and commuter boxes shunted along. Then the Harbor peeled off to my right— tourist kiosks, mid-day families, chain restaurants pretending to be quaint. No gleaming lights yet—it was midday—just people with lunch and shopping bags.

I kept driving until the pretension ran out. The Harbor's gloss stopped a few blocks in and the road went mean quick: rust, concrete, the sort of places you only go if you got business you don't want overheard.

The road hunched toward the water, and the Potomac lay flat and wide to my left, a gray ribbon that split Maryland from Virginia. Barges bumped down its back like tired beasts and cranes kept watch like bored sentries. The water made the whole place feel like an edge—one side clean, one side dirty—and I was cruising on the dirty side.

The industrial strip itself looked tired and mean. Two-story brick warehouses leaned into the road, windows punched out, loading docks yawning. Chain-link fences sagged under razor wire; pallets lay in piles like forgotten work. The air tasted of oil and old money—no shine, no mercy.

Warehouses crouched low, windows punched out, loading docks yawning, paint peeled off corrugated sheets. Chain-link fences sagged under razor wire; pallets lay in piles like forgotten work.

Empty lots where dreams went to die—cracked and half-swallowed by grass. The kind of place you come to if you want to hide a secret or bury a crew.

I drove the strip with the windows down, slow and low, feeling for lines and exits. I wasn't hunting scenery. I was picking terrain, looking for the cleanest place to make the ugliness happen. There were options—a cold-storage plant with long concrete corridors that would echo a fight like a drum; a loading-dock complex with ramps that wound up to a roof I could use for overwatch; a half-collapsed mill that would make bodies and debris part of the weapon set; and a three-story brick warehouse with interior mezzanines. All of them had teeth.

The SUV backed off a little as I slowed, not dumb enough to tail bumper-to-bumper in daylight. Good. Let them give me space. I watched the mirror and acted like I didn't. Routine makes people careless.

I stopped outside the three-story brick place. Old freight elevator at one end, metal catwalks along the second level, mezzanine offices with broken windows, a big open bay where pallets used to stack up. Vertical space meant options—choke points on stairs, lines through the mezzanine, a shaft you could use to funnel men. It fit my taste for surgical work. I killed the engine.

Before I climbed out, I slid my hand to the back of my jeans and eased the Glock into the holster I had rigged there. It was the one I had lifted from Zeke's crew back in Ashwood. I had smuggled it past the cops when I left town. I hadn't carried my own sidearm from the ranch because I didn't know I would be walking into a hornet's nest. Ashwood taught me otherwise. Now, facing a well-armed Baltimore crew, a handgun was the bare minimum.

I stepped out, locked the truck with the clicker, and fumbled my phone like I was dialing someone I was supposed to meet. "Yeah. On my way," I said into the metal, slow and deliberate, then gave a conspiratorial nod as if confirming a rendezvous. I slipped the phone into my pocket, nodded again—just to be seen—and walked to the yawning dock door.

Inside, the warehouse smelled of dust and oil and the hot metal scent of long-unused machinery. Daylight came through broken panes in slatted beams, striping the floor with hard lines. The main bay opened wide, the concrete floor scarred with old tire tracks. A freight elevator sat cold at the far end; a crooked metal staircase siphoned up to the mezzanine where a run of offices looked down over the bay. Catwalks traced the second level like ribs. Wooden pallets formed cover and blind spots; a half-stack of crated pipe made a decent little barricade.

I moved quiet, feeling the geometry of the place—sightlines, blind corners, the ladders that would let a man vanish. I worked my way along the shadowed aisle between stacked pallets, keeping low, breathing even. My eyes mapped exits: the front bay, the side-door delivery, the stairwell that climbed to the mezzanine. I wanted the high ground.

I climbed the narrow metal stairs to the second level and found a gap in the mezzanine where old crates had been pulled back. From there I had an elevated field of fire, choke points below, and a quick route to drop down and take a man by surprise.

I settled behind a stack of damp, oil-streaked carpet rolls, the coarse fabric muffling my outline. The Glock rode against my spine, warm and ready. I checked the slide, heard the click in the quiet, and let the light rake across my face once before I melted back into shadow. I checked both boot knives—edges clean, balance true.

I rolled my shoulders, flexed my wrists, cracked my neck left and right. Quiet readiness. The calm before the storm. The kind of still that made your blood hum.

The warehouse breathed around me, patient as a beast. I waited.

Outside, Torque and his boys were waiting—nervous energy on four wheels. I caught the faint crunch of gravel through the broken panes. They waited five, maybe six minutes, then the SUV doors creaked open. Footsteps spread out. Game time.

Three came in through the front—standard muscle types, black shirts, cargo pants, Uzis out front. These guys weren't screwing around. One wrong move and I would have a spray of 9mm coming my way. Every take down would have to be decisive. Final.

Footsteps creaked on the floor below. They moved like men who had been coached on how to look dangerous: deliberate, practiced sweeps, muzzles sweeping glass and shadow.

The other two stayed outside near my truck—Torque and one extra, both trying to look like they knew what they were doing. They didn't.

Inside, the air turned thick with boot scuffs and breathing. The three on the floor moved slow, weapons slicing the shadows, checking behind everything—rusted drums, pallets stacked with busted pipe, an old forklift sitting crooked on flat tires. Their footsteps echoed soft but steady on the concrete. The first guy crouched to peek under a workbench; the second swept the aisle behind a row of oil drums. The third—taller, leaner—cut toward the staircase, scanning the mezzanine with that cheap confidence men buy with numbers.

I watched him climb, step by slow step, until his head rose into my sightline. He paused to check the mezzanine, sweeping his Uzi left to right. Bad angle—he couldn't see me tucked behind the rolls of carpet. When he came within range, I moved. Silent. Fast. My arm wrapped around his throat, steel flashed once. He jerked once, twice, then sagged like wet laundry. I eased him down so the metal stairs wouldn't groan.

I left him where he fell, slid over the rail, and dropped down to the floor below. Boots kissed concrete. No sound.

The second man was close—moving between a set of crates, muzzle twitching with every breath. I matched him step for step in shadow, closed the distance. When he stepped past a stack of old tires, I slipped in behind him. One hand clamped his mouth, the other drove the knife up and under the jawline. A wet pop. He twitched and went limp. I eased him down, pulled the blade free, wiped it on his shirt.

Still no shots fired. Two down. One more inside.

I moved toward the side door, hugging the walls. The third man had gone out to check the perimeter. Through the broken pane I saw daylight glare, heard the faint buzz of a fly. Then the door creaked open again. He stepped in—careless, his Uzi held low, eyes not seeing, thinking everything was tidy because two men were clearing inside.

He saw me half a second too late. His arms started to rise—too slow. I threw the knife from the hip, watched the steel spin once before it sank into his gut with a solid *thunk*. He staggered, dropped the muzzle, and that was all the window I needed. I was already moving—closing the distance fast, my left-hand knife out and forward. I hit him center mass, blade angled up. His finger twitched on the trigger, a short burst of 9mm slapping the walls before he crumpled against me and went still.

That burst had rung the alarm. The two outside were moving.

I pulled my knife free, grabbed the Glock, and made for the front door at a sprint.

Outside, sunlight hit hard. One of the gunmen was rushing forward, weapon up. I didn't hesitate—three quick rounds, center mass. The impact folded him backward, feet tangled under him before he hit the ground with the stupid surprise of a man who had miscalculated his opponent.

Torque panicked. He had been hiding behind my truck, then stood up and started blindly spraying the lot with his Uzi, his body still half-hidden behind the pickup, only his hand and the gun showing. I could see the barrel of his Uzi shaking, the muzzle dancing like a drunk. He sprayed lead in every direction except mine. Rounds clanged off metal, shredded air. It wasn't the controlled fire of a combat veteran; it was the nervous spray of a man used to paper and ledgers, not combat.

I didn't flinch. I walked toward him, Glock steady. When I reached the hood, I sighted on the glint of the Uzi's barrel and squeezed once. Steel snapped, the Uzi flew out of his hand and clattered to the asphalt, fingers shredded by the blast.

He screamed—high and thin—stumbled back, clutching the shredded mess of his hand, eyes wide with that kind of disbelief people get when they realize death has their scent. His face went white with a new kind of fear: the realization that his math couldn't fix this.

I walked up to him slow, smoke drifting from the Glock's barrel, the echo still rolling through the dead strip. He stared at me like he had seen the devil.

I wrapped my hand around Torque's neck, fingers digging in hard enough to make him gag. His pulse hammered under my fingers. I drove the Glock hard into the side of his temple, felt his skull tremble beneath the barrel. Cold metal, the press of finality. For a half-second I wanted to end it—one clean pull, one scumbag off the board.

I didn't take it. Torque had a ledger in his head. He knew manifests, routes, names. Kill him and you burn the map. Keep him breathing, and he told you where the bodies were buried. He was a pencil pusher, not a battle-hardened nut who would sit on a bullet like some kind of brass idol. He would crack easy.

I eased the muzzle away. "You and I are going to have a long talk," I said, my voice low and dry.

CHAPTER 26

I kicked Torque's legs out from under him. He hit the gravel with a sick, hollow thud, wind squealing from him. I moved quick—frisked him, hard hands over ribs, down the waistband, the armpits, the collar. Found a stack of cash folded tight and a black flip phone.

"Stay down," I told him. "Don't move."

He stayed still enough—except for the little whimpers that made his face twist.

I hauled one of the dead gunmen and dumped him just inside the front door of the warehouse. There wasn't much chance of a nosy passerby poking his nose in, but you never know.

I walked back to Torque, grabbed him by the collar like he was a stray, and hauled him up. He went like a puppet on a wire, eyes huge and wet. I shoved him inside the bay and planted him in the center of the mess—four bodies, with old oil and fresh blood staining the floor like an ugly map. He looked at them like he had never seen men die before. Terror made his face melt.

"Listen, Captain, you know I'm an active U.S. soldier," he squealed. "We're—we're both soldiers. You can't—you can't kill an American soldier."

I looked at him, then at the four bodies on the floor.

"You're a disgrace to the uniform," I replied, my voice cold and sharp. "Hiding behind rank and running dope. I left you breathing not because you're a soldier, but because you've got teeth I need to pull."

The terror was real in his eyes. But I was just getting warmed up. I dragged him to an oil-stained workbench and slammed his left wrist down on the scarred wood. The metal rattled under his arm. I pressed the tip of the knife flat across the middle finger of his left hand until he flinched and the skin went white around the blade.

"Listen to me," I said, cold as winter. "You say one more word about being a soldier—one more pathetic 'I'm-a-soldier' line—and I'll take what's left of your fingers off. You hear me? Your right hand's already fucked up." I let the knife press a little harder, feeling the tremor in his hand. "I won't fuss about how pretty it looks. I'll do it clean, one by one."

He made a sound like a dog. His teeth showed. Blood welled where the blade kissed skin.

"Is that clear?" I asked.

He whimpered. "Y-yes—sir."

My voice tightened, the officer's edge cutting through the threat. "When I ask you a question, you'll give me a clear answer. Not that mushy noise."

"Yes, sir," he said, louder, sharp and broken.

I let the blade slide a fraction away and tightened my grip on his collar until his Adam's apple bobbed.

"Here's the deal," I said. "You answer my questions. You give me names, manifests, routes, who handles what, who's paid, where they stash product. You'll keep breathing. You stop being useful—even one lie—and I put a bullet in your head. Is that clear?"

He stared at me, eyes huge and glossy. His voice came out small, that practiced cadence the terrified

find when they learn the shape of the bargain.
"Yes, sir."

"Good," I said. "We start now."

I thumbed my phone on and hit record, setting it on the corner of the table so the mic faced Torque. The screen glowed pale in the dusty air, catching the tremor in his chin. I kept my knife in one hand, my other hand stayed tight on his collar. I wasn't giving him the room to start spinning some heroic bullshit about loyalty or orders.

He knew it too. The earlier scare had done its job. His right hand was mangled, his left under threat of mutilation by my knife, and four of his buddies lay cooling a few feet away, their blood soaking into the oil-streaked floor. Reality had a way of making men honest.

"Talk," I said.

He swallowed hard, his Adam's apple bobbing like a golf ball in his throat. "It—it was Colonel Harlan," he said, the words tumbling out quick, scared. "He runs the whole thing. Always did."

I didn't say anything. Silence was better than threats. It made men fill the gaps with their own fear.

Torque kept going. "Reaper and Shade set up the links—contacts, routes, all that—out of Afghanistan. Contractors, loaders, handlers, whoever could be bought. They already had the connections from their time in the sandbox."

He looked up, like he wanted to see if I believed him. I didn't move a muscle.

"When they needed someone to keep the manifests clean, they brought me in," he said, his voice small now. "I was... good with logistics. Good with hiding things. Numbers. I made the paperwork match the payloads."

"Keep talking."

"They used body bags mostly," Torque went on, staring down at the table. "Medevac flights. Nobody checks a bag marked 'Killed in Action', not unless they want to lose their job. They'd vacuum-seal the bricks—real tight, foil wrap, double layer—then shove them into the cavity or line the stretcher frame. I swear to God, sometimes the bodies weren't even real soldiers."

He said it like he needed me to know he wasn't *that* bad. That somehow desecrating a fake corpse was better.

I didn't let him off the hook. "You said 'mostly'. What else?"

"Ammo crates," he said quickly. "Gear boxes. Anything headed back stateside marked 'decommission' or 'return to depot'. They'd build false bottoms, seal the dope under the base plates. I'd make sure the manifests matched, so no one noticed the weight."

The warehouse felt colder suddenly. It wasn't just the air. It was the rot underneath every word. These weren't street pushers. They were ghosts in uniform, poisoning the same country they had sworn to defend.

Torque's voice cracked a little as he kept going. "They even moved it through embassy shipments once or twice. Diplomatic pouches. Nothing gets checked there. That was Reaper's idea. Harlan said it was genius."

I could feel my pulse ticking in my jaw. "Who handles the manifests now, back in the sandbox?"

He hesitated. Too long. I pressed the knife a little harder into the finger under the blade.

"Name," I said.

"Sergeant... Sergeant Brett Corman," he stammered. "They looped him in after I got pulled back stateside."

"Pulled back stateside?" I asked, quiet.

Torque realized the second the words slipped out. Both of us knew he was talking about the time after Ryan was killed. His eyes widened, the panic blooming across his face like a flare. He was terrified of what I would do to him. He tried to grab the sentence back with a liar's reflex.

"It was—rotation. Routine," he stammered, breath too quick. "Colonel Harlan pulled us back. Just—routine rotation."

"Pulled *us* back. Who's *us*?" I asked, exerting control to keep my voice level.

He opened his mouth but nothing came out. His face told me everything. They weren't rotated. They were extracted. Pulled off the board fast before anyone could start connecting dots. Before I could. Before Ryan's blood had even dried in the sand.

I didn't say a word. Didn't move, didn't blink. Just looked at him. Hard. Quiet. The kind of look that made a man's eyes find the floor and his tongue forget its tricks.

The room seemed to have gotten smaller. Outside, the air in the bay tightened. You could hear the river like a far-away clock. Torque's hand trembled where it lay on the bench. The man was unraveling under the pressure and it was ugly and honest and exactly what I needed.

He shoved his face up like he couldn't stand the weight of the silence. "Jesus," he whispered. "I'm—God, I'm sorry. I swear to God, I didn't know at first. When the news came out—when they said—" He choked on it. "I wished I'd never touched it.

Every damn day I wished I hadn't signed on. But once you're in, you don't just walk away." He bowed his head like a man asking the sky for forgiveness.

His voice was thin. He kept saying sorry like it was a prayer. Real sorry, not the kind that buys you time. Real remorse. It pissed me off and it made me cold at the same time.

"Save the rehearsed guilt for the chaplain," I said. "Look at me."

He flinched but lifted his head. His eyes were red, not from the blast, but from whatever had been eating him alive. "I wish I hadn't joined it," he said, the words tumbling out like nails. "I didn't know— I didn't know the scale at first. I just— numbers, manifests, make it work, do the job. You know how it is."

"No, I don't know how it is. I took an oath and kept it sacred in my heart."

"I know. You were right—I'm a disgrace to the uniform. A coward. I followed orders because I was scared, not because I was following a chain of command. Once I got in, I didn't have the guts to walk away. Stahl and Wade... they'd make you disappear if you even thought about walking. And Harlan—Harlan's not a man you cross. I'm ashamed. Honest to God, Captain, I'm ashamed."

"Cut the pity party," I snapped. "Who did it? Who killed them?" I asked. Short. Officer's tone; no room for his softening.

He flinched, then forced his eyes up. I saw the confession in them before the words came.

"Stahl and Wade," he said, voice raw. "They— they rolled in like they were friendly. They brought uniforms. They lobbed frags into the little room where Captain Ryan Blaze and his men were talking with the Afghan source. Two grenades. Enclosed space. It was a meat grinder. Then they cut anyone who moved down with automatics. It was quick. Brutal. Stahl... he talked about it later, like it was a job. Like he'd bagged something big."

"He called Harlan," Torque added, voice going thin. "Told him he'd fucked it up— bodies, shrapnel, rounds... it would point right back at them. Harlan told him what to do. Told him to call it in as a request for fire. Told Sloane to scrub the logs, wipe comms, erase the audio. Harlan pulled the strings and made the strike look like a panic call, like the Captain lost his nerve. That's why they pulled us back—pulled the whole crew—to keep things tidy."

Torque's jaw worked around the confession. He swallowed hard and went on, quieter now. "After we got back, Harlan moved fast. He arranged discharges for Stahl and Wade—paperwork, early separation—so they weren't sitting on active duty where anyone could start asking questions. Got them out clean so they could focus on running the business stateside. But he kept me in place. He needed someone inside the logistics system who could keep the heroin flowing and the manifests clean. I stayed because he needed me to keep the lanes open."

Then he went quiet again. Wouldn't look at me. The recording was still running—his voice, every filthy detail, saved to a file that would not die quietly.

Outside, the Potomac moved on, indifferent. Inside, the truth sat on the table between us, ugly and heavy.

CHAPTER 27

I stepped out of the warehouse into the heavy stillness of late afternoon. The air smelled of rust, hot concrete, and the faint chemical stink that never really left old industrial zones. Sunlight slanted through broken warehouse windows, turning the dust into lazy gold motes that hung in the air. Out beyond the fence line, the Potomac gleamed dull and indifferent. The city skyline shimmered in the haze—clean glass and commerce not far away—but here, the world was silent and forgotten.

The silence was a relief. My head was running on fumes and rage. I needed space to think, to let the fire cool just enough so I didn't walk back in and put a round through his skull out of sheer principle. My head felt like it had been caught in crossfire—too many revelations, too much filth, and one steady, cold conclusion: Torque wasn't lying.

Everything Torque said lined up perfectly with Mark's video. The timing, the way the cover-up was orchestrated, and what came after. Stahl and Wade pulled the triggers. Harlan orchestrated the cover-up. And the quiet pencil-pusher sitting inside—he was guilty, but in a different way. Torque might have been a coward, but he wasn't lying. I had seen enough interrogations to know when a man was bluffing—and when he was bleeding truth. Torque had bled plenty that day.

That meant I had three names carved into my skull now, and they weren't leaving till I put them in the ground: Stahl, Wade, Harlan.

I leaned against the hood of the pickup, looking at the empty road beyond. Shade was the closest. I could almost smell him. Echo had his phone on the radar. Shade had also bit into the bait I dangled in front of Harlan about meeting a source at Lincoln Memorial at 2000 hours. If luck held, I would have his throat in my hands before the night was done.

Reaper was still buried somewhere deep, hiding in the smoke. It would take more digging to get him out.

Harlan, though... he was a different kind of hunt. I didn't want to straight up kill him. That would be too easy on him. I didn't just want to end him; I wanted to dismantle him. I wanted to watch the light drain from his eyes while he saw everything he built—his money, his network, his reputation—burn piece by piece and crumble to ash. Only then would I finish it.

That kind of ending took planning. Patience.

I was still thinking about how to do it when I heard footsteps behind me—hesitant, dragging, like he was afraid the sound alone might earn him another broken finger. I didn't even turn. I knew it was Torque. The guy walked like a man unsure if he was welcome anywhere, especially around me.

He stepped out, his shoulders hunched like a man walking into a storm he couldn't avoid. He stopped a few feet away. "Captain," he said, voice small and tentative. "I told you everything you wanted."

I turned then, slow. Met his eyes. "No. You told me what I *asked*. Don't ever confuse that with what I *want*."

He swallowed. "And what do you want?"

"Blood," I said simply. "All of it. Every drop from the bastards in your rotten circle."

Torque nodded slowly, like he had been expecting that. He looked smaller—just a thin man in a sweat-darkened T-shirt, skin gray from fear and guilt. The clipboard soldier.

"Captain, when I said I regretted being part of Harlan's operation... that wasn't an act. I wasn't just trying to save my skin. I meant it. I—."

I cut him off with a look, and he shut up for a heartbeat. I had heard every kind of repentance before—most of it bought cheap at gunpoint.

I stared at him for a long beat, my face giving away nothing. "Save your breath," I said finally.

He took a small step closer, hands trembling slightly. "Just hear me out, Captain. Please."

I said nothing, just waited.

"I know words don't fix what I did. But I need you to understand something. I wasn't the one who killed your brother, but I know what I did made it possible. The drugs, the logistics, the cover—I helped build the machine that chewed up good men. What I did... it cost you your blood, your family. That's an unpardonable sin."

He looked down at his hands. "I can feel your anger, Captain. And I get it. It's not like the violence I've seen in Harlan's world—not the kind those gangsters do for money or fun. Yours... it's righteous. You're not killing for kicks. You're killing for something that was taken."

That got me quiet. His words hit closer than I liked.

Torque went on, voice lower now. "My father was a minister in Lubbock. Hellfire-and-brimstone type. Used to quote James 4:17: *'Therefore, to him who knows to do good and does not do it, to him it is sin.'* Silence can be just as evil as violence." His mouth twisted bitterly. "Guess I took that lesson and burned it. If he saw what I've become, he'd turn in his grave. He also liked to quote Romans 6:23: *'The wages of sin is death,'* and I figure that tab's about to come due."

He gave a short, broken laugh that didn't sound much like laughter.

For a second, I didn't say anything. I just looked at him. The same man who had been shaking like a leaf not twenty minutes ago now sounded like he had just found Jesus in that godforsaken place. I had seen plenty of men beg before—most of them just trying to save their own skins. But this felt... different. Maybe he had finally looked in the mirror and didn't like what stared back. Maybe guilt finally did what bullets couldn't—broke him clean through.

My own anger pulsed steady under the surface. I had spent months hunting ghosts, and now the flesh-and-blood version was standing right there, quoting Scripture with a trembling voice.

I scrubbed a hand across my jaw and exhaled. "You find salvation out here, Sergeant?" I asked, my tone halfway between mockery and curiosity.

He shook his head slowly. "No, Captain. But I finally stopped lying to myself about needing it."

That line hung in the air for a long beat.

I looked off toward the horizon—the clean, distant skyline glowing under the sun—and felt the divide between that world and this one widen. Ryan's face flickered behind my eyes, then faded, leaving only that familiar cold burn in my chest.

The facts Torque had given me were solid. He hadn't once tried to steer me off course. I decided to give him rope—whether he climbed with it or hung himself was up to him.

"All right," I said finally. "Let's say I buy that you're not full of shit. What've you got in mind?"

Torque's eyes lifted, a flicker of something alive in them for the first time that night. "First off, let me make this clear—I know I'm not getting any free rides. You're not the kind to give me one and I'm willing to do whatever time they give me to start with a clean slate."

The guy was saying all the right things. I looked at him, waiting for him to go on.

He drew a long breath. "I want to help you bring Harlan down. Every last piece of his operation—I'll help you burn it to the ground. You might think I'm doing this just to save myself—maybe I am, partly. But I'm also done being afraid. I've lived under Harlan's thumb for years. He owns me. I'm not proud of that. But that ends now. And I can still do what's right."

He straightened a little, squaring his shoulders like a man trying to remember what standing tall felt like. "You're the first man I've met who can finish this, Captain. I wish I had a chance to meet your brother when he was investigating all this. I've been a coward my whole damn life. You give me a chance to make this right, I'll take it. Whatever it costs."

He straightened as he said it—still pale, still trembling, but with a trace of something steady beneath.

His words hung in the cold air between us, sharp as the echo of a gunshot.

I didn't answer right away. Part of me wanted to laugh at the idea—the cowardly quartermaster turning penance into partnership. But another part, the one that understood how monsters were made, saw something different: a man trying to claw his way back to the light, one scar at a time.

Torque might just be my way to smoke Harlan out.

"Careful what you promise," I said finally, voice low. "Redemption's a full-time job. And I don't hand out second chances easy."

He met my eyes and nodded like a man taking an oath.

"Understood, Captain," he said, all earnest shoulders and shaking hands. He squared up like a recruit about to recite the creed. "I get it."

And then Torque began revealing intel about Harlan's operation—exactly what I needed to drag Harlan out of the shadows and into the open.

CHAPTER 28

Torque took a breath like he had practiced the line. "There's an opportunity tonight," he said. "Big one. Dover. A shipment coming through."

My ears pricked. Dover AFB, Delaware. The Air Force Base was the largest air freight terminal in the Department of Defense, handling the bulk of east-coast cargo and military arrivals. Plane offloads, pallets, medevac runs. If you wanted to move a shipment that had to look legitimate, Dover was where it came to be processed into the system. Close to the ports, easy to redirect into private yards, and miles from the kind of scrutiny a big city brings.

"It routes the usual way—Bagram to Ramstein to Dover," he went on, fast. "That's the chain."

Most military transport flights out of Afghanistan in 2015 originated from Bagram, stopped in Germany, primarily Ramstein Air Base, before continuing to the US to land in Dover AFB. This was turning out to be really interesting.

"Go on," I said.

"This one isn't your usual Medevac padding or a couple of bricks hidden in stretchers. This load's heavy, the kind you don't just hide in a stretcher; you hide in the guts of the shipment. It's equipment crates, arms returns—huge crates, pallets the size of cars. False bottoms, inner cavities. You could hide a lot in there. You do the math, Captain." He looked like a man trying to swallow the numbers. "Almost two tons. Wholesale, that's near two hundred million.

Street—five times that. Harlan's betting his future on this one. It's his ticket to owning the East Coast."

I didn't interrupt. Two tons. The number punched the air out of me. Two tons buys armies. Two tons bought Harlan an empire if he pulled it off.

"That's why Harlan called me to Andrews this morning," Torque said. "Wanted to go over the logistics a final time. Wanted the manifest routes airtight. Everything needs to go like clockwork to make sure extraction happens before the official chain ever touches the crates. That's my job tonight—rig Bills of Lading, change consignee names, mark pallets as 'secure hold', route them to a private bonded yard instead of normal processing. I'll schedule which trucks and teams handle the offload, bring in a contractor who owes Harlan favors. By the time the manifest gets entered, the payload's already gone."

Torque rattled through it, fingers sketching routes in the air like a man tracing smuggling lanes. I listened. The devil lived in details, and Torque worshiped details. Bureaucratic sleight-of-hand was his trade—ugly, precise, corrosive.

"If you'd used that brain for something honest," I said, shaking my head.

He gave a short, sour smile. "Should've. Enlisted to make something of myself. Should've kept clear of Harlan. He strings men up like marionettes. But one thing I realized today, and it gave me a big kick—he's scared of you."

"How's that?"

"You spooked him at Andrews. I didn't know till after that you were the guy who single-handedly took out Shade's crew last night, made Shade tuck his tail between his legs and run," he said, chuckling. "The second you left, Harlan told me to stick to your tail, never lose sight until he figures out what to do next. I told him I wasn't Jason Bourne—so he sent his boys with me." He jerked a thumb toward the bodies on the floor.

"Who are they?" I asked.

"Local Baltimore crew. Did dirty jobs for Shade. Offing people, making them disappear... things like that."

He went quiet a beat, then forced the pitch back up. "Listen, Captain—if you stop Harlan from moving that shipment, you're going to hurt him real bad. He promised supply lines to crews from Baltimore to Boston, took a lot of advance cash. Hit that stash tonight and every buyer he owes will look at him and wonder if their supply's vapor. His backers eat their own when the money vanishes. It nukes his retirement. Right?"

"Right. They won't take time turning on him if he doesn't deliver," I said, trying to process all that he had revealed.

I laid it out for him straight. "What you told me—it's priceless. Exactly what I needed. But we don't just smash this with a crowbar. It has to be handled smart. We need to come up with a solid plan."

He nodded like a man relieved someone said it out loud. "I know, Captain. I know."

As I got my thoughts together, I told him to sit tight, walked to the truck, grabbed the first-aid kit from under the seat and pulled out gauze and disinfectant. Torque held out his right hand like a kid with a busted knee. The skin was shredded, ragged and dark with blood, a testament to the force with which a single bullet can tear a gun out of a man's hand.

"Hold still," I said, and started dressing the wounds—clean, quick, methodical. Bandage over blood, tape to hold. My hands moved on autopilot, the same hands that had fixed worse things in worse places.

He flinched once, then went steady. "Captain," he said, "thank you."

While I worked the tape, my head sifted through options. Torque's detail about Dover was the kind of lead that made a plan possible. But it wasn't enough to light the fuse by itself.

I couldn't stroll into Dover AFB with a bullhorn and demand a seizure. I was too low on the food chain. A Colonel's word would drown mine in one phone call. If I showed up and made accusations, a man in a J3 office could file a complaint and make the whole thing a bureaucratic circus. I would end up in an MP interview and the evidence would go into a box to rot.

There were two sensible plays. One, bait Harlan's men when they moved the stash and torch the whole load. Smashes and pyres, quick and messy—effective, but leave a lot of loose ends and a mess of bodies that a guy like Harlan could bury in other men's files.

Two, get the consignment interdicted at the airbase. That would be neat. Permanent. Seized by legitimate authority. Have law and paper finish what my hands started. Take the product, take Harlan's power and make his name radioactive.

But that second option required more than a shotgun and a grudge. It needed a heavyweight who could call the right people, make the DEA and base command do what needed doing the same night. There was one man I knew who carried that kind of weight: James Davis. Deputy Director of Operations at the CIA.

I had a history with Davis. The man owed me a life. Back when I was an Army Ranger, before Delta, I had pulled Davis's daughter Madison out of Taliban hands. After that, Davis moved me jobs that bent the rules; when I went to Delta I ran ops that dropped from his desk. He owed me, and more importantly, he had the clout to get men on the tarmac with warrants and teeth, and that too on a timeline measured in hours, not days.

But I wasn't going to call Davis on rumor. I wouldn't drag his office into a joke. If Torque was spinning a yarn to save his skin and I dragged Davis into it, the fallout would be ugly for a lot of people who didn't deserve it—and I wasn't interested in being the reason a federal director got humiliated.

I needed iron on the tail: flight numbers, ETAs, cargo markings—the cold facts that would let Davis make the call and not get burned.

Torque seemed to have some kind of a sixth sense as he watched me with those scared, earnest eyes. "Write it down, Captain," he said suddenly. "Everything. Flight number, tail number, ETA, manifest codes, pallet count—everything. If it's real, you'll have what you need. If it's not... then you can gut me right now. Remember I just quoted James 4:17. Well, I'm trying to do the good now."

He reached into his jacket with his left hand and produced a small notepad. He jabbed a pen across the page and began rattling numbers and codes—fast, precise, automatic. I didn't look at the paper yet. I listened to the rhythm of his voice: manifest numbers, consignee names, a bonded-yard tag, the contractor's company name. Detail after detail stitched the story together.

The more he spoke, the less my gut clawed at doubt. He wasn't inventing stuff on the fly. The specifics were there, hard and ugly. Good enough to call Davis.

Then Torque paused, eyes going somewhere else for a beat, and said something that stopped me cold. "There's one more thing," he said. "If you want a real hammer, I can tell you where they keep the stock they hold for distribution. It's where they break pallets and stage the packages for local moves. It's locked up in a warehouse south of Baltimore. Well-guarded. A guy like me couldn't dream of hitting it. But you're Delta. You could make the door open and stay open long enough to wreck the place."

The guy was full of surprises—a never-ending source of information. This latest intel was exactly what I needed to make sure Davis wouldn't get tripped. And it would drive the final nail on Harlan's dreams.

When I finished bandaging, I slid the tape tight and folded the excess. Torque's hand looked less like a ruin and more like an instrument that might still play.

Torque looked at me then with the kind of earnestness that made guilt look like a uniform you could take off. "Captain," he said, "I know how this looks. Me suddenly turning Santa and giving out free goodies. My old man threw James 2:17 at me a lot: 'Faith by itself, if it does not have works, is dead.' Maybe this is my work. I'll make it count."

I let the Bible line hang there and said nothing. The Scripture didn't change anything, but it gave the man small ballast. It was almost funny—his sermonizing and my strapped Glock—but I kept my face like a slab. But I heard the sincerity in his voice and, for better or worse, I believed him enough to use him.

Torque had given me a map. Now I had to turn it into a trap. I felt the plan lock into place like a bolt sliding home.

I slid the phone out of my pocket. Time to call in a favor. A favor I had earned in an Afghan canyon full of gunfire.

CHAPTER 29

I called Davis. The line clicked once, and his voice came through.

"Captain Blaze," he said. Then his tone shifted, softer, carrying a weight you didn't usually hear from a man who commanded the world's most secret wars. "I heard about Captain Ryan Blaze. I'm sorry. He was a good man. A damn good one."

That hit me harder than I expected. We hadn't spoken since Ryan went down. "Thank you, sir," I said, keeping it short. "He was the best of us."

The silence after that stretched thin, then Davis pulled it back to business like flipping a switch. "What's on your mind, Captain?"

"I'm in D.C.," I said. "I've got something big—time-sensitive, critical. Can't talk about it on the line. I need to bring it to you in person."

There was no pretense. No "what's this about?" He was never the kind to waste words. "Can you make it to Langley?" he asked, his tone back to clipped command mode.

"I can be there in forty minutes."

"Good. Give me your license plate. I'll have security wave you through."

I read it off, hearing the scratch of his pen on the other end.

"Got it. See you soon," he said, and that was that.

I hung up and turned to Torque. "Get in the pickup."

He obeyed fast, without question. I took the SUV he and his goons had rolled up in, drove it into the yawning mouth of the warehouse and shoved it behind a stack of pallets until it looked like it belonged there. No point in leaving a conspicuous vehicle in a dead lot. Curiosity and cops had the same appetite. I wiped my prints, closed the metal door, locked it, and walked back to my truck.

Torque sat stiff in the passenger seat, clutching his bandaged hand like a relic. He cleared his throat. "Uh... Captain? Where are we going?"

"CIA headquarters," I said, starting the engine.

His eyes widened, and for a second, I thought he might try to open the door and roll out. But he just nodded, silent, staring straight ahead.

I shifted gears. "Harlan expecting a call from you?"

Torque swallowed. "He said to call if something happens. Otherwise, just tail you and keep him posted."

"Then he won't notice anything," I said.

Torque nodded again. "Right. Because nothing out of the ordinary happened." He paused, glanced at me, then added, "Except all the guys I came with are dead, and I've decided to change sides and go straight."

I almost laughed. "Right," I said flatly. "Nothing to report."

He grinned weakly, a flash of gallows humor before we fell into silence.

We pulled out of National Harbor, the late afternoon sun burning low through the haze. I took I-295 north, the road stretching long and gray between green strips of industrial scrub and old brick buildings. The city crept up in the distance—glass, traffic, and too many flags.

Torque sat quiet most of the way, rubbing his bandaged hand like he was trying to pray through it. Every so often, I would catch him glancing at the rearview mirror, as if expecting Harlan's men to rise from the dead and tail us.

The turn onto the George Washington Parkway came easy. The Potomac slid along our left, smooth and cold-looking under the fading light. By the time we crossed into McLean, the world had gone quieter—suburban money, heavy trees, and security fences disguised as landscaping.

Langley. The CIA's headquarters sat back in the woods like a secret built into the earth—no high towers, no neon signage, just calm, methodical authority. It was less a fortress and more a campus of iron and protocol: badge readers, barriers, men with earpieces who learned how to look at you without being seen. You didn't find it unless you were meant to. Wide driveways, perfectly trimmed hedges, and armed men who looked bored until the moment they weren't.

As we rolled up to the main gate, the guard booth door opened. A guy with a square jaw and a ballistic vest stepped forward, already looking down at a tablet. "Captain Blaze?" he asked.

I nodded. He glanced at the screen, then waved his partner to lift the gate. The heavy barrier rose, and he gestured us through. "Straight ahead, sir. Visitor lane."

No fuss, no delay. Someone on the loop had already told them to expect us.

The compound swallowed us—redbrick buildings, clean glass, and parking lots that looked like they were drawn with rulers.

A plainclothes escort stepped out from another checkpoint, wearing a blue blazer and a badge clipped to his belt. "Captain Blaze?"

"Yes."

"Director Davis is expecting you. Follow me."

He led us to a parking area near the main entrance. I shut off the engine. Torque followed me out, blinking like a man seeing daylight for the first time. We passed through a layer of reinforced glass doors that sighed shut behind us. Inside, the lobby gleamed—quiet floors, soft lighting, a long reception desk manned by a woman who looked too calm for someone surrounded by the ghosts of a hundred covert wars.

She looked up as we approached. "Captain Blaze. Director Davis said you'd be coming."

"Ma'am," I said with a nod.

She printed two visitor badges and slid them across the counter. Torque just stared, mouth half open, taking in the flags, the seal on the wall, the buzz of analysts in suits gliding past security doors.

"Close your mouth, Sergeant," I muttered. "You've got nothing to worry about. At least not yet."

Torque smirked. "Thanks for the comforting reassurance, Captain."

We sat. The building hummed the way something monumental hums—air handlers and filtered light and the soft whir of a thousand small, important things. Torque kept his head down, fingers worrying at his good hand. I looked at him, then at the badge in my palm, and felt the plan tightening like a noose with teeth.

We didn't have to wait long—less than two minutes, maybe less. The sound of quick footsteps came from the corridor, and then I saw him.

Nate Foster. CIA analyst, poster child for caffeine and overwork, but right now he looked fresher than I had ever seen him.

"Axel!" he called out, a broad smile cracking his face.

Before I had even fully stood up, he closed the distance and pulled me into a hug. Not a handshake. A full-on, two-arm, bear hug.

I froze for a beat—last time I saw Nate, he was shaking in a Syrian ghetto, about to be executed by ISIS on live stream before I pulled him out. He had been pale, jumpy, and nerdy enough to quote geopolitics mid-rescue.

Now he was solid, confident, even casual. He stepped back, clapping me on the shoulder. "Man, it's damn good to see you. And... Axel, I'm really sorry about Ryan. I mean that."

"Thanks, Nate," I said quietly.

He nodded, then noticed Torque standing awkwardly behind me.

"Sergeant Wade," I introduced him. "Temporary assignment."

Torque shot me a look that said *temporary what?*, but I ignored it.

Nate smiled and gestured for us to follow. "Director's waiting for you. Come on in, Captain."

Nate led us down a long corridor lined with glass offices and muted carpet, the kind of place that smelled like coffee, printer toner, and secrets. He stopped at a smaller room, dropped Torque in there with a cup of coffee, and said he would be back in a bit. Torque looked like a kid about to meet the principal. I told him to stay put. He gave me an unenthusiastic nod.

I closed the door behind me as we walked to the next conference room to meet Davis.

CHAPTER 30

Nate walked me into a bigger conference room—mahogany table, three chairs, a wall screen looping satellite feeds on mute. Davis was already there, leaning into his laptop with that signature intensity that made junior analysts sweat through their suits.

Late fifties, blond hair touched with gray, face like weathered sandstone. He stood when I came in and for a second I almost didn't recognize the man—there was something in his face that loosened the stern line I had always seen on him. He took my hand in a grip that was firm and, for once, a little warm.

"Blaze," he said, the faintest glint of emotion in his eyes. "I'm sorry about Captain Ryan Blaze." The words weren't a formality. They carried a weight. That flash of something human in him made the room narrower for a second.

"Thank you, sir," I said quietly. I kept it short. Davis wasn't the kind to do long condolences. Neither was I.

He snapped back to business like a switch. "You've got my attention. What have you found?"

I got straight to it. "There's a drug smuggling operation running out of Afghanistan. Heroin pipeline, big one. It's coming into the U.S. through military channels."

Davis frowned slightly. "Go on."

"It's being moved under official manifests—military flights. I've got intel on a big shipment due to arrive at Dover AFB. Took off from Bagram and is currently in Ramstein. Scheduled to take off in an hour. Wheels down in Dover at 0200 hours."

That got his attention. Nate, standing by the screen, looked up from his laptop.

"Dover," Davis repeated. "That's not your usual trafficking route."

"Exactly," I said. "Which is what makes it perfect. Nobody's going to question a C-17 touching down at a U.S. military base. But this one's carrying two tons of heroin."

Both of them straightened up. Even Nate stopped typing for a moment.

Davis's tone hardened. "How confident are you in this intel?"

"High confidence," I said. "Sergeant Wade—the guy I brought in—handled logistics for the smugglers. He gave me flight numbers, cargo details, and manifests. I don't flash a name without cross-check, but you'll want to see this data." I pushed the notebook across the table.

Nate nodded, eyes scanning the screen like a man decoding the Matrix. He ran the numbers while Davis watched both of us with the patience of a man who had seen too many lies try to look like truth. The room hummed with low tech sounds—fans, distant servers, a building breathing around secrets. Nate's fingers moved through validation, cross-referencing tail numbers, flight plans, chain-of-custody notations.

I could see the tension leave his shoulders fractionally as things matched up. "Everything matches," Nate said, glancing between us. "Flight manifests, cargo weight, destination—all clean on paper, but the timing and authorization codes are... off. Blaze's guy isn't lying."

Davis's expression softened into something like a half-smile. "Good work."

"I wanted to loop you in early," I told him.

He leaned back, steepling his fingers. "If this is real, and sounds like it is, we seize it on the tarmac. DEA takes custody on American soil. We'll need signatures, warrants, a judge willing to listen at stupid hours, but I can move that if the intel is solid. We keep it clean—legal chain, warrants, the whole show. You understand the risk of doing this without paperwork?" he asked.

"Yeah." I told him my plan—confirm a smaller cache first. "I'll give you a final green light once I've confirmed one smaller bust tied to this same network."

Davis leaned forward. "How small?"

"About two hundred pounds," I said.

"Two hundred pounds? That's not small at all."

I gave a thin smile. "Compared to two tons, it's pocket change."

He nodded once. "What's your plan?"

"I'll personally verify the stash. Once I confirm it's real, you can send in DEA. That'll give us probable cause and evidence chain for the main sting tonight. You could then move the machinery: warrants, a DEA task force, base command cooperation. I know that's the only way to make a seizure stick."

He took that in, then looked up. "Does this connect to Ryan's death?"

I froze for a beat. Davis always saw more than most.

"Yeah," I said finally. "It does. But I'm still putting the final pieces together. All I can tell you right now is—it's being run by someone high up."

Davis's eyes sharpened, but he didn't press. I wasn't giving him the name yet. Not until Harlan was done breathing.

"Once I confirm the smaller bust, the sergeant becomes our state witness. He was the Quartermaster—handled the supply chain end of it."

"How'd you recruit him?" Davis asked, a smile ghosting across his face like he knew the answer would be more interesting than the question.

"I talked to him," I said. "Persuasively. He saw the light."

That earned me a quiet smirk from Davis, like he didn't believe a word, but wasn't going to bother asking.

"I better get moving," I said. "Need to check out the smaller cache before it moves."

"Want to share location details?" Davis asked.

"Not yet. Safer if I do this solo. But when I give you the signal, I'll need every resource you can put in play to make the airport sting airtight."

Davis stood and offered his hand again. "You'll have it."

We shook. Then he left the room, leaving Nate to see me out.

Nate closed his laptop. "Hold on a sec. Someone from D.C. drove over to see you. Said it was important."

I frowned. "Who?"

He didn't answer—just grinned and stepped out. A minute later, the door opened again.

She walked in.

Madison.

She moved with the kind of quiet grace that made the room slow for her—long blonde hair, green eyes so vivid they looked like a light. She had that same steady, disarming presence she had always had. Smart. Kind. The kind of kind that nearly cost her her life in Kandahar.

She stopped two paces away from me. "Axel," she said softly.

"Madison," I said, a little stunned.

Then without a beat she stepped forward and hugged me. It was one of those rare, whole hugs that landed warm and solid. I stood there for a beat, surprised by how normal it felt.

One hell of a day for hugs, I thought: first Nate, now Madison. But between the two, hers didn't exactly feel like something to complain about.

She pulled back, her eyes finding mine—green, sharp, and full of something that looked a lot like concern. "I'm so sorry about Ryan, Axel," she said softly.

"Yeah," I said, voice low. "Thanks." I hesitated. "I got your voicemail. I just... wasn't in a good place." I didn't offer anything more. I didn't need to.

"I figured," she said gently. "You don't owe me an explanation."

She told me she had moved to D.C., taken a break from the relief work—the hotspots, the long drives, the places that ate kindness for breakfast. When Nate told her I would be at Langley, she had dropped everything and come over. "Figured I'd say hello," she said.

Madison looked different now—still beautiful, but steadier somehow. She said she had moved to D.C. a few months back, taking a break from the relief work—the war-torn hotspots, the long drives.

"Figured I should stay somewhere that didn't require a flak jacket to buy groceries," she added with a faint smile. "I was writing freelance pieces for the Chronicle from overseas... ended up joining them full-time when I got back."

"Reporter now?" I asked. "Guess that explains why you're still running toward trouble."

She shrugged. "Old habits." Then she added, "When Nate got word you were coming to Langley, I dropped everything and came straight here. He knew I'd kill him if he didn't tell me in time."

That actually made me smile—a real one this time.

We caught up for a couple minutes—surface talk mostly. Her apartment, her new beat, how strange it was living in a city where people fought with words instead of guns. She laughed, and for a moment the weight in my chest eased. But she could read people too well—and she could tell I was on the clock.

"You should go," she said. "You've got that look—like you're already halfway gone."

She was right.

Before I could turn, Madison asked quietly, "This thing you're chasing... it's about Ryan, isn't it?"

I paused. I didn't want to pull her into this mess, but there was no clean way to dodge the question. "Yeah," I said. "It's about him."

Her eyes shifted—soft, but wary. "His death... it wasn't an accident?"

I met her gaze. "No. Took me a long time to piece it together. He was murdered—by a drug-smuggling ring run by American soldiers."

Her eyes widened. For a second, she didn't breathe. "Oh my God!" she whispered. "Do you think you can get them caught? Sent to prison?"

I gave a small, humorless smile. "They've buried their tracks deep. The law won't do much more than slap their wrists—if that."

Madison looked down, then back up at me. "So what are you planning to do?"

"What I was trained to do," I said quietly. "Take out the bad guys."

She studied me for a long moment, eyes searching for something human under the steel. She exhaled slowly, torn between horror and understanding. "You know, a few years ago, I'd have tried to talk you down. I used to believe everyone could be saved... that forgiveness fixed everything." She hesitated, voice trembling slightly. "But maybe some things shouldn't be forgiven."

"They shouldn't," I said flatly. "Some men aren't broken—they're built wrong. Evil's in the wiring. You can't fix that. You can only cut it out."

Her eyes glistened, the conflict in them clear. "Axel... if there's anything I can do to help—anything at all—I'll consider it a privilege. I haven't forgotten that I owe you my life."

I shook my head. "You don't owe me a thing, Madison. But... I appreciate the thought."

Her hand brushed my sleeve, lingered a second too long. "Just be careful," she said, voice low. "Don't lose yourself in this."

I nodded once. Didn't want to say it out loud that part of me was already gone.

Then I turned and walked off, leaving her in the pale light of the hallway—her silhouette caught between worry and something that looked a lot like belief.

By the time I got back to the truck, the clock was ticking loudly in my head. Two hours to hit

Harlan's stash before I could give Davis the green light. The Potomac blurred past as I pulled away from Langley and pointed the truck north toward Baltimore.

The mission was clear. Everything else could wait.

CHAPTER 31

I ran the layout of the warehouse over in my head as Torque talked and I kept my hands on the wheel. He painted it in clipped strokes, like a man reading an inventory of sins.

"It's a freight-forwarding front," he said. "Import broker look. Nobody walks in without a reason. Two doors—front for the paper, back for the trucks. Cameras on both. Front door's locked; keypad, but the guards inside usually open it. Two guys posted just inside. A guy or two behind the counter. Back door opens only for trucks. Inside's a converted garage. That's where they keep the stash."

"How many men?" I asked.

"Ten, give or take," he said. "Three up front, the rest in the back. Rotations change with the shifts."

Everything he said tracked with the map Echo had pushed over the feed when I sent him the address. Echo's overlay had matched cameras to beams and public ingress points. I hadn't told Torque that I had double-checked. Torque had been right so far; had earned the benefit of a small measure of trust. Didn't mean I wasn't hedging my bets.

Torque watched my face. "That's...a lot of guys, Captain. How you thinking we do this?" His voice had that mixture of fear and hopeful bravado that people get when they try to convince themselves they are brave.

I kept my hands steady on the wheel. "You walk me past the guards like you belong. You ask for your buddy in the back. When I give the nod you take a seat in the lobby and don't twitch. I go back. You keep your head down."

He gulped. "So... you're saying I hold the front? Me? Captain, didn't you just see my fighting skills when you whupped my ass? I'm the guy who gets nervous if the coffee's too hot."

"You didn't hear me. You just lie low. I'm the one taking out those guys."

"Right, you've got like an assault rifle back there," he said hopefully, glancing at the back. "Might get a bit noisy, but I guess we've got other things to worry about."

"Nope. No fireworks. No slaughter. I don't want homicide on the scene. We subdue, secure, call it in. Let the cops do their job and confiscate the stuff. I don't want a murder scene. It'll mess up the plan."

He looked so nervous I almost felt bad. "You're seriously going to go in there and take down ten men with nothing. I mean, you're Delta and all, but... all due respect, Captain, but that's either the bravest stupid thing I've ever heard or the stupidest brave thing."

"We do it fast, surgical. There's a baseball bat in the truck if I need it. Otherwise it's hands, knives, timing. Comes down to surprise, speed, overwhelming violence. Surely you must've picked something from CQB training at some point, Sergeant?"

"Close quarters battle?"

"Yes."

"Look at me, Captain, and take a guess."

"I guess that's a no. Anyway, don't worry about it. Like I said, lie low. Stay where I tell you. I'll take the men down hard enough to keep them from getting up, but not dead. Then we call it in."

He rubbed his bandaged hand and let out a half-laugh. "Right. Not a worry in the world. Got it, Captain. I'll text my mama—she's never going to believe this."

"Don't tell your mama anything," I said. "Keep the texting to a minimum."

I let that settle between us. The plan was fragile and precise; it would take timing and luck and the kind of violence I preferred to keep measured. And now that I was getting close to what I had been hunting all these weeks, there was so much pent up energy inside me that I was looking forward to an outlet.

We fell into a silence of engines and road noise. The river wove away to our left, gray and indifferent.

My burner suddenly buzzed on the dash, a low vibration that cut through the silence. This was the burner I had lit just hours ago—only Echo and I had that number. I didn't expect other calls. I frowned.

I glanced at the screen. The number looked familiar, but my brain didn't pull the file right away. Some half-buried memory stirred, and then faded again.

I thumbed the accept button, popped the earpiece in, and said, "Yeah."

A voice came through—lazy, cocky, and unmistakable. "Damn, Cowboy, took your sweet time pickin' up. Thought you'd gone dark on me."

For a split second, I forgot to breathe. Then I actually laughed—something I hadn't done much of lately. "You gotta be shitting me. Ninja? Didn't think I'd hear that smart mouth again this side of a war zone."

"The one and only," he said, with that grin I could hear over the line. "Ninja Man himself. You miss me?"

Ninja was the call sign of Staff Sergeant Buck Conway. Fast with a blade, faster with a wisecrack. His nickname came from the black-inked ninja across his back and the hand-forged nine-inch blade he carried like it was an extra limb. Lethal in a fight, loyal in a storm. We had run dozens of ops together, side by side, in more sand and smoke than I cared to remember—and somewhere along the line, he had become more brother than teammate. One of the few men I would trust to guard my six in hell.

I leaned back in the seat, still shaking my head. "Hell, Ninja. How the hell did you get this number? I just lit this burner a couple of hours ago."

He chuckled. "Come on, boss. You think you're the only one who talks to Echo?"

That made me smile. "Should've told Echo to keep that big mouth of his shut."

"Yeah, good luck with that. You ever try shutting him up? You'd have better odds wrestling a grizzly with a toothache."

I could practically see his smirk. For a second, it felt like old times—sand, sweat, and gun oil between the jokes.

"So," I asked, "what's the occasion? You guys parked at Bragg?"

I guessed the reason Ninja was stateside was the team was at Fort Bragg, North Carolina. Officially it's the headquarters of the 1st Special Forces Operational Detachment–Delta, though you won't find that name on a sign anywhere. It's where we trained, rebuilt, and sharpened the edges we had dulled overseas.

He laughed. "You guessed it. Whole team's back at Bragg for the week—same grind, endless drills. We were gonna swing by your ranch this weekend, but command tossed us some R&R. I'm down in Gainesville visitin' my folks, figured I'd check in on the legend himself."

Gainesville. Virginia. About forty miles west of D.C. Close enough to trouble if you knew where to look.

"So you just *called* Echo?" I asked.

"Yeah," he replied, "but the little gremlin was actin' cagey as hell when I asked about you. Got all twitchy when I brought up your name—like a kid caught with a nudie mag. Took a bit of my charm to get him talking."

"Charm? That what we're calling interrogation now?"

He laughed. "Echo knows he's catching hell next time he sees you."

Then his voice changed—lower, steady, the edge that came out when things got real. "So tell me straight, Cowboy. You finally hot on the trail of Ryan's killers?"

There was no dodging this one.

"Yeah," I said quietly. "I'm close."

A pause, then the sound of him exhaling. "That's the way to go, brother," Ninja said, his voice now solid steel. "Knew you wouldn't let that one go once you caught the scent."

"Wasn't ever gonna," I said.

"Didn't think so." He paused again, then, "So where do I meet you?"

"You don't," I told him. "This one's personal, Ninja. I'm not dragging you into it."

"Save it," he cut in, sharp as his blade. "We may not be blood, Cowboy, but you know how this works. Brotherhood ain't just a word—it's a pact. For life. You fight, I fight."

That one hit like a punch to the gut. There was no arguing with him when he said it like that. I sighed.

He must have sensed me wavering, because he shifted gears with a grin you could almost hear. "Besides, you can't rob me of the chance to kick some ass again. We been sittin' on our asses in Bragg for a week, doin' training drills and PowerPoint briefings. I'm itchin' for a real fight in Baltimore."

I rubbed a hand over my face. "You know about Baltimore too?"

He chuckled. "Ears to the ground, boss. And a few friendly satellites in the sky."

"Jesus," I muttered.

He laughed. "I'm in D.C. tonight, gotta head back to Bragg tomorrow. So how 'bout we raise a little hell together again?"

I still tried to hold back.

"Come on, Cowboy," he said, voice dropping into that old familiar rhythm. "One last dance, for old times' sake."

I leaned back in my seat, stared out at the dim lights ahead, and exhaled. There was no winning this one.

"Fine," I said. "Meet me at the gas station a mile from the site. How soon can you be there?"

"Oh, I'll beat you to it," he said, smug as ever. "Already in Baltimore. Figured you'd try to talk me outta it, so I parked my ass here before you even picked up."

I shook my head, smiling despite myself. "Still a pain in my ass, Conway."

"Love you too, boss."

The line clicked off.

Torque was staring at me from the passenger seat, brow raised like he had just watched me summon a ghost.

I looked at him and said, "You can breathe easy. We just got another Delta operator in the game."

Torque let out a slow breath, some of the tension slipping from his shoulders. "That's good news."

"Yeah," I said quietly, eyes fixed on the road ahead. "Good news."

But in my head, the laughter faded. Every call, every move, every hour—I was getting closer.

I could feel it. The target was near.

CHAPTER 32

The sun had begun to slide low, turning the hard edges of the city into gold. It was just about 1700 hours—rush hour coughing up workers in suits and women in heels, cars folding into the arteries like a swarm heading for the exits. Horns stitched the air.

We cut across the beltway and aimed for the Curtis Bay industrial area—south Baltimore, where the warehouses sat like old teeth. The route funneled us deeper into freight territory: loading docks, stray pallets, chain-link fences topped with wire. Streetlights winked on against the early dim, and commuters streamed toward Metro stops.

Torque rode shotgun, restless. He kept talking, half to keep his hands busy, half to keep his eyes off the rearview. He pointed out spots as we passed—names and signs like a map to trouble.

"South and west sides are the big flows," he told me. "Corner stores, barbershops, laundromats—places that look normal unless you know what to look for. Fronts for cash drops. Docks handle the imports. You hit the right block, you find the pipeline. Harlan ran product through pockets like that."

I listened more than I spoke, scanning the blocks we passed. There were signs the city had been chewed on and spit out—boarded storefronts with graffiti like signatures, furniture on curbs waiting for someone to claim it or torch it, a mural that tried to be pretty under a sheen of grime. Once in a while, a strip club or a shuttered grocery blinked neon. Outside it, clusters of men in hoodies hung around. Eyes flicked toward us and away.

Torque pointed out landmarks like a nervous tour guide. "Baltimore's got sectors," he said. "You hit the west and you're in the middle of the market—low-level guys feeding higher-level crews. East side has folks who manage imports. North... north is where the hitters live, muscle mostly. They run the streets like landlords. Harlan's crew? They fit right in. They started by moving product through a few of these pockets."

I kept my hands on the wheel, letting his chatter fill the cab like static. Torque's own voice calmed him; talking kept fear on a leash. As the blocks narrowed and the buildings grew squat and industrial, Torque's drumming got faster. He started glancing at his phone like it might sprout answers. Sweat collected at his temple. He was a live wire.

There was a reason he was so jumpy. Right after my call with Ninja, Torque's phone lit up—Harlan on the other end. He looked at me like the world had just dropped a live grenade in his lap. I told him to take the call and play it cool: tell Harlan he was following me and moving through D.C. Torque gulped, answered, and sounded as natural as he could. Harlan bought it and the call ended. Since then his nervous energy had been ratcheted way past normal.

"You good?" I asked.

He exhaled, too loud. "It's not the warehouse, Captain. I can handle the warehouse. It's Shade, Reaper, Harlan—when they find out I flipped, they'll kill me. They'll do it slow. Make an example." He rubbed the inside of his forearm like he was putting out a spark.

I looked at him, watched the way his hands trembled against the dash. There was no swagger in what I said next, no chest-thumping bravado. I said it like I was stating something about the weather.

"None of them will live to see tomorrow."

The words landed cold and clean. No flourish. Just a statement of fact. Torque watched my face like a man reading a verdict.

"You sure?" he asked, voice thin.

I nodded. "Yeah."

He looked at my face then, searching for the lie people always tried to hide behind their eyes. All he found was resolve. He let out a breath the length of a small prayer.

"Good," he said finally. "Because—I don't want to die like that. Not for Harlan's trash." His fingers curled into the seam of the seat. "I'll—if I gotta do time for what I did, I will. I'm done with them. I want out. I want to—start over."

"You'll do your time," I said. "You'll pay what you owe. But this is the only way you make it possible to rebuild. You help us bury this crew, close this chapter, then you do the rest the right way. Court, plea, whatever. Clean slate after the debts are settled. That's your shot."

He tightened his jaw. "I'm ready. I'll take whatever comes."

We rolled into the part of Curtis Bay where the buildings were squat and industrial and the sun didn't reach much of the concrete. A freight train clattered on a nearby track and the vibration ran up through the steering wheel. Shadows pooled under awnings. A rusted sign swung on a factory that hadn't cared for its name in years.

The gas station I had picked, about a mile from the warehouse, sat like a pale lighthouse in the gray evening—pumps under a flickering canopy, a rectangle of fluorescent light, a couple of sedans and two pickups hunkered near the convenience door. I eased the truck into a parking spot.

Ninja's truck stuck out before I even killed the engine. A black ninja, painted on the tailgate like a bad tattoo, stared back at me like a joke with teeth. If the paint job didn't give it away, the man in the bed did—propped on a toolbox, one boot hooked over the tailgate, grin doing most of the talking.

Ninja was all angles when he moved. He flipped over the side and landed on catlike feet. That motion—smooth, silent, efficient—made the name fit. Around five foot ten, wiry at about 175, Ninja didn't look like much until you knew what he could do. When he keyed in on a target, he turned into a different machine: silent, surgical, lethal. Delta ran through him like a language he spoke without accent.

I climbed out. "Cowboy," Ninja greeted me, all teeth showing. "Miss me?"

"Keep asking me that and I'll make you sleep in the toolbox," I shot back.

I nodded at the ninja on the tailgate. "Is that a family trademark now? You trying to collect royalties?"

He laughed. "Gotta represent, boss. You gonna complain? I left room on the bumper for your name."

I punched his shoulder. "Keep it, man. It's uglier than you."

We traded easy shit for about half a minute. Torque watched from the pavement, hands jammed in his pockets like he was holding himself together.

Then Ninja's face shifted. The grin tightened. The joke thinning, the blade coming back into focus.

"So what's the play?" he asked, voice small and professional.

I introduced him to Torque. "This is Sergeant Wade," I said. "Wade, Ninja."

Then I laid it out like I always did—short and flat. "We walk in with Sergeant Wade," I said. "Guards know him. He gets us inside. There's a front office with a couple of guards and maybe two other guys. Behind the office is a converted garage where they store their stash. We clean out the front first—quickly and silently. Then walk into the back and take out the guys in there. Nobody gets a radio call out."

Ninja's eyes tagged Torque like a predator smelling fresh meat. A look of question formed—how did this guy know the runners?—but he shut it down when I shook my head, a tiny, tight motion: don't ask.

"Copy," Ninja replied. "How many inside?"

"Ten, give or take," I said.

He shrugged like it was Tuesday. "One of those easy days, then. Rules of engagement?"

"Non-lethal," I replied. "We take them out, but leave them breathing. Hand it over to the cops after that."

"Roger that. The plan's tight," was all he said.

Torque looked like he might throw up. He volunteered to use the restroom before we moved.

Alone, Ninja raised an eyebrow. "You think he's solid?"

"He was the quartermaster," I said. "Ran logistics for the shipments—Afghanistan into here. Handled routes, cash flows, stash rotations. Grew a conscience when I took out his pals and made him see the light. Flipped sides. He's with us now."

Short facts. No mercy.

Ninja whistled low. "So we ain't... you know—wringing his neck afterward?"

"No." I didn't like it, but the calculus was clean. "We put him in front of the law. Hand him to the state as a witness. He helps us take the whole damn network down. He pays his debt in court, not in the street."

Ninja nodded, the motion quick. "Smart. Less mess." Then his voice grew cold. "And Ryan's killers?"

"Three targets. Harlan, Shade, Reaper."

Ninja finished the thought for me: "They're not seeing tomorrow."

I nodded. No swagger. Just agreement, an iron exchange between men who kept promises with blood.

He smiled, small and sharp. "You handle the hunt. I'll be wingman. I clear the chaff, keep the angles clean."

He looked ready. So was I.

Torque reappeared from the convenience store, hands in his pockets again, jaw set. He met my eyes and gave the slightest nod, the kind a man gave when he decided life was worth the gamble.

We got into my truck and moved out—no more jokes, no more small talk. It was time to take another big swing at Harlan's empire.

CHAPTER 33

The warehouse sat like a quiet lie—a dull office tacked onto a corrugated box of a building. A shipping-company sign out front that promised freight-forwarding and nothing more. A single roll-up door gaped black at the side, a line of pallet racks visible through the slats, and the front office was a dull little box of glass and cinderblock with a faded logo above the door.

People who drove by would imagine invoices, stamps, and a bored guy behind a counter. They wouldn't see the kill-switches, the stash rooms, or the men who used polite business hours to move poison.

We rolled to a stop in the parking lane. Torque's stance changed as he slid out from the truck. He moved into the role he had rehearsed. Gone was the jittery man in the cab, replaced by the guy who had walked these doors a hundred times. He stepped to the keypad and punched the numbers like it was muscle memory. Nothing happened. He tried again. Nothing. The pad stayed dark.

Torque hit the buzzer. The camera's red eye blinked hard.

Torque looked up, square to the lens, and said, "Open the fuckin' door."

The latch clacked. The door swung inward and a big man filled the frame—beefy, barrel-chested, a short-barrel shotgun lowered but ready in his hands. He blocked the doorway like a gate and didn't smile. Torque kept his face flat.

"What's up with the lock?" he asked.

The big man shrugged. "Reaper changed the combos. Beefed up security. Orders."

Torque's jaw tightened. "I'll take that up with Reaper. Move."

The man didn't flinch. He looked past Torque, at Ninja and me.

"Who are those two? I've been told not to let unknowns in," he said.

I watched Torque for the microsecond before he snapped—authority snapping out like a steel cable. "Don't you fuckin' know me?" Torque barked. "Call Kruger to the door."

That name made the guard step back an inch and grumble as he scuffed the concrete to let us pass. Torque breathed like someone coming off a sprint. He had pulled it together. Become the man he needed to be.

Another big guy stood just inside the entrance, an Uzi slung on a strap across his chest. The office area had a counter up front, two men and a computer behind it. One was dumb muscle, wide shoulders, the kind of man whose first answer to everything was force. The second, a slightly leaner version of his partner, while certainly not looking like a philosopher, did at least have the acumen to be going through a spreadsheet on the computer screen.

Torque slid behind the counter and leaned over the keyboard, making soft talk—anxious small talk that worked as a mask. He jabbed at the screen, asked about invoices, glanced at a schedule.

That was our cue.

Everything after that moved in clean, brutal choreography.

I stepped right and drove my shoulder into the shotgun guy's sternum like a battering ram, driving him back off balance. My palm found his chin and I snapped his head back, slamming it against the wall behind him. Once. Twice. The third time did the trick. The wall shook with the impact as the man crumpled, arms flopping uselessly, unconscious before his fingers could find the shotgun strap.

At the same time, Ninja had moved on the other big guard by the door before the man could raise his Uzi. A hard palm to the throat stopped the breath; a hooked elbow cracked into the jaw. The guard doubled up and Ninja finished it with a sharp, practiced neck strike. The man slid to the tile like someone letting go of a rope—out cold.

After taking out the first guard, I didn't stop for an instant. Before the big guy had begun to slump to the floor, I saw the dumb muscle behind the counter lunge toward the shotgun by the corner. I cut across the counter and flipped over the edge, my forearm driving into his throat—to shut the air off—and he gagged. My knee drove into the side of his knee and it gave. He hit the deck with an oath. Before he let out a howl, I finished with a blunt palm to the back of his head, driving him face-first into the tile until his body went heavy and limp.

Ninja rolled through at the same time as I did, flipping his body over the counter. He drove a knee straight up into the computer guy's back while catching his wrists in a vice. The man tried to curl away; Ninja twisted, dislocating the shoulder clean with a quick wrench. The cry died into a gurgle as Ninja bashed the man's skull against the desk face-first—one hard, measured strike—and the man slumped, lights out.

The front office went from loud menace to dead silence in under ten seconds.

Four men, four solid knockouts. No fancy flourishes—just clean, brutal mechanics. And no shots fired—that was the plan. If the guys at the back heard gunfire, the whole place would go live and the plan would go to hell.

We went through the knocked-out men quickly, looking for guns. We dumped what I found on the shelf behind the counter: two Glocks, an Uzi and a shotgun.

I popped the bolt on the Uzi, let the mags clatter out. Ninja broke the shotgun open far enough to dump the shells and wreck the action. The four men on the floor weren't getting up anytime soon, but I didn't trust miracles. The last thing we needed was one of them snapping back and pinning us with gunfire from behind while we cleaned house in the back.

I handed a Glock to Ninja and nodded. He weighed it in his hand, ready.

Torque got the nod. He moved to the door, slipped the bolt, and eased it open. A wave of sound hit us—hard rock thumping. No wonder no one came checking when we banged heads of their pals against the walls in the front. But still, a gunshot wouldn't have blended.

We stood in the threshold and took it in. There wasn't any wild party going on back there. Just bored men going through mechanical tasks, the music giving some respite from the boredom.

The storage area was a long, squat hall. A central strip of LED lights hung overhead. Everything under them looked too sharp: pallets stacked shoulder-high, rows of metal shelving forming tight aisles, a forklift parked like a sleeping beast to the right.

To our immediate left, under a single dangling work light, a battered folding table held the packet line: glassine envelopes, tiny zip-lock baggies, a digital scale, a heat sealer, and a pile of bulk bricks wrapped in brown tape. Two men hunched there, one scooping and weighing, the other sealing and stacking. Fat stacks of small packets were already laid out in neat piles, waiting to be bagged.

At the far end, a steel roll-up shutter waited for trucks—its teeth sealed and heavy, the obvious route for big deliveries and quick exits.

Off to the right, set into the wall, was the strong room: a reinforced door with a keypad and a thick metal frame. Inside that safe-room they kept the serious stuff—bricks of product wrapped in brown tape, and the firepower they needed for their turf wars.

There were six men in total. Two at the table cutting and sealing; one bagging into contractor sacks; a muscle seated on a stool by the shutter, toting an Uzi slung on a strap; a watchman by the column staring into his phone; and a ledger guy near the strong room.

Six men, spread tight enough that a single ripple could toss them into each other.

Ninja and I split up without talking—a nod and we moved like shadows between pallets and shelving, because that's how you stayed quiet and alive. Torque stayed by the entrance. He had done his part; this one wasn't his to run.

I moved low between the pallets, eyes on the guard by the shutter door. Ninja was ghosting to the left, keeping his profile tight against the columns. Two armed guards were our first problem. Mine stood near the shutter door, leaning on a steel pipe like a bored bouncer at a dive bar. He was glancing at his phone, head down. Perfect.

My hand brushed against a crowbar lying on a crate—cold steel, solid heft. God's little gift to improvisation. I picked it up, shifted my grip, and closed in behind the guy, quiet as smoke. Across the room, Ninja ghosted behind the other guard near the column. I gave him the hand signal—two fingers forward.

As Ninja moved toward his guy like a whisper, I swung. The crowbar cracked against the guard's skull just above the ear—a clean, ugly thud that dropped him like a sack of wet meat. I caught him before he hit the floor. He was out cold, but breathing.

But the noise was enough to blow my cover.

The three at the folding table jerked upright—one still holding a heat sealer, the other two lunging for their pistols on the table. I was already drawing mine. The time for keeping things quiet was over. Glock up, front sight on target.

Two sharp cracks echoed across the hall. Both rounds hit clean—one man spun backward, clutching his shoulder, the other howled as his right arm went limp. The third froze mid-step, hands in the air, face white. Smart guy.

I closed the distance fast. One elbow strike to the jaw—lights out. Then I kicked the table aside and cracked the next guy across the temple with the Glock's frame. The last one got the butt of the gun straight to the nose. Four men down, none of them dead. Just how I wanted it.

Across the room, Ninja was already standing over his two—both sprawled, limp and breathing through broken dreams.

"Clean," he said.

"Mostly," I replied. "Get Torque. Have him scrub the cameras. Don't want our faces turning up on Baltimore PD's greatest hits."

Ninja nodded and vanished toward the front office.

I stepped over the unconscious men and headed to the strong room. The keypad door was already cracked open—the boys had been busy inventorying product. Inside, it was all business: shelves stacked with vacuum-sealed bricks wrapped in plastic film and brown tape, each stamped with black dagger logos. Two hundred pounds easy. Enough to make a city forget its own name.

But what caught my eye wasn't the dope. It was the C-4. On the bottom shelf sat a stack of military-grade C-4 blocks, clean, fresh, each paired with a handful of detonators and digital timers. I stared for a second. Someone was planning something a hell of a lot bigger than moving smack.

I grabbed one block, slipped it into my crossbody bag. I knew exactly what I was going to do with it.

I pulled out my phone and called Davis.

"Got the bonus prize," I said. "Two hundred pounds of H, give or take."

"That's enough to make the DEA dance," Davis replied. "I'll push buttons, get Dover AFB ready for the late-night drop. You just stay off the grid."

"Copy that." I hung up and went back to the front office. Ninja was there, wiping his hands.

"Cameras wiped clean," he told me.

"Good," I said. "Time to call the cops."

I grabbed an unlocked burner phone off one of the unconscious goons, and dialed 911.

When the dispatcher answered, I pitched my voice rough and panicked. "There's a shootout between rival gangs. They're killing each other in here!"

I looked at Ninja and gave a small nod. He raised the Uzi and let off a short burst into the air—loud enough to make the dispatcher scream for backup. I rattled off the address and hung up.

"Time to move," I said.

I wedged a cinder block under the door and tipped the handle so it would hang open like an invitation. Let the uniforms walk in neat and quick—let them gawp at the mess and find the bricks, the bags, the C-4. The faster local boys saw the strong room, the sooner Harlan's whole house of cards started to topple.

We piled into my pickup and rolled out just as the sirens started wailing in the distance—flashing red and blue lights tearing toward the scene we were leaving. Another piece of Harlan's empire gone up in smoke.

The time was 1830 hours. I was acutely aware of each passing second until zero hour.

Torque stared straight ahead, jaw working. Ninja hummed under his breath. I kept my hands on the wheel and the thought in the front of my head: Shade. Lincoln Memorial. 2000 hours.

Shade would be hunting the mysterious "source" —the ghost I had fed him. He was walking to a kill he didn't know was for him.

No heroics. No mercy.

Just the quiet business of ending a hunter. Making sure Shade never hunted again.

Menace sat in my stomach like a second heartbeat. I was on my way to an appointment I couldn't miss at any cost.

CHAPTER 34

The drive back south to D.C. was quiet—the kind of quiet that sat heavy on your shoulders and let your thoughts run wild. I dropped Ninja at the same gas station where we had linked up earlier, so he could grab his truck and trail me to D.C. He slapped the roof of my truck before walking off to his vehicle.

"Try not to start the fireworks without me," he said.

"No promises," I told him, trying a smile that didn't manage to reach my eyes.

Once he pulled away, I turned my truck toward I-95 and let the engine stretch its legs. The sky was deepening into that dull amber that leaks over the horizon before the night takes full hold. Baltimore slid away behind me, just another scarred skyline full of broken glass and half-dead dreams.

The road was busy—trucks, sedans, minivans loaded with office drones heading home, everyone chasing their own version of peace. A few beat-up sedans weaved between lanes like they had somewhere very important to be. I kept my pickup steady at seventy, the low hum of the tires the only sound I wanted.

The highway lights flicked by in rhythm, white-yellow-white-yellow, and my mind started doing what it always did after a mission—unwinding, dissecting, rebuilding. I thought about this city we were heading into—the nation's brain and its rot, sitting side by side like conjoined twins.

D.C. was all glass towers and white marble, monuments that pretended permanence while the real work happened in rooms without windows. You couldn't drive through it without feeling the weight of power—and the stench of what came with it.

Guys like us had bled in every corner of the world for those polished floors. And men like Ryan had paid for it with their lives.

The farther I got from that warehouse, the quieter it felt. But the silence didn't bring peace—it just gave the ghosts room to talk.

Ryan's voice drifted up first. It always did when I was headed into something that felt personal. He had a way of getting under my armor without even trying.

"You ever think maybe we're fighting other people's wars?" Ryan had asked me once, somewhere outside Kandahar, both of us sitting on the hood of a Humvee under a moon so bright it made the sand glow.

I had looked at him and said, "Sure. But the bastards we're fighting don't seem to care whose war it is, as long as we bleed for it."

Ryan had laughed, that deep, easy laugh of his. "You gotta stop reading Nietzsche, man. You're starting to sound like one of those philosophers with a rifle."

"Hey, you're the one who made me read that damn book. I didn't even know how to spell his name."

He grinned, shook his head, and looked out at the desert. "Well, at least out here, you know what the rules are."

"Yeah," I said, "rule one: don't get shot."

He laughed under his breath. "Rule two: make sure the other guy does."

I looked over at him. "Hell of a way to find clarity."

"Dude, I've got even more clarity for you. We're like Uncle Sam's janitors. Cleaning up everyone else's mess. And you know what bugs me—nobody even remembers our names."

I smirked. "Nah, man. Janitors get holidays."

He grinned. "Still better than a nine-to-five job. Out here, at least you know who the bad guys are."

That line hit harder now than it used to. These days, I wasn't so sure the bad guys were only out there. Some wore suits and had security details. Some gave orders that turned men into ghosts.

Now Ryan was gone, and I was driving toward one of the men responsible for it.

The closer I got to D.C., the more the skyline sharpened. The glow of the Beltway turned the horizon into a band of gold. By the time I merged onto the George Washington Memorial Parkway, traffic had thinned out and the city lights shimmered through the trees along the Potomac. The river ran dark and silent beside me, mirroring the city's reflection—beautiful from a distance, rotten underneath.

Once I hit Arlington Memorial Bridge, the skyline opened up—the Washington Monument a white spear stabbing the sky. The Lincoln Memorial came into view through the trees—white, perfect, eternal. The Reflecting Pool stretched out in front, dark as oil, catching the glow of the Washington Monument like a blade cutting the sky. The monuments looked peaceful from a distance, like they guarded something worth protecting.

I turned down Ohio Drive and coasted toward the lot south of the Memorial. It was mostly empty at this hour, just a few tourists finishing selfies and a couple of joggers ghosting through the dusk. The city had that strange calm before full night.

I rolled into a space with a clean sightline of the steps leading up to Lincoln. Seconds later, Ninja's truck eased in beside me, his headlights cutting through the dark like searchlights before switching off.

I sat there a beat, watching the marble glow in the twilight, thinking about all the words carved inside that monument—freedom, honor, sacrifice. Words we used to believe in.

Tonight, I was going to write my own—in blood.

Before heading out toward the Memorial, we went over the plan one last time. It was the kind of talk that didn't need many words—two men who had done this dance too many times before.

Ninja leaned on the hood, arms folded, scanning the shadows. "So, the good news is they don't know what the source looks like."

"Yeah," I replied. "That's our one advantage."

"Means they'll follow you like lost puppies till you lead them where we want."

"Yeah. I'll wander around. Let them think I'm waiting for my source. Give them plenty of time to make visual contact. You hang back—high ground, long eyes. Start picking out the players. I'll reel them in behind the Memorial, into those trees. Quiet zone, no tourists, no cameras. When they step into the shadows, we hit."

The advantage we had was simple: Shade and his crew had no idea what the "source" looked like. They only knew Captain Axel Blaze—the guy they were supposed to tail until he led them to the target. That ignorance was the bait. I would make sure they saw me. I would give them a show—walk slow, look distracted, the perfect mark. They would think they were hunting me while I would be drawing them into their own kill box.

The space around the Memorial made the job easier. Too open for a sniper. Too many tourists. Shade would have to get his hands dirty, send men on foot. I would use that. Let them follow me through the open, right into the trees behind the monument where Ninja would be waiting—quiet, patient, lethal. And then we would hit.

Ninja's voice was quiet. "How hard?"

"Lethal," I said. "Blades. Close and clean. These guys will be coming heavy. If bullets start flying, Shade runs. I'm not letting him run tonight. And a firefight a mile from the White House brings every cop and fed in a fifty-mile radius—swarm, contain, and we're dead in the middle."

"Copy. Silent and lethal."

Ninja didn't need to ask what I planned to do when we got Shade. He already knew.

"You sure about leaving Torque in the truck?" was all he asked.

"Yeah," I said. "He's not part of this dance."

Ninja leaned back, expression unreadable. "You trust him?"

"It's not about trust. Torque's out of options. He knows he keeps breathing only if I take out Harlan and his crew. Or else, he's a dead man walking."

We both went quiet for a moment. The hum of the city rolled in with the breeze, mixing with the faint slap of water from the Reflecting Pool.

Finally, Ninja looked at me. "Alright, Cowboy. Let's dance."

We split then—me heading down the walkway toward the steps, him fading into the dark like he had never been there. The marble columns rose above me, pale and watchful, as I stepped out into the open.

This was a different kind of hunt—the prey was being led to believe that it was stalking the predator.

This time, the gloves were off. Rules of engagement: Lethal.

Out there in the darkness, Shade was waiting, thinking he was closing in on a target.

He didn't know the truth. He was already walking into his own grave.

CHAPTER 35

I walked out of the lot and cut across the lawn, boots crunching the gravel path. The south face of the Memorial rose before me—white stone turning the last light into something cold. Traffic on the Parkway hummed behind me; joggers ghosted past; a vendor folded his cart and moved off. The air smelled faintly of river and old stone. Each step was a small rehearsal—casual hands, loose shoulders, the face of a man who had nowhere urgent to be.

The Reflecting Pool soon came into view, a black ribbon of water at the foot of the monument, glass-slick and still, except for a slow ripple where a goose had bothered the surface. The Washington Monument stabbed the sky behind it, a pale spear reflected in the pool. People clustered at the far edge, taking pictures, laughing like everything was still simple.

I stopped at the base of the steps and looked out over the pool. Lights from the city winked across the water. Tourists' silhouettes drifted past. For a second I let the quiet sit in me like a loaded magazine.

Ninja had already moved. He had vanished up the front steps a few minutes earlier and taken an elevated perch where he could read the open space. We were on real-time: tiny Bluetooth earpieces, voices in the dark.

"I've got eyes on a couple guys already," Ninja said, low. "Over by the far bench. Eyes stuck on you like they're trying to memorize your profile.

One's leaning on his phone like he's waiting for a cue."

"Copy," I answered. I kept walking, cool, giving the men ample time to spot me. I intended to be seen. I wanted them to log my gait, my jacket, everything that would make them think they had spotted their mark.

I climbed the front steps slow. Tourists glanced at me as if I were part of the scenery—an indifferent figure moving toward the statue.

"Two more," Ninja said a beat later. "Can't see Shade yet." He had already looked hard at the mugshot I had shown him—Shade's face burned into place. "They're pairing up, moving about twenty yards behind you." His tone was patient but sharp. He knew what to look for.

I reached the top and lingered at the columned portico, hands in my pockets, the world laid out below. I waited long enough to let anyone who had followed settle their pace, then pretended to check my phone, made a show of taking a call—like the source had finally called. Then I pocketed the phone and moved quickly inside the Memorial toward the statue of Lincoln.

Lincoln sat enormous and quiet at the far end—a stone man folded into thought. The statue's eyes seemed to measure the country and find it lacking. Marble knees, a clenched jaw. The stone face looked kinder in this light than I felt.

My earpiece lit up. "Shade just stepped into view," Ninja's taut voice came through the earpiece. "I've clocked eight men in all, including Shade. They're spread out—three up front, five trailing."

Time snapped into place the way a broke spring snaps—instant and final.

“Copy,” I said. “Time to move. Head to the trees. Head on a swivel.”

“Roger that. Watch your six.”

I came down the marble steps with some urgency, like a man on his way to an important appointment. The men that had followed me were easy to pick out now, heads turned just enough, shoulders angled like hunters who had smelled what they wanted. Shade stood back a step from his crew, jacket unzipped, chin down, watching like a hunter who had already imagined the kill.

Inside me, something cold and animal tightened. For a second, the thought of squeezing the life out of Shade with my bare hands flashed through me—clean, simple, final. It burned hot and stupid and utterly irresistible. I shoved it down. Not here. Not yet. Patience did the real work.

I barely looked at him. Let him believe I didn’t know who he was.

I skirted the monument, phone at my ear again for show, talking like a man with a schedule. The trees waited at the northwest corner—about fifteen of them packed tight, trunks like pillars, branches lace-knotted high overhead. They made a black wall against the night, dense enough that you couldn’t see more than a few feet into their belly. The ground beneath was dark with leaf mold; the trunks stood shoulder to shoulder like sentries. It was the kind of shadow that ate light and left only shape and sound.

As we closed, the eight men fanned out the way hunters do when they want no surprises. They spread in a loose ring—eyes forward, boots soft on the path—covering every foot of ground so a man inside would have to walk into an open net.

They weren't idiots; they carried guns, sure, but their orders were explicit: no shots unless absolutely necessary. This place was too hot—right in the city's center of power. A firefight near the monuments meant immediate federal response, helicopters, uniformed swarms. They knew that. They also knew that pulling triggers here would invite a net they couldn't slip through.

That restraint suited me fine. It made them predictable. They had to remain quiet. It made them easy to take apart one clean, silent piece at a time.

The men thought they had boxed the trees. They had made themselves a perimeter with no blind spots. I watched them move and felt the mesh tighten like a noose. They didn't know the trap was designed to close inward.

I moved into the trees like a shadow that belonged there. The trunks closed behind me. The city's noise became a distant sound. My breath stayed even. Ninja slipped in beside me, all motion and intent, and we fell into the rhythm we had practiced a thousand times: two hunters, two instruments.

Two of Shade's men stepped off the perimeter and followed me like bloodhounds. They were too eager, too sure. I let them think the trees had swallowed me. They cut between trunks, boots soft on the leaf litter, voices low and clipped. When they were a body-length past me, I moved.

My first strike was a whisper. A low swing, the heel of my hand into a throat—hard and precise. He folded, reflex lost to shock, air leaving him with a wet sound. I didn't give him time to breathe. I grabbed the back of his head with one hand and his chin with the other. One powerful clockwise jerk and the man's neck snapped. He was gone in an instant, eyes dull, face slack.

At the same instant as I moved, Ninja's blade slid across a second man's throat. It was all clean mechanics—grip, angle, exit. The guy's knees buckled and he hit the ground without a sound.

The other six tightened their ring, boots sweeping the perimeter, voices getting spiky. They had spread out enough to think they still had the trees contained. That was fine. Containment was just geometry until someone came through the mesh and tore it open.

We moved between trunks, behind roots and low hanging limbs. Ninja was a ghost, appearing at an angle I hadn't watched and collapsing a throat before a body could realize the world had changed. My blade was an extension of a long, practiced motion: slip an arm around the neck, pull the head to the side, and plunge the blade in. Nothing more than a soft gurgling sound. And then—silence.

We worked the ring clockwise, then counter—two cuts, a shove, a twist, and a man went down. One guy lunged for a sidearm, not knowing that Ninja was behind him like the shadow of death. He drove a knife into the base of the man's skull in a motion that used more weight than grace. The drop was quick.

No shots. No calling cards. Just men collapsing into the leaf mold like sleep.

Their training didn't help. Up close, under a canopy that swallowed sound, training was a thin illusion. A man's hand could go slack on a gun quicker than he could think of calling for help. We kept it surgical: throats slit, necks broken with clean jerks.

We were efficient and brutal. We didn't savor it—we made space. We closed down the ring until only Shade's shadow remained.

Shade was out there—pacing, calling to ghosts that weren't answering anymore. He moved closer, checking his six, shoulders tight. The faint wash of streetlight caught his face for a second. I could see beads of sweat. Smell his fear.

His voice had gone from confident to brittle. That's the sound of a man realizing he is alone. He went tight when the men stopped answering. The confidence left his shoulders first, then his jaw. Panic is a small, ugly animal; it makes men make bad moves.

He moved like a man who had to do something. He drew. I saw the crease of his jacket, the way his hand rolled to the inside pocket. He pulled out a gun: an H&K MP7 automatic, compact and mean, the sort of weapon that belonged to men who wanted a lot of punch without a lot of bulk. Chambered in 4.6×30mm armor-piercing rounds, it was built to cut through soft protection and leave clean holes. Small gun with lethal intent. I couldn't let him follow through on that intent.

Shade raised the gun and scanned the shadows. He wasn't fast enough.

I had been half up in a low branch, a shape concealed by shadow, when he moved. Then I dropped. My boots hit his back like a hammer, driving him face-first into the dirt. The MP7 flew from his hands, clattering across dead leaves. He grunted, tried to roll, but I already had my knee jammed between his shoulder blades, my forearm pressed across his neck. He bucked, kicked, caught air.

I drove his chest down into the earth, and slid one hand behind his head. The blade was there in my other hand—cold as judgment, a fingertip of steel tracing the tender line at the base of his skull. He tried to twist, panic making him clumsy, but my knee anchored his ribs. I felt the pulse at his throat like a tiny drum under my fingers.

"I heard you've been looking for me," I whispered, the menace in my voice making his blood run cold.

That got him. His body went rigid, eyes darting sideways like he could somehow see me through the dark. I didn't give him time to speak. The flat of my hand came down behind his ear—one sharp, practiced strike. He went limp instantly, lights out.

I sat on him for a beat, chest heaving, knife still at the ready. Months of hunting, weeks of false trails and sleepless nights—and finally, I had one of Ryan's killers right under my knee. I let the thought settle in, slow and heavy.

CHAPTER 36

I sheathed my blade, bound Shade's wrists and ankles with paracord, then dragged him through the trees toward the lot. His keys were still in his jacket. I thumbed the remote—heard the chirp and saw headlights blink about fifty yards out. That was his ride.

I dumped him in the back seat, face down, tossed a tarp over him, and slid behind the wheel. Engine turned over smoothly. Black SUV, tinted windows—the usual hitman starter kit. I pulled out slowly, headlights off until I hit the street, then blended with the traffic across Memorial Bridge.

Behind me, the city stretched out like a corpse in moonlight—D.C. skyline cold and sterile beyond the river. The Lincoln Memorial stood across the water, a ghost in white marble. I turned off onto a dirt track near the Potomac, eased the SUV down until the road vanished into trees and mud.

I killed the engine. Silence. Just the whisper of the river moving steady through the dark. Somewhere beyond the trees, half a mile away, lay Arlington Cemetery spread out like a field of quiet white—row after row of marble markers under black sky. I thought about Ryan for a second. Maybe that was fitting.

Shade was still out cold. I hauled him from the back, dumped him on the ground, and leaned against the hood, watching him breathe.

There were two reasons I hadn't ended him with the others. One was the simple, human thing: I wanted him to know why he was about to die. Not as bloodsport, not as theater—he needed to know that he had killed fine Marines, the best of soldiers, simply for a few wads of dirty cash. Bad choices. He needed to think about them.

The second reason was practical and colder. I had a very short timeframe to get to Reaper. Torque didn't have a clean lead on him. He had fragments, hints and rumors that could take the whole night to chase down—if they even led anywhere. Reaper had also dumped his phone—the one Echo was tapped into.

Reaper had become a shadow inside Harlan's network. Only Shade and Harlan were the ones in regular contact. If I couldn't find Reaper before Harlan's operation at Dover went sideways, the bastard would vanish into the wind.

I looked down at Shade—hands and feet bound, mouth taped. The thing I kept turning over in my head was simple and ugly: this was the man who put a bullet in Ryan's back. Mark Kincaid next, wiped off the board so the story could look tidy. Dana and Jesse would have been next on the list if his luck had held that night—collateral he would have burned without a second thought.

Shade wasn't crooked; he was hollow. There was no light in him to redeem, no corner of decency to bargain with.

Guys like him made the oath I had taken taste like a lie. Ryan and I signed up to be the blunt end of a system that buried monsters so the innocent didn't pay with their lives. We trusted that service meant something—that the people we bled for would at least pretend to be on the same side.

But when your own side—Shade, Reaper, Harlan, men wearing the same colors you had bled under—turned a gun into a politics of profit and used the law like a curtain to hide behind, the old rules didn't fit anymore. You had to find your own justice.

Shade moaned and blinked. He was waking up. He came up in a ragged breath, eyes darting, trying to piece together the world. Panic crept over his face as his eyes tried to figure out the shape above him. All he could see in the darkness was my face reflecting the faint light of my phone screen—a ghost in the dark. He sucked a breath through the strip of tape and whatever confidence he had brought out of the city started to crack.

I talked like someone reading a report. Flat. Clinical. "Corporal Darius Wade. Demolitions specialist. Wired to make things go away." I let the words hang. "You like blowing things up, tough guy?"

He tried to answer through the tape. Nothing but muffled nonsense came back.

"What was that?" I asked, sarcastic and slow. "Never mind. As I was saying: a disgrace for a U.S. soldier—running product, working with the Talis, shooting Marines in the back. That's a long list of bad decisions. You know the military punishments for that?" My voice wasn't a question.

He made another muffled sound.

"Oh, sorry," I said, and ripped the tape off his mouth in one violent motion. It peeled skin with it and he screamed, raw and immediate.

He spat and tried to scramble away. "You don't understand—you got it wrong—I left with an honorable discharge—" He tried to bluster, to make the soldier's paperwork matter as if it cleared a ledger of murder.

"Honorable discharge, huh?" I said. "That settles everything, right? That makes murder fine?" I let the derision sit in the air.

He glared, trying to scare me. "You don't know who you're fucking with."

"That's the new line?" I asked. "Now we're using threats?"

He tried to square his voice. "If anything happens to me, you'll have the East Coast's most ruthless mafia on you." He spat the warning like a talisman.

"Is that so?" I said. "The most ruthless mafia?" I let the question hang while something colder than the river moved through me.

I crouched next to him and pulled three objects from the tarp and set them where he could see: a wrapped block of plastic explosive that I picked from the warehouse, a small detonator-looking device, and a cheap digital timer.

"You know what those are?" I asked. "You know what they do when they're put together?"

His tough act slid off him like wet cloth. He stared at the block, the detonator, the timer. His eyes flicked between them like a trapped animal reading a trap.

"What do you want?" he rasped, voice shaking like he had swallowed gravel.

I kept my voice even. "Now we're talking. Where will I find Sergeant First Class Marcus Stahl. You guys like calling him Reaper, right? Trying to make him sound meaner than he is?"

He tried to puff himself up. "You think you can take on Reaper? You've got any idea the kind of muscle he runs? He's not some corner boss—he's heavy. You're out of your depth."

"There we go on the threats again. Well, never mind."

I ignored him and assembled the explosive. Then I tapped the timer until the digits lit up and held the screen up so he could see the countdown begin.

"You've got two minutes to start being useful," I said, as I began to count, soft and precise, into the dark: "120… 119… 118…"

He looked at the digits and then at my face, and whatever swagger he had managed to pull back evaporated again. His voice came out small.

"OK, OK. I'll tell you. He'll be at the Sovereign Hotel. In Rosslyn. The nightclub—Gilded Vault. 2200 hours tonight."

I had no way of knowing if he was just jerking me around.

"You expect me to take that at face value?" I asked, and I leaned closer. "I don't believe you." I let the silence stretch and the numbers tick down. "100… 99… 98…"

Panic broke him open then. He practically screamed. "I'm telling you the truth! The Black Dagger Syndicate owns the place. There's a meeting at ten—mob bosses from the East Coast, buyers who fronted Harlan money. They're all coming in. I swear—please—"

"Which East Coast mobs?"

"New York, Philadelphia."

"What's Reaper's cellphone number?" I kept the pressure high.

"He switched to a new burner today. I don't remember it off the top of my head but it's in my phone. Please—check it. It's under his name."

I picked up the phone I had already taken from him. While Shade was out, I had pressed his thumb to the sensor and opened it like a man reading a confession. Contacts showed two entries under Reaper: the old burner Echo had tracked—and a second, newer number. I turned the screen so the glow matched his face and held it up.

"You sure?" I asked.

He swallowed, throat raw. "Yeah, that's the one."

Shade's voice had that break in it—something primal, the sound a man makes when the lies run out and all that's left is fear. I could tell he wasn't lying anymore. Fear had stripped him clean.

The timer was down to 55 seconds.

I didn't say a word. I just reached down, pressed the tape back across his mouth, and smoothed it tight so it sealed his last plea in place.

He started squirming, mumbling something behind the gag. But I was done listening. I yanked his jacket open. His eyes went wide when he saw what I was holding. I slid the explosive device inside his chest pocket, tucked it neat, and zipped the jacket back up like I was buttoning a body bag.

Then I turned and walked away.

His muffled cries followed me for a few steps, high and desperate, but then got swallowed by the night, fading under the crunch of gravel. I didn't look back. Guys like Shade didn't deserve a last look.

The night air felt cold and clean after all that noise inside my head. Shade's SUV sat under the trees, black and still, like it was waiting for its owner to never come back. I had wiped my prints from every inch of it earlier—steering wheel, door handles, even the mag release on the rifle sitting up front. Inside were the guns, the half block of C-

4, and all the pieces the cops would need to write it off as another idiot playing with explosives.

An "accidental detonation", they would file it under. The universe, for once, would balance itself out.

I kept walking toward the water. The Potomac shimmered dark and glassy under the city lights. Across the water, D.C. pulsed like some restless beast—sirens in the distance, headlights streaking across bridges. From here, it looked peaceful. But I knew better.

The calm was a lie. Underneath, things festered—men like Shade, Reaper, Harlan. Parasites chewing through the bones of everything we were supposed to stand for. Snakes dressed like men, scumbags who smile while they bleed you dry. The kind who shoot good men in the back and sleep like babies after.

The system was supposed to catch them. Hell, that's what Ryan believed in. That's why he wore the flag. Why I wore it. The system says justice takes time—but time's the one thing the innocent never have. When the system falters, when the law trips over its own red tape, someone's got to step up. Someone who's not afraid to get his hands dirty.

You don't wait for justice. You make it happen.

Someone has to step up, clean house, make the ledger right again.

Tonight, there would be one less name on that list.

The blast rolled through the trees a heartbeat later. Like a sudden breath from hell—loud, bright, final. It echoed off the river, and then the world went quiet again.

The tombstones at Arlington, just beyond the tree line, looked like a jury in the moonlight. The rows of white stones caught the moon. There was something morally wrong in the ledger, where real soldiers' names were tarnished by the rot created by men like Shade. For a second I felt something shift, like justice rolling back onto its axis.

I didn't look back. Just kept walking, one steady step after another, into the dark.

CHAPTER 37

The pickup was waiting where the dirt track met the edge of the Memorial Bridge, engine cold, windshield fogged from the night air. That ninja decal on the tailgate grinned back at me as I approached. Subtle as a brick to the face. But fitting. Violence wearing a smile.

Ninja sat behind the wheel, one arm resting on the door, eyes steady on me. Torque sat silently in the back, face pale in the dash glow.

I slid into the passenger seat. Ninja looked at me once—didn't speak, didn't have to. His question was in his eyes.

"Shade won't be killing anyone else," I said, voice low. "Ever."

Ninja nodded once. "That him going up in the fireball?"

"Yeah," I said. "That was him."

He didn't flinch. Just turned the key, engine grumbling to life like an old warhorse. "Where to, boss?"

"Place called Sovereign Hotel in Rosslyn," I replied, twisting around in my seat. "Torque, you got anything on this place?"

Torque leaned forward. "Yeah. Real high-end joint. Harlan funneled a lot of money into the nightclub they run outta there—place called *Gilded Vault*. All velvet rope and champagne, but underneath it's just another front. They push product through the club crowd, wash the money clean through the hotel's books. Gives the Syndicate a straight line into D.C.'s nightlife—

lawyers, lobbyists, sugar daddies with offshore accounts. All the filth in suits, partying like saints."

Ninja glanced at me. "So, evil got itself a VIP list."

"Pretty much," Torque said. "Harlan wanted to make it look legit. Reaper's crew handles distribution. Keeps things quiet and shiny for the city folks."

I nodded, mind working. "Shade said something before he went out. There's a meeting tonight. East Coast mob bosses. All under one roof."

Ninja whistled. "That's a lot of guns and egos in one nightclub. You planning on crashing that party?"

"If I have to," I said.

"Then I hope the place has valet parking," Ninja muttered.

Torque shifted in the back seat. "I've been in that place a couple times. Daytime only, when it's dead. Way above my clearance level, though. Reaper handled all the night ops himself."

"Figures. Well, let's go check it out," I said looking at Ninja.

Ninja gave a short nod and started rolling, tires crunching gravel as we climbed onto Arlington Boulevard, the city lights bleeding back into view. The Rosslyn skyline glowed ahead—looking calm and innocent, like the quiet before a gunfight.

I squinted through the windshield, trying to work out how we could make a low-key entrance to the club without Reaper's crew locking on to us the second we walked in. My fingers came up and, half-absentminded, I pulled out my phone.

A message from Madison blinked on the screen: "*In the office if you need me to pull anything. Or anyone.*"

It read like an offer and also like a promise—*I'm still here. I've got your back.*

For a second, I smiled. That message suddenly solved the problem I was grappling with.

Ninja glanced at me. "You good?"

"Yeah," I replied, sliding the phone away. "We might have to tweak the plan a little. Can you pull up over there for a minute?"

He eased the truck against the curb, engine idling low. My mind was already piecing it together. Getting into *Gilded Vault* wasn't going to be a walk in. Not with Reaper's men guarding a mob summit. Two guys like Ninja and I walk in together, and we would light up their radar before we even hit the bar.

But a couple of guys with a good-looking woman like Madison with them, looking like they belonged there? That was a different story.

If we wanted inside, we would need to look like just another pair of high-rollers out for a good time. Which meant we would need cover—distractions. The kind that turned heads and lowered guards.

And there was the problem of where to stash Torque while we went after Reaper. We couldn't take him to a place where everyone recognized him. And I couldn't just leave him sitting in some random diner.

Madison was the only solution I could think of, who could help solve both problems.

I looked out the windshield, watching the lights of Penn Quarter flicker in the distance. "Hang on," I said to Ninja. "Gotta make a call."

I opened the door and stepped out, cool air cutting against my face.

My thumb hovered over Madison's name for a moment before I hit call. When she picked up, she sounded a little surprised. "Axel? Didn't expect you to call. No, scratch that, actually, I was kind of expecting it. Everything OK?"

"Mostly," I replied. "Where are you right now?"

"At my office. Downtown. K Street. Pulling in a late shift tonight. Like I said in my message: *in case you need me to pull anything*," she said. "Why? You need backup or a coffee?" Her laugh was light, but there was curiosity under it.

"Still trying to figure it out," I replied.

"I'm sure I can help with that. What's it all about?"

"I'll tell you in a sec. Do you know a place called Gilded Vault?"

"The nightclub in the Sovereign Hotel? Yeah. I've been there a couple times—clients, openings. It's—fancy. Rooftop, velvet ropes, the whole scene. Why?"

"Uh... I need to get inside without setting off every bouncer and security camera between me and the VIP room," I replied. "Me and Ninja walking in alone? That's a neon sign reading *suspicious*. They'll watch us the second we pass the rope. We need cover."

She laughed—soft, a little incredulous. "Are you asking me out, Axel?"

"Not exactly," I replied, trying to figure out how to put it.

Before I could make up some lame excuse, she cut me off. "OK, seriously—what do you need?"

"If you go with us, I guess we can walk in as regulars, not two guys who have 'trouble' stamped on their foreheads. I need to be able to move around freely in there. Can you do that?"

"Yes, of course," she replied, suddenly turning serious as she realized what it was all about. "I'm game. When?"

"In half an hour?"

"Sounds good. Anything else I can do. Feel free."

"Actually, there is. There's this guy I need kept safe for a few hours. He's a crucial witness. I need a place for him to stay low, safe in an anonymous setting."

"Is he in immediate danger?" Her tone went flat—professional, real fast. Not surprised, not shocked. Just efficient.

"Yeah," I said. "High threat level. He won't last wandering the streets."

"I can lock him in a conference room," she said without hesitation, her voice carrying calm competence. "Locked door, card access. Security won't let anyone barge in without a name on the list. I can put him there, no problem. I'll sign him in as a consultant or vendor so he has a legitimate reason to be there. He'll be safe."

"Sounds perfect. I'll be at your office in half an hour—2100 hours."

We hung up and I pocketed the phone. The plan was beginning to take shape in my head.

I climbed back into the truck and shut the door. Ninja glanced at me, eyebrows lifted—like he was waiting for the punchline I hadn't told him. I laid it out quick, telling him how we would take Madison along.

"We get in like customers," I said. "Madison fronts us. We look like we belong. Once inside, we scope the place, find Reaper's perimeter, and figure a way into the back rooms without waving flags at the bouncers."

Ninja made that face like he was trying to place a memory. "How come we never got these kinds of ops in Delta? All we got was 'slam and clear'." He grinned briefly, then dropped it. "Alright, so what's the plan?"

I shrugged one shoulder. "Honestly, I don't have a clear plan until we see the lay of the place and the security. We fly in, we look, we decide. It's old-school recon before you punch a hole in a map."

Ninja gave me that crooked smile he used when things looked dangerously fun. "Sounds like one of our Delta ops after all," he said. "Half plan, half winging it."

I couldn't help the brief grin that slid across my face. "Yeah," I said. "Winging it sounds about right. But we were the best at improvisation, Ninja."

"Yes, boss. Can't argue with that," he chuckled.

"Torque," I turned to him, "I've arranged a secure place for you to sit tight until we've got Harlan out in the open."

His head jerked up. "You sure? I can—"

"You're safer staying put," I cut in. "We'll keep Harlan guessing until the last minute. We want him to feel the pressure. He'll have to move, go himself to oversee the Dover shipment."

Then I gave Torque a task he wasn't exactly kicked about. "Call Harlan. Tell him everything's on track. Make him feel like his plan's running smooth. Keep him confident."

Torque's shoulders stooped like a man who had been asked to take a hard punch. To him, talking to Harlan felt like walking into a lion's mouth.

"OK," he finally said, taking a breath.

He swallowed hard and took the phone from me. I watched the way his hand trembled when he put the burner to his ear like he was picking up a noose.

Harlan answered with that clipped tone that belonged to men who gave orders and expected obedience. Torque played it straight. "Colonel. I'm still following the Captain as you asked."

Harlan's voice was a blade. "I was expecting Shade to check in. He's not answering? Where's he?"

Torque hedged. "Don't know, Sir. I'll try to reach him—"

Harlan cut him off. "You better. Everything in place at Dover for tonight?"

"Yes, Sir. All the manifests set. Crew, planes, timing—good to go." Torque tried to make it sound like certainty.

"Good," Harlan replied slow and cold. "Because if anything goes wrong tonight, it'll be the last mistake you make. You hear me? Be at Dover by midnight. Two hours before the flight. No excuses."

"Understood. I'll be there."

Torque ended the call and let out a breath that sounded part relief, part triumph. The little victory showed on his face—he had done what Harlan wanted to hear.

"You alright?" I asked.

He let out a breath that might have been a laugh, maybe a sob. "Yeah. I'm... that's it. He told me to be at Dover. He thinks he's in control. I... I don't have to take that from him much longer."

There was a satisfaction in his eyes—like trapping Harlan made the whole night worth it.

I looked at Ninja. "Time to head downtown."

He grunted, flicked on the signal, and peeled off Arlington Boulevard, heading back toward D.C.

CHAPTER 38

The night was clear, traffic thin—just the low hum of the engine and the gleam of headlights rolling over the Potomac. The Memorial Bridge opened up ahead like a dark ribbon over black glass. Lincoln's statue loomed ahead—calm, stoic, the old man watching over the mess his city had become.

We didn't stop. Just rolled past, tires whispering on the asphalt. We hit Constitution Avenue, weaving through the late traffic, headlights streaking past the monuments and marble ghosts. D.C. at night always looked clean from a distance—like the city was pretending it didn't know what was hiding underneath.

At 18th, Ninja swung north, the buildings tightening around us—rows of glass, steel, and stone pressing in, the heartbeat of the capital buried under too much concrete.

Once we crossed Pennsylvania, the streets changed character—brighter, busier, meaner. Downtown D.C. after dark was a strange animal: suits and hookers sharing sidewalks, black Suburbans idling beside food trucks, too many people pretending they were running the world, but everyone pretending not to see each other.

Neon signs reflected in puddles, horns echoed between the facades, and the smell of street food hung in the air like the city's after-hours perfume. The city looked clean on the surface, but you could feel the rot humming underneath if you knew where to listen.

Ninja pulled up outside the Washington Chronicle building—a mid-rise slab of glass and old ambition wedged between two newer towers. The kind of place that looked like it had seen better decades, back when journalism still smoked cigars and drank bourbon at its desk. The name was stenciled in bronze letters above the door, giving the feeling that truth was still printed somewhere inside. Behind the glass, a security guard in a gray uniform sipped bad coffee under too-bright lights.

I pulled out my phone and called Madison. "We're parked right out front," I said. "Red F-150. You'll see us."

"Got it," she said. "Be down in a minute."

A couple of minutes later, the lobby doors opened, and there she was—scanning the street. She wore dark jeans, a cream sweater that caught the streetlight, and a navy coat that framed her like she'd stepped out of a magazine by accident. Her hair was loose, falling over her shoulders in soft waves. She looked simple. Effortless. The kind of stunning that didn't even try.

I caught myself staring longer than I should have. Even in the mess I was knee-deep in, she had that calm way of making the world stop clenching its fists for a second.

And just like that, a flash of memory hit—Ryan, back in Kandahar, grinning like a devil after I had pulled Madison out of that hellhole. "How come you get the rescue-the-pretty-blonde gigs, and we get stuck chasing rats through caves?" he had said.

I had laughed, told him it was pure luck. He had called it bullshit. We had clapped shoulders and split off to our next suicide runs.

The smile that crept up on me died just as fast. Ryan was gone now. Murdered. And every mile I drove, every breath I took, was heading straight toward the men who did it.

I shook off the memory like dust from an old photo and stepped out of the pickup. Madison met me halfway on the sidewalk. She didn't waste time with greetings.

"We should move the truck into the underground lot," she said. "There's a side entrance off the alley—less visibility. You said your contact's in danger, right? Better no one sees him stepping out."

Smart. I nodded. "Makes sense. Let's go."

"Hop in then. Get the middle seat. I'll take shotgun," she ordered.

I gave her a look. "Seriously?"

Truth was, I had never sat in the middle before. In my world, you were either behind the wheel or riding shotgun with your weapon angled out the window. The middle seat was for the guy who didn't have a job yet.

She smiled. "Dead serious. I'll need to talk to the security guy at the parking entrance."

Couldn't argue with that. I slid in.

She smiled mischievously: "Don't worry, Captain Blaze. I won't tell anyone you let someone else take shotgun."

As she got in, her eyes fell on Ninja. "Sergeant Buck Conway, isn't it? Didn't expect to see you here," she said giving him a bright smile.

Madison knew all the operators by name. It had been four years since our team rescued her, but she clearly hadn't forgotten anyone's name.

Ninja looked like he had just been promoted. "You remember my name?" he asked, his grin stretching wide.

"Of course. I couldn't possibly forget the heroic soldiers who saved me from the Taliban," she said warmly.

Torque shifted in the back seat, the compliment about heroic soldiers landing on him like a reminder he surely wasn't one. His face folded inward—half guilt, half shame. He sat stiff in the back, looking like he wanted to disappear into the seat.

I didn't comment. I just gestured toward him and said, "Sergeant Wade. He's the one who needs to lay low for a bit."

Madison gave him a polite nod, no judgment in her eyes. She had that gift—making people feel human, even when they didn't deserve it.

She pointed toward a narrow turn beside the Chronicle building. Ninja steered the pickup in, the headlights bouncing off the brick as the truck eased down the ramp. There wasn't a security guard, just a barrier. But it did need Madison to lean out her window, swipe her keycard, and the steel gate hummed open with a low groan.

"Park near the elevator," she said. "Less foot traffic."

Ninja drove us down into the bowels of the parking lot while Madison guided him toward a secured section. She moved fast, efficient. A minute later, Torque was tucked into a glass-walled conference room with blinds drawn and a thermos of coffee on the table. It wasn't much, but it was safe—and for now, that was enough.

When she came back, I opened the passenger door for her like it was 1950 again. She arched an eyebrow, amused.

"Chivalry, Captain Blaze? Or are you just dodging that middle seat again?"

"Call it tactical courtesy."

She laughed—a low, genuine sound that didn't belong in the kind of night I was having—and slid in. I followed, shut the door, and nodded to Ninja.

"Let's roll. Rosslyn."

"Roger that," he replied.

We rolled out of the underground and back into the city.

We drove west along K Street, the city lights sliding off the windshield in streaks of white and gold. The deeper we got out of downtown, the thinner the traffic became, replaced by the rhythmic hum of the city easing into its midnight lull. Foggy Bottom slipped by on our left—those gray government buildings standing tall and watchful, still lit like no one ever went home. Out here, Washington's soul felt quieter, colder. You could almost feel the power thinning out as you left the capital's marble spine behind.

We hit I-66 and cut across the Theodore Roosevelt Bridge, the Potomac sliding dark and silent beneath us as we moved out of D.C. into Arlington. The water caught the city's reflection—Capitol dome glowing faintly in the distance, the Washington Monument like a ghostly spear through the skyline.

Madison sat quietly, watching the lights fade behind us. I could tell she was trying to read me, but I wasn't offering much. I was only seeing the fault lines in D.C.—those quiet edges where power changed hands and blood washed off easy.

"Just so you know," I said finally, eyes fixed ahead, "you might actually get a story out of tonight, Madison."

She turned her head slightly, those green eyes catching a streak of neon. "A story?"

"Yeah," I said, eyes on the road. "The Sovereign's hosting more than overpriced cocktails. There's a meeting upstairs—New York, Philly mob bosses. They're in town to see the big prize themselves."

"What prize?" she asked, voice low.

"Heroin. Two tons of it. Shipment's coming in tonight. These guys put up serious money for a taste of it."

Her gaze hardened. "How much?"

"My guess is about fifty million. Advance payment."

Madison exhaled sharply, disbelief flashing across her face. "And you're telling me this *now*?"

"I didn't have confirmation," I said. "Even now, it's just the word of one man. But word like that travels fast in this city. So hang tight. Stay alert. Me and Ninja'll make sure it doesn't go sideways."

She smirked faintly, shaking her head. "Never a shortage of thrills when I'm with you Delta guys."

From the driver's seat, Ninja grinned. "We aim to entertain, ma'am."

Madison laughed once under her breath. Then the car went quiet again, the weight of what was coming pressing down like a loaded chamber.

As we came off the bridge into Arlington, Rosslyn rose ahead of us—steel and glass towers glowing blue and silver under the streetlights. The air felt cleaner here, the skyline sharper, all modern lines and quiet money.

The Sovereign Hotel came into view like it owned the skyline. Twenty floors of mirrored arrogance. The kind of place where senators cheated, lobbyists toasted their sins, and mobsters pretended they were businessmen. Its black-glass façade reflected the streetlights, turning them into a glittering snarl. Up top, the Gilded Vault nightclub pulsed with light and bass—exclusive, overpriced, and perfect for a man like Reaper to disappear into.

Before we got out, I sent a message to Echo, asking for a data sweep on the Sovereign—guest list, staff, building plans. Priority was Reaper, a.k.a. Marcus Stahl.

I knew we were walking into a place crawling not just with Reaper's syndicate, but also tough guys from other East Coast crews. We couldn't afford to act too cocky.

Echo's message came back within seconds. "Copy, Cowboy. Pulling hotel security feeds and scraping metadata. Give me a few."

Inside, the lobby hit us with warm air and money. White marble floors, gold-trimmed elevators, and a crystal chandelier that looked like it could fund a small war. A piano in the corner was playing something soft and expensive. Madison looped her arm through mine, laughing at something I didn't say. Ninja walked beside us, grinning like he owned the place. To anyone watching, we were just three people out for a night of bad decisions and good whiskey.

But my eyes were working overtime. By the front desk, two guys in leather jackets sat too still—eyes scanning, hands near their belts. Another leaned by the bar, pretending to text while keeping one eye on the door. Packing heat. Probably concealed carry, maybe subcompact Glocks. Their posture said muscle, not guests. Could have been Reaper's crew. Could have been one of the mob entourages. Either way, it smelled like trouble.

We stopped by the elevator, our reflections staring back from the gold-tinted doors. Madison looked calm. Ninja looked like he was itching to break something. I adjusted my jacket, scanning again.

Reaper was in this building somewhere. We were about to walk straight into the lion's den—smiling all the way.

CHAPTER 39

The Gilded Vault didn't just look expensive—it looked untouchable. The entrance was cordoned off with black velvet ropes. Two big guys blocked the entry of anyone looking borderline questionable. Broad shoulders, clean suits, comms in their ears. Their eyes flicked over us once, recognized confidence when they saw it, and let us through without a word.

Inside, the place hit like a sensory overload. Gold and obsidian décor. Glass walls reflecting the skyline. The bass from the DJ booth thrummed through the floor, slow and hypnotic. Waitresses in sequined dresses weaved through the crowd carrying trays of champagne and bourbon neat. The air smelled like perfume, cash, and control.

A chandelier made of interlocking gold bars hung above the dance floor, catching the light like fire. The crowd was a mix of high-rollers, politicos, and predators in tailored suits. The kind of people who smiled with their mouths but not their eyes. Madison played her part perfectly—elegant, unreadable. Ninja and I blended in behind her, just two ghosts in the noise, scanning faces for the one we came to find.

We moved through the noise, the crowd splitting just enough for us to pass. Madison's hair caught the gold light like fire. Ninja and I scanned the corners, casual but alert, letting the place wash over us—music, perfume, and the faint metallic scent of trouble.

We found a table near the edge of the lounge, half in shadow, half in the glare of the dance floor lights. I grabbed a bourbon—no ice. So did Ninja. Madison went with something clear and expensive. The bouncers near the bar looked bored, one scrolling his phone, the other doing lazy head-checks over the crowd. Nothing about this place screamed "mob summit". Too open, too loud, too public. If there was business going down, it wasn't happening out here.

I leaned back in my chair, eyes drifting to the elevators across the room. "Not exactly a high-level summit vibe," I muttered.

Ninja smirked. "Maybe they're conducting business between dance tracks."

Before I could respond, my earpiece buzzed. Echo's voice cut through the noise like a scalpel. I pressed a hand to my ear to drown out the bass.

"Talk to me," I said.

"Been running through the floor plans," Echo reported. "I've also piggybacked into the hotel's security system. Got facial recognition scraping every camera feed I can reach. But so far, no visual on this Reaper guy."

"Maybe he's holed up somewhere," I said. "Office, back room, something locked down."

"That's what I'm thinking," Echo replied. "But his phone pinged. It's definitely inside the building. I can't get a tighter fix, though. Could be anywhere from the lobby to the roof."

I took a slow sip of bourbon, scanning the upper balconies. "Alright, what about movement? Anything out of place?"

"Yeah," Echo said. "Nineteenth floor. Cameras show five heavy types guarding the elevator entrances. Three at the main elevator and two at the service elevator at the back. All of them look like they're packing. Cameras show elevators are bypassing the floor—none of them are stopping there. Looks like the whole floor's on lockdown."

"That's probably where they set up shop. That could be our summit," I said. "What about the roof?"

"Gimme a sec… Yeah, right, so there are a couple of armed guards up top. Nothing else. Roof's got a helipad but no bird sitting on it."

I checked my watch. 2135 hours. Shade said the meet would kick off at 2200. Twenty-five minutes to go.

I ran the options in my head. Pulling a guy from the club was a fantasy—first I would have to ID the right body, then neutralize him without a scene, then find a private corner to pry answers out of him. That took time I didn't have. The nineteenth-floor option sucked as well: five armed men at choke points meant that bullets would fly the second we tried anything decisive. Once shots cut loose, the floor would go into lockdown and I would lose my chance at grabbing Reaper.

The roof was the only clean play. Two guys, exposed, out in the open, away from civilians. If I could get them fast, I could make them talk before anyone even noticed.

I told Echo as much. "What about accessing the roof? Main elevator go all the way?"

"Hold on, I'll check," he said, coming back a few seconds later. "Access is keycard-locked—employee-only. I can try an override, but it'll take a few minutes."

With the clock ticking, a few minutes felt like a lifetime. I didn't have that luxury. "Copy that. I'll call you back," I said, and cut the line. That left the old-fashioned option: steal a keycard. Old, ugly, reliable.

I looked at Madison and Ninja. “I need a keycard. Now.” No explanation. They didn’t ask for one. That was the shorthand of people who had accepted danger as a menu option.

Ninja’s eyes flicked the room like a predator’s. He pointed to a waiter weaving between tables, a belt loop heavy with service keys and a hotel swipe card clipped to the hip. “There,” he said. “Madison, run a bump on him. I’ll snag the belt.”

Madison moved like she had practiced clumsy elegance all her life. She drifted past the waiter and bumped his shoulder with the precision of someone who was a pro at friendly collisions. And then came the soft, apologetic smile and a “Oh my God, I’m so sorry.” The man froze, charm booted into emergency mode. While he gaped at her face, Ninja leaned in like a shadow and, with fingers smaller than they looked, palmed the card from the holder on the waiter’s belt.

It was surgical. The waiter didn’t even move until another table needed more champagne. Half a beat later Ninja dropped the card into my palm. It was warm from his hand, glossy with hotel logo crap.

I didn’t have time to savor the little victory. “No time to explain,” I told Ninja, tucking the card into my jacket pocket. “You two—stay put. Five minutes. Be ready to move.”

Ninja cracked a grin that didn’t reach his eyes. “Five minutes, boss. We’ll keep the audience entertained.”

I clipped the card between thumb and index finger and walked off toward the elevators with every muscle tuned to the job. I could hear the club thump behind me; it was softer now, like distant artillery.

The elevator doors opened and a bunch of people got out. I stepped into the empty elevator, tapped the keycard against the reader, and pushed the button for the rooftop. The card worked like a charm. The doors closed and the elevator moved up.

It hummed as it climbed, that low, mechanical growl that always sounded like a countdown. I rolled my shoulders, flexed my wrists, feeling the tightness in my knuckles. The bourbon warmth was long gone—now it was just focus and the rush of blood through my veins. If anyone was up there, they weren't going to see a polite visitor.

The doors slid open with a soft chime.

I didn't expect the roof to be so well lit. Bright floodlights along the perimeter threw hard white light across the concrete, cutting sharp shadows against the helipad markings. The city spread out below—D.C. in the distance at night, a sprawl of power and secrets, all glowing like sin.

The wind was biting, carrying that high-altitude chill and the faint thrum of music bleeding up from the club below. HVAC ducts lined one side, their metal skins rattling against the wind. To the left, a red beacon flashed atop a steel railing near the helipad. Two men stood near it, silhouettes solid and squared—the kind of stance you only got from years of carrying a gun and expecting to use it.

They noticed me as soon as I stepped out. Their hands drifted to their jackets, but they didn't draw. My confidence did its job—confused them, made them hesitate. Predators didn't expect someone to walk toward their teeth.

"Evening, boys," I called out, tone casual but cold. "Reaper sent me up to make sure things are squared away before the bird lands."

They looked at each other, uncertain. One spoke, rough Baltimore accent. "Who the hell are you?"

I kept walking. Slow, deliberate steps crunching against the rooftop gravel. "Who the fuck do you *think* I am? You think I'm up here for the goddamn view? I'm with the New York crew. Now get Reaper on the phone and ask him where the fuck's Shade."

The taller one frowned, his hand still buried inside his jacket. The shorter guy shifted, uncertainty written large on his face. He pulled his hand out—no gun, just reaching for his phone. That was my cue.

I moved before he blinked.

I closed the gap in three strides. My left hand snapped out, slamming into the wrist of the taller guy's gun arm just as it cleared leather. His fingers went slack from the impact, and I drove a palm strike up into his jaw—hard enough to rattle teeth and drop him to one knee. I pivoted with the motion, grabbed the back of his head, and brought it down into my rising knee. The crack of cartilage and bone echoed over the hum of the city. He went limp, weapon clattering out onto the roof.

The second guy fumbled with his phone, eyes wide. I hit him before he could even think of swinging. I jammed my elbow into his throat—once, clean and deep—then grabbed a handful of his jacket, turned, and used his own weight to throw him over my hip. He landed flat on the concrete with a sound like a dropped sandbag, air shooting out of his lungs. He tried to roll, wheezing, but I stomped down on his chest to keep him there.

The first guy groaned behind me, trying to rise. I didn't give him the chance. I twisted, stomped the side of his knee, and felt the ligaments tear. He howled once before I silenced him with a short hammer-fist to the temple. His body went slack, dead weight on the roof.

I turned back to the other one—the one under my boot. He was awake. I had made sure of it. I eased off the pressure just enough to let him breathe. His eyes flickered with panic and pain, blood running from his lip.

"Good you didn't go to sleep like your pal," I said quietly, crouching down beside him. "I need you awake for this part."

He tried to speak, but all that came out was a wet cough.

"Save your breath," I told him, voice low and steady. "You've got some talking to do."

CHAPTER 40

I kept my boot on the man's chest like a punctuation mark—heavy, final. He was still coughing, ribs working like bellows, that wet rasp that meant his lungs were pissed off at me. Up close his breath smelled like booze and fear. I leaned down close enough so he could see the intent in my face—calm, cold, patient.

"I kept you awake for a reason," I said, my voice low and flat. "Answer quick and maybe it's your lucky night. I won't break any bones if you don't make me." I let the threat hang there like a blade. He blinked, face twisting, trying to judge whether I was bluffing. I didn't let him look away.

"If you're thinking of trying to play tough guy, take a look at your partner," I added, nodding at the man splayed out like meat across the gravel—jaw caved and leg crooked, face a map of smashed bone and missing teeth. "You'll go down a lot worse than him. Do you understand?"

The sight had the effect I had planned—panic punched into his pupils. I grabbed his hand and curled my fingers around his middle finger like it was a bar I planned to snap.

"Let's talk," I said.

His jaw clenched with the sound of defiance and he spat: "Fuck you."

I knew he had to try once to see if I was bluffing. I didn't make him wait. I snapped the finger and heard the small, sharp crack. The finger folded where flesh and bone weren't meant to fold and he howled—an animal sound cut off by cold air.

I didn't flinch. "You can howl all you want. "There isn't anyone up here to clap for you."

I held him with the broken finger hanging useless, then closed on his index finger the same way, no hesitation, because dead time was where men got clever.

"Try it again," I said.

His face went white in a way that said he realized he had chosen wrong the first time. "No—no, I'll tell you. I'll tell you whatever."

He hustled the words out like they were life rafts. I kept the pressure on while I spoke, asking the questions clean and fast. "When's the meeting? Where?"

He stammered, throat working. "Ten. The chopper lands at ten. They go down to the nineteenth. Meeting's there."

"Where on the nineteenth? How many men down there?"

I watched the calculation cross his eyes. I didn't like the look. I broke the index finger with a quick twist, just to remind him that hesitation cost bone. The sound of it separating was small and sharp against the wind.

He screamed, then spilled fast: "About ten men on the floor—hard cases. Big apartment at the end of the corridor. Third door on the left." His words tumbled out like someone afraid of losing them to the wind.

"What's your and this other guy's name?" I asked. I couldn't care less about their names but knowing them might come in handy later.

He looked a little surprised at the question, but knew better than to take too long to answer. "I'm Granger and he's Barry," the man blurted out in a hurry.

"Where's Shade?" I asked just to be sure if these guys were wondering about where he had disappeared.

"I don't know. I swear. Shade's gone dark and Reaper's been going nuts trying to raise him."

That was everything I needed. I drove my fist into his jaw hard enough to take the light from his eyes. He went limp, out cold.

Before I let him stay that way, I put the heel of my boot to the outside of his ankle, twisted until the joint protested and gave. No flourish, just efficient ruin. It was ugly and loud—just the kind of afterthought that made sure he wouldn't be a problem if he came round in the wrong place.

I sat back on my heels and listened to the city breathe around us. I checked the watch light—2140 hours. Felt the clock ticking through my bones. Twenty minutes. The window was closing fast.

I frisked the two men, emptied their pockets, and tossed their guns into a hidden nook by the elevator shaft. Their expandable batons stayed hooked to their belts. I yanked both free and felt the cold steel thump in my palms like a promise. The sticks folded out with a practiced snap—no batteries, no faff, just physics and force.

I checked the rooftop once more: the helipad, the city's veins of light, the two bodies curled like shut books. Then I moved for the elevator, boots on concrete, senses on a hair trigger, the night air still humming with the memory of violence.

I swiped the keycard, hit the button for the elevator, and waited. It was time to use the ace up my sleeve—Shade's phone. That little phone would smoke Reaper out of whatever hole he was hiding in.

When the doors slid open, I stepped inside the empty car and called Echo.

"Echo, I'm going to send Reaper a few messages—give him a reason to move. Watch the nineteenth. If he moves, catch him on camera and let me know."

"Copy, Cowboy," Echo said. "Eyes on Nineteen. I'll queue the feeds and watch for movement."

"Good," I said, ending the call as the elevator hummed down toward the 20th.

The doors opened to the muted thump of bass from the nightclub. Blue lights strobed across polished floors and half-drunk faces. I pulled out Shade's phone, opened his messages, and typed:

"*You in the hotel?*"

Barely two seconds later, the screen lit up with an incoming call. Reaper. He had taken the bait. I stared at the caller ID for a moment, then killed the call. No way I could fake Shade's voice—not with a guy like Reaper.

I cut the call and fired a text. My thumbs moved fast, keying in a message: "*Being followed. Barely made the lobby. Unknown guys—armed. Think it's the same crew that's been hunting me. Hiding. Can't talk. They're watching.*"

The reply came quick, curt, and cold. "*Is it that dead Marine's brother?*"

My blood rose when I read that. But I knew I had to be patient. "*Don't think so. Look like mob guys.*"

"*Stay put. I'm coming down with my men.*"

Perfect.

The pieces were moving. And Reaper was walking straight into my trap.

I pocketed the phone and scanned the room. The bassline rolled through my chest as I walked toward the table where Ninja and Madison sat. She looked calm but alert; Ninja had that thousand-yard readiness in his eyes.

I set Shade's phone on the table like it was evidence and handed one of the batons to Ninja. He palmed the metal, felt the balance, flipped it once between his fingers, and nodded.

I looked at Madison. "You should go. Things are going to blow up fast. Sorry for springing this so suddenly."

She gave me a steady look. "Don't worry about it. I figured this might happen. No surprises. Forget about me and focus on what you need to do. Are you closer to Ryan's killers?"

I let that mission-face settle like a mask. "Close enough to touch them."

She nodded like that was everything. For a second, I let myself believe she might actually walk. I watched her, calculating risk. Even if she stayed—and knowing her, she probably would—the club was the safe place. All the fireworks would go off upstairs. She wouldn't be in the line of fire. That was the calculus that let me move.

Echo came back on my ear, voice calm and fast. "Cowboy—Reaper's coming out a door on the nineteenth. He's with four men. They're waiting on an elevator."

"Copy. They're headed for the lobby. Confirm when they're moving," I replied.

I nodded to Ninja. We rose as one.

I squeezed Madison's hand once, hard. "I'll see you later," I said, before walking out with Ninja, headed for the elevator.

"They're headed down," Echo added a beat later.

“Scramble the security feed on nineteen and the roof,” I said. “Overwrite the feeds—confuse the loop.”

Echo confirmed he would seed noise into the cameras and loop the footage. That would make us ghosts, with cameras just showing an empty area.

We had just gone dark—there wouldn’t be any footage of what we were about to do.

CHAPTER 41

Ninja and I stepped into the elevator. The air inside felt thick, heavy with the kind of tension you only get before violence. I pressed the keycard against the reader, then hit the button for the 19th floor. The light blinked red once, then green. The doors began to close.

"Good," I muttered. "Keycard still has juice. If that floor button was locked out, we'd still be standing here like a couple of tourists."

I glanced at Ninja. He was rolling his shoulders, that hungry look in his eyes—the same one I had seen a dozen times before a fight.

"There'll be five guys waiting outside when these doors open," I said quietly. "Guns holstered, probably relaxed. We keep it silent. No shots. No mess."

He grinned faintly. "How hard we going?"

"As hard as it takes."

"Sounds like fun."

The elevator slowed, the floor indicator lighting up nineteen. We moved into position—Ninja on the left, me on the right. Both of us leaning slightly, bodies loose, heads tilted, balance a little off. Two party guys who had lost their way.

The bell chimed. The doors slid open.

Five men stood waiting—three up front, two behind. All of them dressed in the usual mobster casual: fitted suits, open collars, shoulder holsters just visible under the jackets. Their hands hovered near their weapons, but their eyes said they weren't worried. Two drunk partygoers didn't exactly scream "threat".

The one in front—built like a dump truck, with a shaved head and neck wider than his jaw—scowled.

"This floor's off-limits," he barked. "How the hell did you even get here?"

I raised my hands, laughing, playing it loose. "Hey, man, we were just partying. Looking for the bar. Pressed the wrong button, I guess. Thing lit up, door opened, boom—we're here."

I pointed back inside the elevator. "Look, the thing lit up on its own. Must be broken or something."

Shaved Head took the bait. He stepped forward, leaning into the elevator to look. The two beside him leaned too, curious.

That was all the opening we needed.

The batons snapped open with twin *cracks*—that sweet, sharp metal sound.

I brought mine up and over, smashing it across Shaved Head's jaw with enough force to pop teeth loose. He crumpled sideways, blood spraying across the elevator wall.

Ninja moved like a ghost—his baton whipped low, smashing the next guy's kneecap. Before the man could drop, Ninja's elbow hammered his throat, cutting off the scream before it started.

The third guard fumbled for his holster. I caught his wrist, yanked him forward, and drove my knee into his gut. The air blasted out of him, and I followed with a baton strike to the side of his neck. He dropped like a marionette with its strings cut.

The two in the back came alive, reaching under their jackets. I didn't let them finish. I lunged out of the elevator, swung my baton sideways, and cracked the closer one across the temple. He hit the wall and slid down, eyes glassy.

The fifth guy got his gun halfway out before Ninja was on him—snatched the pistol from his hand, spun it, and pistol-whipped him so hard his head bounced off the doorframe. He dropped like a sack of bricks.

The whole thing took maybe eight seconds. No shouts, no shots, just the wet sounds of bone and flesh meeting steel.

I stepped over the bodies, breathing steady, eyes scanning the hall. All five were down—knocked out cold. Ninja gave one of them a solid kick in the ribs for good measure.

I glanced at Ninja. "Fun enough for you?"

Ninja gave a small grin, twirling the baton once before collapsing it with a snap. "Yeah. Quiet, too."

But we didn't have any time to take it easy. The clock was ticking, and Reaper had to be hitting the lobby any second now. Once he looked around and didn't spot Shade, he would start blowing up the guy's phone again. That gave me maybe two, three minutes before things got noisy.

I crouched beside one of the bodies and checked his pockets. Found an apartment keycard. Perfect.

"Grab the guns," I told Ninja. "We're not done yet."

We moved fast. I scanned the corridor—no cameras we hadn't already looped, no movement. I pushed the keycard into the reader, light turned green, and the lock clicked. I pushed the door open slow, muzzle-first, my gun angled high. We went in low and tight, corners first, slicing the pie like we had done a thousand times before.

The apartment was big—penthouse suite style. Plush furniture, city lights bleeding through sheer curtains, soft music humming from hidden speakers. We cleared each room fast, tight angles, covering each other's backs. No one inside. Just silence and the faint chemical bite of heroin in the air.

"Clear," Ninja muttered.

"Yeah," I said, scanning the room. "But look at this."

A table near the window was stacked with about ten pounds of heroin wrapped in cellophane. Pure, uncut, bagged tight and waiting for shipment. And right beside it—guns. Handguns, shotguns, and three M4 carbines with suppressors and fresh mags. Someone was planning for a long night.

I picked up a Glock, racked the slide, checked the chamber—good to go. Then grabbed an M4, three mags, and suppressors for both. The M4 felt right in my hands. Balanced. Familiar. Like coming home. I also grabbed a flashlight and slid it into a pocket.

We dragged the five unconscious bodies inside one by one, stacking them against the wall like broken mannequins. I took a quick look back before shutting the door. Five broken men, a table of heroin, and a small armory—the cops would have a hell of a day when they busted in there.

Back at the elevator, I hit the call button and looked at Ninja. "You head back to the club. Stick close to Madison."

He gave me a flat look. "You're kidding, right? You want me to babysit her?"

"Madison's not gonna leave," I said flatly. "And if Reaper's guys check security footage and see her walking in with us, she's a target. You know what that means—she's leverage. We can't have her getting snatched."

Ninja smirked, but there wasn't much humor in it. "You just feeding me a line to get me out of the way? 'Cause I get it, man. This Reaper thing—this is personal. Just like Shade was."

I gave him a small nod. "You know me too well."

I was heading to the roof to finish Reaper and anyone with him. Even though Echo had scrambled the security feed on the nineteenth and the roof, this was a public place—too many eyes, too many variables. I wanted to leave no trace, but plans don't always go how you want them to go. If the cops pulled anything back to us, I would take the fall. I wasn't going to let Ninja get nailed for my mess.

We stepped out into the hall, boots soft on the carpet. The elevator chimed open, and we got in. The silence was heavy between us—no more words needed.

When the elevator doors opened, he clapped me on the shoulder. "Get the bastard who killed Ryan."

"Count on it," I said, then added: "I couldn't have done it without you."

Ninja gave me a nod and stepped out toward the nightclub. His shoulders were squared, eyes sharp.

I watched him go, then hit the button for the roof. The doors closed again, sealing me inside the mirrored box.

Just me now. Me and the hunt.

The M4 hung tight against my chest, the Glock sat warm in my hand, and my mind was locked on one name—Reaper.

Time to finish this.

CHAPTER 42

Reaper's message came through on Shade's phone—short, angry, and loaded with attitude. "*Where the fuck are you?*"

I stared at it for a second, then typed back: "*Made it to the roof. Up here with Granger and Barry.*"

Didn't take him long to respond. "*What the fuck? I'm coming up.*"

I smiled coldly and typed: "*I'll be waiting.*"

The phone dimmed in my hand, screen going black again. I tucked it away and looked toward the elevator. Reaper had gone down to the lobby with four men. That meant five targets coming up.

The smart play would have been to stand right here by the elevator, M4 leveled at chest height and pointed straight, and hose the whole bunch the second the doors slid open. A quick burst, clean sweep, five bodies. Easy.

But I wasn't there for easy. Reaper needed to *see* it coming. Feel that cold, creeping terror in his gut when he realized he was being hunted. I wanted him to die knowing *exactly* who had come for him and why.

Ryan deserved that much.

I knew from the schematics Echo had sent me that the light controls for the roof were tucked behind the elevator shaft—out of sight. Perfect place for me to wait.

I moved around the back of the shaft, boots silent on the concrete, and keyed my mic. "Echo, you got eyes on Reaper?"

"Affirmative," he said, his voice calm and quiet in my ear. "He's still in the lobby. You want me to call it when he moves?"

"Yeah," I said, resting one hand on the main switch. "Tell me when he gets into the elevator, and when he's coming up. I'll handle the rest."

"You got it, Cowboy."

I closed my eyes tight and pressed my free hand against them, shutting out every trace of light. The move wasn't random—it was deliberate. Force my eyes to start adjusting early, prep them for the darkness I was about to create. The world went completely black behind my eyelids, and I focused on slowing my breathing.

A few seconds later, Echo came back on the line. "Reaper's in. He's got four with him."

"Copy that," I said quietly. "Let me know when he passes the twentieth floor."

I could almost hear Echo's fingers tapping on his console. About ninety seconds passed, long enough for the faint hum of the building to settle into a rhythm.

"Elevator just passed twenty," Echo said.

"That's all I need, brother," I replied. "Sign off and keep the channel cold."

"Roger that," he said, his tone softening. "Be careful, Cowboy."

The line went dead.

I stayed crouched behind the shaft, one hand still over my eyes, the other resting on the switch. Then I heard it—the *ping* of the elevator arriving.

I didn't move.

Doors slid open with a hiss. Boots shuffled onto the concrete. Muffled voices, five in total, one of them gruffer and sharper than the rest.

“What the fuck’s goin’ on?” the voice snapped—angry, confident. Reaper.

I didn’t need to see him to know it.

I stayed motionless, head low, listening. Then came the sound I had been waiting for—the *ping* of the doors closing again, the elevator gliding back down. The five of them were locked in up there now, boxed in under an open sky with no exits.

I flicked the switch.

The roof went pitch black.

Instantly, chaos hit. Voices rose, confused, nervous. Shoes scuffed, weapons clicked as they tried to orient themselves. A second ago, they had been cocky. Now they were blind and vulnerable—rats in a maze they couldn’t see.

It takes human eyes two to three minutes to adapt to darkness. Like walking into a movie theater straight from the afternoon sun—you are blind as a bat for a while.

But me? I had already done my time in the dark.

I opened my eyes. The world bled into faint shapes and shadows, enough for me to see outlines—the movement of men who thought they still had control.

I moved low and silent, gliding through the black like smoke.

This wasn’t just tactics anymore. Killing the lights was a message.

I was dragging Reaper into the dark—his dark—and that’s where I was going to end him.

Reaper’s gruff voice cut through the dark like a blade. “The hell’s goin’ on with the lights? Check it out!”

His tone was all fury and command—the kind of voice that made men move without thinking. I heard boots scraping concrete as two of them peeled off, muttering curses, groping their way toward the back of the elevator shaft—toward me.

They were pissed, blind, and stupid. In their rush, it didn't even occur to them to pull out their phones for light. That's the thing about fear—it eats your logic first.

I waited behind the elevator shaft, crouched low, one hand wrapped around the grip of the collapsible baton. It was already half-extended, cold steel in my hand. My breathing was steady, heartbeat slow, the kind of rhythm that only comes from years of killing in silence.

The first silhouette rounded the corner, just a faint blur against the dim glow from the city lights bleeding through the rooftop glass. The second followed right behind him, trying to act brave.

I thumbed the baton open. *Crack*. The steel shaft snapped out to full length with that familiar sound—clean, fast, final.

"—What the—" was all the first guy got out.

I swung upward in a tight arc, driving the baton upward with all my weight behind it. The baton connected under his jaw with a sound like splitting firewood. His head snapped back, jaw splitting wide, teeth scattering like loose gravel. He dropped instantly, legs folding under him like a marionette with cut strings.

The second guy froze for a half-second, too slow to process what just happened. I pivoted on my heel and drove the baton sideways, hard into his temple. The strike landed with a solid *thunk*, the kind you feel in your wrist more than you hear. Bone gave way. His knees buckled, body jerking once before crumpling silently onto the concrete.

Both men went down without a sound, except for the soft thud of dead weight meeting concrete.

I eased back into the shadow of the shaft, heartbeat steady, listening. Up front, the others hadn't seen a thing—but they had sure as hell started to *feel* it. The air changed. The kind of silence that makes men's throats go dry.

"What the fuck was that?" one of them called out.

"Rico? Jay? You hear me?" Reaper's voice was sharper now. More alert. The tone of a man who just realized the game changed and he wasn't in control anymore.

I raised the M4, braced the stock against my shoulder, and peered through the scope. Even with minimal light bleeding in from the city below, I could make out faint outlines—three silhouettes near the far side, near the air-conditioning units. Two closer to the front, one standing back, still as stone. I slowed my breathing and studied each one.

Reaper was easy to spot. He stood in the middle, a head taller and built like a goddamn tank—six-four, around two-twenty five, all muscle and menace. Square jaw, wide shoulders, that predator stillness that never really left him. The kind of man who didn't just walk into a room—he filled it.

My finger hovered near the trigger. I could take the shot—end it clean, quiet. But that wasn't the plan.

One of the silhouettes twitched near the far side of the roof—one of Reaper's men finally getting smart. I saw the faint glow of a phone screen light up his face as he fumbled with it, trying to bring up the flashlight. Rookie mistake. The city lights behind him outlined his body like a damn target poster.

I didn't even think about it. Muscle memory took over.

I brought up the M4, the suppressor already fixed, selector set to semi. My cheek pressed against the stock, crosshairs settling on his arm.

Pffft.

The 5.56 NATO round punched through the dark, whisper-quiet, and hit him right around the elbow. The impact almost tore his forearm in half. He let out a strangled scream, phone clattering to the ground.

Before he could even fold over, I sent a second round into his knee. *Pffft.*

He went down like a sack of concrete, clutching what was left of his arm, howling in pain.

That did it. Reaper and his last guy opened up, firing wild into the shadows where they had seen the muzzle flash. Rounds zipped and sparked off the metal around the elevator shaft, but I was already gone—slid two steps left and tucked behind a steel duct.

They were shooting ghosts.

I came around the opposite side, fast and quiet, brought the rifle up again. The second guy was standing a little ahead of Reaper, scanning the dark, gun trembling just enough to give me a clear silhouette.

Pffft. Pffft.

First round took him in the shoulder—his gun spun out of his hands. Second round nailed him in the left knee. His leg folded, and he went down screaming.

Reaper turned toward the sound, weapon up. But before he could squeeze the trigger, I stepped out just enough for my voice to cut through the dark.

"Don't even breathe too hard, Reaper. Next bullet goes right through your chest."

I could hear him freeze—boots scraping faintly on the roof gravel. His gun hand wavered.

"Drop it," I snapped, the kind of tone that carried weight even over the wind.

He hesitated.

So I squeezed one off—deliberate, controlled. The round snapped past his boot and sparked off the concrete, an inch from his toes.

"Next one takes your ankle off," I warned.

That did it. The rifle clattered to the ground.

I moved in slow, keeping the M4 leveled on him. His chest was heaving, eyes darting around in the dark. I could feel his confusion—the same kind of primal fear you see in animals when they realize they are not the hunter anymore.

"Who the hell are you?" he growled. "What do you want?"

"Shut up," I said, stepping closer. "Get down."

He didn't move fast enough for my liking. So I did it for him.

I jammed the muzzle of the rifle into his gut and drove forward with my shoulder behind it—hard. The air blasted out of him in a grunt. He staggered back, lost his footing, and I followed through, sweeping my right leg behind his knees. His balance broke, and gravity did the rest.

He hit the ground flat on his back with a heavy *whump*, the sound of a man who just had all the fight knocked clean out of him.

Now it was just me, Reaper, and the dark.

CHAPTER 43

I stood over him and watched the recognition roll across his face like a tide. The city lights painted my features sharp and ugly in his pupils. He didn't ask who I was. He already knew.

"Was that you messin' with Shade's phone?" he asked, voice rough with surprise and something that smelled like fear.

"Take a guess," I said, letting the silence hang like a noose.

"Is Shade dead?" His question was small, like he was trying to steady himself with facts.

"Yeah."

For a second his face went slack, then he asked, quieter, "You know everything?"

"Yeah."

"Kincaid's flash drive?" He sounded like he was testing the bones of the world to see if they still held.

"Yeah." I let the word hang there. Even in death, Kincaid had outfoxed them. That fact felt like cold justice in my mouth.

He muttered something about Dana—like a bitter aftertaste. The word slipped out rough and ugly: "That bitch fooled Shade—"

I didn't wait for the rest. I kicked him hard in the ribs, hard enough to take the breath clean out of him. He gasped and curled.

"Say that again," I warned, letting the anger sit cold and heavy. "Say it and I'll make you eat the word."

He glared up at me, teeth bared, but went quiet. I stepped closer, voice low. "She had balls and brains enough to make sure the truth didn't die with Kincaid. More than all you scumbags put together."

The barb landed; his face tightened.

"The video don't mean shit," he snapped back, trying to angle for bravado. "It's one man's word against ours—won't hold in court."

"What makes you think I'm taking you to court?" I said, each syllable a blade. For the first time, a shadow of proper fear slid over his features. It tightened the muscles in his neck.

"Turn over," I ordered. "Now. And don't make me ask twice."

He flipped onto his stomach but then tried to needle me. "Too pussy to look me in the eye, huh? Gonna shoot me in the back like some coward?" he jabbed.

I ignored the bait. I put my boot on his back and leaned my weight into it, the heel pressing into the center of his spine. I started patting his upper body—chest, shoulders, collarbones—routine, mechanical, covering pockets, feeling seams.

"I got a snub-nosed in an ankle holster—right ankle," he said, almost too casual, like he wanted to be helpful. I kept moving, but the little smirk in his voice told me the truth: he was trying to steer my hands away from somewhere he didn't want them checked. Classic misdirection.

I played along. I reached for his right ankle, fingers practiced and sure, and then I brushed the left ankle casually with the back of my hand. Tape scraped under my knuckles. A sheath sat there, taped and ugly against his calf. I felt the outline of a blade. I ignored it, let him believe he had fooled me.

I thumbed the snub-nosed free from the right ankle and tossed it across the roof into a dark corner. It hit concrete and rolled to a stop. The knife stayed secure against his left calf where he had thought it would.

I stepped back and he rolled to his back, eyes still burning with hate. He tried to shove one more taunt into the dark: "You can act tough with a gun in your hand, but you don't have the balls to face me one on one."

I let the silence stretch. I had been waiting to hear the exact things he spat—because I had already decided I didn't need a gun to end him.

"If it's one on one, you'll die the same way your brother did," he said, hissing the words like a promise.

I had been waiting for him to say it. I had already decided I was going to take him apart bare-handed.

I eased the magazine out of the M4, thumbed it free, and slid it into my pocket like I was putting my wallet away. I propped the rifle against a low concrete wall, muzzle up, as casual as leaning a broom against a shed.

Then I looked at him and said, flat and steady, "Get up. Let's do this man to man."

As Reaper pushed himself to his feet, he gave me an evil smirk and said: "Fell for it like a sucker. I'm going to break you."

He was on his feet, looking like a bull ready to charge, chest heaving. He was built like a human tank—massive shoulders, barrel chest, forearms like slabs of meat. The kind of guy who had won most of his fights by crushing the other man under pure size and fury.

I stayed loose, on the balls of my feet, hands up and open. My heart rate stayed low, breathing steady. Let him come.

He charged—arms swinging wide like hammers. I sidestepped left, pivoted on my heel, and drove an elbow into his kidney. He grunted, more surprised than hurt. His arm swept back like a bear swatting flies. I ducked under, felt the air stir past my head, and came up with a jab to his ribs. He stumbled back, snarling.

Reaper swung again, slower now but still dangerous. Every move carried the weight of a man used to ending fights with one blow. I gave him nothing to hit—sidestepping, pivoting, giving him angles instead of targets. His fists hit nothing but air and frustration.

I kept my distance because I knew what he could do if he caught me. He could crush a man by sheer will; I had to make sure he never got the chance.

"Come on," he snarled, spittle flashing in the dim rooftop light.

I smiled. "You're gonna need a bigger hammer."

He roared and lunged. I shifted right, sank a short right hook into his midsection. It landed solid—air whooshed out of him. He doubled slightly, left hand clutching his abdomen. That's when I saw it.

The tell. His right hand slipped low toward his ankle. I caught the glint before the steel cleared leather.

He came at me in the same breath, lunging with a blade flashing upward in a vicious arc meant to gut me. I twisted out of the swing and felt the wind of the knife miss my gut by inches.

"Yeah," I said coldly. "Knew you'd try that. Snake like you doesn't have the balls for a fair fight."

He didn't answer—just turned and slashed again, faster this time, blade whispering through the night air.

I slid a hand down to my boot, drew my own knife—black handle, matte edge, balanced and beautiful. Ryan's gift to me when I made Delta. I would use that to take out Reaper.

"Big mistake," I warned. "You just stepped into my classroom."

A voice echoed in my head. "*Cut the lines, kid. Take the limbs. Own the fight.*"

It was the voice of Adriel. He had worn the title of Navajo warrior like a quiet badge and ran the foreman's patch on the ranch after dad died. He had taught Ryan and me how to butcher a hog and how to butcher a fight—same hands, different end.

Reaper swung wide again. I parried the strike, metal kissed metal, and I stepped inside his reach—close enough to smell the sour sweat and adrenaline. The first cut I made wasn't pretty; it was precise. I slashed his forearm across the tendon, a shallow, surgical arc that opened him and turned his wrist into a useless lever.

He spat and tried to swing, but his grip faltered. I drove a second cut across the meat of his thigh, deep enough to nick the tendon that ran under the muscle. He staggered, knee wobbling.

He still had bulk and fury. He shoved me with a shoulder like a freight car and my ribs lit up, but I kept my center and let the force run past me. I chopped at his elbow next—hard, clean—and felt the snap of ligament give like a cord cut. His knife arm jerked where it should not have.

Ryan's words were steady in the back of my head: "*Go for the levers, Ax. Take the limbs. That's where a big man falls apart.*"

Reaper tried to compensate, jammed his good arm into me, and I used his momentum. I rolled inside a swing, slashed under the knee that still held him, and felt tendons give with a wet, honest rip. His leg folded like a chair with broken bolts. He howled, a raw animal sound, but pain wasn't enough to stop him from flailing.

I took a shallow wound across my bicep—steel kissing skin—and let it sting. Pain was information; blood was a compass. I answered with a quick, precise cut across the back of his other wrist. The blade found the soft spot at the base of his thumb and severed the control line. His hand went from instrument to a flapping weight.

He lunged blindly, knife useless in a hand that no longer obeyed. I moved in, closed the distance, and twisted my blade into a final, practiced arc across his lower thigh and calf. Tendons that had held him upright were gone. He pitched forward like a puppet with its strings cut.

He dropped to one knee, growling, bleeding, still trying to swing that knife like sheer hate could hold his body together.

I stepped in close, blocked his hand, twisted the wrist, and wrenched. The blade clattered across the concrete, spinning off into the dark. I followed up with a headbutt—sharp, brutal.

I finished it by slipping a hand behind his neck and using his remaining motion to send him face-first into the concrete. He hit with a sick, bone-sounding thud and tried to scramble, but his limbs were traitors now—jerking and useless. I had cut too deep—severed what controlled them.

I stood over him, chest heaving, blade still warm in my hand.

He glared up at me, panting, blood streaking his mouth. I wiped my blade on his shirt, then slid it back into its sheath.

"Class dismissed," I declared.

Then I grabbed him by the collar, hauled his deadweight across the concrete, and dragged him to the low wall facing the helipad. He was heavy as sin, but he wasn't fighting anymore. I propped him up there, back against concrete, arms useless at his sides.

CHAPTER 44

I checked my watch—2158 hours. Two minutes to zero hour. The plan was about to finish writing itself. I felt the night squeeze down to the width of a barrel.

I walked to the area behind the elevator shaft and turned on the roof lights. Then I walked back and picked up the M4 carbine from where I had left it propped against the wall, felt the weight settle into my hands like a returning friend. I dug the mag from my pocket, slid it home with a sharp click, and racked the charging handle to make sure the first round would kiss the barrel. Selector on semi, suppressor still on. Ready to whisper death.

A couple of minutes later I heard it before I saw it—the whine of rotor wash cutting through the city noise. A low thrum built in the distance and became a hungry roar. Rotor wash hit the roof long before the bird came into sight—air like a fist, bits of grit whipping across my face. The chopper's silhouette cut the skyline, swept into position above the helipad with the nose into wind, skids hovering just inches off the concrete.

I leaned down and jabbed my heel into Reaper's ribs, hard enough to remind him he was still on the clock. He squinted up at the whine of the blades with hate-filled eyes.

"That's your pals," I said, loud enough for him to hear over the downdraft. "Your gangster boys are coming in for the big meet. Guess what—they aren't getting jack. The millions they fronted? Gone. And when that happens, Harlan's going to be eating shit for dinner. Your empire's about to piss itself into confetti."

Fear had finally settled into his eyes. "What are you gonna do?" he asked, throat raw.

I told him. "Kincaid told me everything—how you set up friendly fire on Captain Ryan Blaze and his Marines—lowlifes like you shot the best of men in the back. Thought you'd gotten away with it. You can't outrun justice—it gets you one way or the other. You got one last surprise coming. Friendly fire's about to come home."

He swallowed. No bravado left in his voice. "What do you mean?"

"You'll see firsthand."

I climbed over the low concrete wall, dropped down behind it, kept my profile low so the crew in the chopper wouldn't pick up a moving silhouette against the city. The bird eased lower, rotorwash pounding, cockpit glazing catching the light from the helipad floodlamps.

I leaned out enough to see the silhouette through the downwash—skid gear settling toward the concrete pad, the cockpit facing inboard, nose drooped, the windshield gleaming under the floodlights. I knew what parts would ruin everything if I hit them—main rotor, mast, tail rotor, fuel vents, engine inlets—so I didn't touch any of that. I didn't want to crash anyone into the crowd on the street below. I wanted chaos, not carnage.

I aimed low. Target: the landing skids and cockpit glazing—hit those and you scare the pilots, maybe crack their view, make them fight for control without sending the bird into a death spiral.

"Your friends are about to get a nasty surprise," I shouted into the dark and then I opened fire.

The first rounds thudded into the starboard landing skid and pinged off the metal. A couple smashed into the cockpit windshield—spiderwebbing the glass, scattering tiny diamonds of fracture across the pilots' view. I kept my bursts short, controlled, aimed to maim and intimidate, not to rip rotors or blow tanks. The chopper bobbed like a wounded animal, rising an inch, then another, hesitant and confused.

Then they got mad and answered.

Automatic rifle fire stitched the air, tracers flashing out of the open door like angry fireflies. The rounds found concrete and HVAC boxes where I had been a heartbeat ago, then found flesh as the gunmen on board zeroed in. The muzzle-flashes lit the roof in angry, strobing bursts.

Reaper tried to scramble, tried to wave them off. He was too slow. He was still slumped against the wall when the lead tracers hit him. Bullets tore through his chest and face, ripped into the meat of his shoulders and throat. Dozens of rounds ripped into him before the pilots could figure which way the shooting was coming from. He convulsed, a ragged sound tearing out of him, and slumped against the wall. Blood darkened his shirt in spreading blooms.

The pilots pulled the nose up hard, rotors chopping, then peeled away like a wounded animal. The chopper climbed fast, downdraft tearing at anything it passed. By the time it was a patch of sound and then gone, Reaper lay still with the city lights flickering off the slick sheen on his face.

I stood up slow and walked to him. He was a sculpture of surprise—blood and shredded cloth, features frozen in one last, shock-shot expression. I dropped the M4 across his chest where it thudded heavy and impotent. The smell of oil and hot brass and old gunpowder hung between us.

I eased my gloves off, turning them inside out like a man shedding a disguise. No prints left anywhere. Echo had the cameras looping; everything looked like a quiet rooftop to anyone watching. Nothing would tie me to the roof.

I dialed Madison. "Call 911. Tell them there's an active shootout on the roof and at apartment 19C on the nineteenth floor. Tell them to send everything. I'll be down in a minute." My words were short, clinical. She didn't argue. She did what I asked her to do.

The rotor wash faded into the city noise. The helipad lights threw long, hard shadows. I looked at Reaper one last time—dead, mouth open, face frozen in a final, surprised expression.

I slipped my hands into my pockets, swallowed the last of the night's adrenaline, and walked to the elevator. The elevator chimed open on cue. I stepped inside and pressed the button for the 20th floor.

The elevator dinged and the doors opened to the same neon-lit roar like nothing had happened up there. Music thumped through the floorboards and into my ribs; laughter and glass and the usual plastic sheen of a place built to make you forget everything except your drink. Nobody here would have heard the roof. Nobody would know the night had been torn open above them.

I stepped out, let my eyes adjust to the half-light, and took in the room. Tables, lacquered wood, glittering drinks, people pretending the music was the only truth. Madison sat at the table, phone to her ear, tone clipped and professional. Ninja was beside her, playing calm like it was a costume he slipped on and off. He looked up when I walked in—question in his eyes, the kind that didn't need words.

He stood and came over slow. "How'd it go?" he asked. Quiet, tight.

"Second target crossed off," I said. "Reaper's killing days are over." I kept my voice low so the bass could swallow it. Didn't want to be loud for the wrong listeners.

Ninja's face hardened. "Friendly fire?" he asked. He already knew the play—I had told him when I asked him to hold position with Madison.

I nodded. "He died getting wiser to the idea." No victory in it. Just the arithmetic of it—what goes around, comes around.

Madison closed her call and came over. "I called the cops," she said. "They're on their way."

That was good. That put another nail in the coffin for whatever Harlan had been cooking—DEA on a roof with bodies and busted concealment? Harlan and his crew wouldn't have a clean story to tell the mob. And if he didn't, Harlan wouldn't be left with anyone he could rely on.

Madison's eyes slid to my sleeve and then to the dark smear on my bicep. "You hurt?" she asked.

I shrugged. "Just a scratch."

"Well, the scratch's bleeding," she said, ripping a napkin and pressing it to the cut.

"I know blood's better inside the body than out, but don't worry—Ninja's truck is basically a traveling trauma bay. He carries enough stuff to staunch anyone he's been slashing with that blade of his."

Madison blinked, eyebrows climbing. "You're kidding, right?"

"Half," I admitted. "But we don't call him Ninja Man for nothing."

She let out a small, doubtful laugh. Ninja rolled his eyes at me.

We walked out together. The lobby hit us with cool air and the light of emergency strobes—blue and red strobing through the glass. Cops were already there, uniforms knotting into clusters, radios spitting orders. Faces turned our way, then back to work.

As we pushed through the doors, the plan kept working in my head. I needed to make sure the last pieces of Harlan's plan fell apart—get to the contractors who would move the smuggled load from Dover to Harlan's warehouse. Torque had given me the details. Once those hands were stopped, the trap would close and Harlan would have nowhere to run.

I felt the tally slide into place. Two targets down. One left.

Time to get Harlan.

CHAPTER 45

The plan had to be surgical. No improvisation. No half-measures. I wanted Harlan standing on a tarmac with no exits, watching law and the mob close around him. This was about engineering a collapse—psychological, operational, reputational—so precise the man couldn't wiggle free.

I wanted him pulled out into the light, cuffed to his own arrogance, watching the empire he had built burn before he could wheedle his way out of the smoke. Same payoff Shade and Reaper deserved—only this time the audience was bigger and meaner.

First move: create motive. Make the boys from New York and Philly think Harlan had already double-crossed them and was planning to run the shipment overseas. If the mafias believed he had taken fifty million and planned to cut them out, they would come looking for blood. And if Harlan believed he was about to be burned, he would have to come himself for the delivery. People in power who weren't used to being exposed get sloppy when they panic. That's the opening you strike.

Echo had already primed the feed. He spun up a network of assets—TOR personas, PGP-signed handles that looked like insiders. He seeded posts on hidden forums, pushed doctored manifests and a fake internal memo that made Harlan look like a man who had skimped the mafias and planned to move the product off-shore.

Echo sent targeted DMs to known mafioso accounts—messages that read like leaked whispers from a cagey lieutenant. Metadata was faked. Exit nodes were spoofed. Everything smelt legitimate enough to make real criminals bite. The trick wasn't to prove Harlan guilty in a court of law; it was to make people believe it enough that they would act on it. Belief moves bodies. Belief makes men show up with guns.

Echo seeded the chatter and the forums lit up like a warning flare. That was the quiet part.

Next I planned to get loud. I was going to pay Gideon Crane a midnight visit. Crane ran Ironbridge Logistics—the man who would take the C-17 pallets from Dover, sign the fake manifests, and shepherd the crates to Harlan's warehouse.

Torque had given me the lowdown on Crane. Harlan used Crane as a contractor shield: Crane's crews showed up with paperwork, loaded the pallets, and drove them off under the cover of "freight forwarding". Crane's trucks moved pallets into a fenced yard, peeled them off into discrete delivery legs, and made sure the right vans took the right loads to storage.

Crane would know the routes, the fake manifests, the truck roll-plan and the names of the mafiosi he had been cashing for. My plan was to make him talk. I wanted the exact playbook—how he would pick up the shipment, which dock teams he relied on, the truck-roll plan, and the names of the mob guys he was dealing with.

My job was simple: plant a live rumor in meatspace to match Echo's ghosts online. Crane would hand that live rumor to the men who carried guns. Echo had made them hang on a ghost; I was going to make them hear it from a man with a face.

Before I paid Crane a visit, I used Reaper's phone to light a fuse. This was the part of the plan that was supposed to make Harlan start shitting bricks and jolt him into moving. I used Reaper's phone and sent a text to Harlan. If the bait was going to work, the message had to look like a man on the run, not some neat, staged provocation. It had to sound real, raw, urgent.

I typed the opener and sent it. "*It's gone FUBAR at the Sovereign. Cops everywhere.*"

That line was a hook—short, ugly, immediate. If Harlan was anywhere near breathing, that text would make him inhale wrong.

The phone rang before the dots faded. Harlan's number lit the screen; he called back like a man closing ranks. I couldn't take the call—couldn't fake Reaper's voice without getting cut to pieces—so I let it ring out once, twice, then cut it. No drama. Just a clean disconnect.

I sent the follow-up as if Reaper were hiding and too hot to speak. "*Can't talk. Up on the roof. Cops all over. Pinned. Text only.*"

That second text did two things: it explained why I didn't pick up, and it telegraphed danger close enough to shove Harlan into motion.

Harlan fired back in two impatient words. "*Copy. Sitrep?*"

Perfect. He was already mentally rerouting—going into problem mode. I sent what I needed him to know and nothing more.

"*Shade and Torque—vanished. Looks like they got taken. Probably a rival crew.*"

That text was the real trigger. Shade's name alone made Harlan's gut lurch; Torque's disappearance was the gear-grinder. Torque handled logistics—if Torque was gone, the Dover run was on a knife-edge.

Harlan's text read like a man trying to stop a collapsing ceiling. "*Which crew? How the hell did you let that happen?*"

I kept the posture of a man who had been hit but was keeping the situation together. That kept him moving without letting him off the hook.

"*They hit fast. Caught us off guard. I'll hunt them when it's over.*"

His snapped back quick: "*Them and whoever ratted out on the Baltimore stash. We've been hit hard.*"

The speed at which things had been moving, I had almost forgotten about the bust on Harlan's heroin stash at the Baltimore warehouse. On a whim, I tossed him a bone to keep him hooked.

"*Baltimore's not totally lost. My guy pulled eighty kilos in a truck. I'll give you the location once the heat's off.*"

That had the intended effect. Harlan perked up. "*That's excellent news.*"

"*Yeah. But right now we're pinned. You need to move.*"

That put the ball squarely in his court: act, or everything unravels.

The reply came thinner this time, panic tucked under control. "*The shipment lands in less than three hours!!*"

Bingo. Time pressure. He had swallowed the hook.

I pushed him where I wanted. "*Get to Dover yourself and take charge of the offload. If you don't, the buyers show up and there's nothing to hand over.*"

Language tight, threat implied. No need to yell about fifty million. No theatrics. Just the shove that made him act.

Harlan cursed, then confirmed. "*Fine. I'll be there. I'll secure it.*"

I felt that little internal click of satisfaction—bingo. He had moved from desk to runway in his head.

The thought of me must have popped into his head at that moment. "*You think Blaze is behind this? He's been snooping—dead brother and all.*"

This wasn't the time for Harlan to overthink. He needed to be kept moving. "*Can't be sure. My money's on a rival slipping in. Turning phone off. I'll call you when I can.*"

Short, sensible, noncommittal—kept him moving but didn't let him loop back and stall.

His last text was a command to himself. "*I'll make the arrangements to take control. Keep me posted.*"

I stared at the screen for a beat. The subtext of everything I had sent had been a single, lethal instruction: go to Dover tonight or lose it all. That pressure wasn't a polite summons. It was a shove. Men like Harlan don't stay in offices when that kind of pressure lands on them. They go walk the tarmac.

I turned off the phone, slipped it into a pocket, and let the cold settle. Echo's chatter would stir the mobs; my texts had shoved Harlan out from behind his desk. All the pieces were where I wanted them.

Time to go see Gideon Crane.

CHAPTER 46

We hit Ironbridge Logistics just past midnight, when the industrial park was dead quiet—just sodium lamps humming and the occasional semi rumbling a mile off. The place was a converted office welded onto a low-slung warehouse, corrugated walls, two roll-up doors, and a single main gate. A chain-link fence circled the property, topped with razor wire.

The guard at the gate wasn't a bored municipal joker—he was a mean-faced man in a wool coat, jaw like a brick and tattoos peeking from his cuffs. The other guys we could see through the glass were the same: hard eyes, cut faces, men who had learned to solve problems with a fist. This surely wasn't a regular transport office.

I killed the lights and eased the truck toward the gate. Ninja had slipped out half a block earlier, ghosting along the shadows at a forty-five from my vector. The plan was simple—quiet entry, quick cleanup, no noise, no deaths. We needed Gideon Crane talking, not bleeding.

The camera on the pole above the guard panned left just as I rolled up. I saw the lens start its sweep toward my truck—then *pop*. The camera froze, glass spiderwebbed. Ninja's suppressed Glock had kissed it clean. The feed died.

The guard straightened and took a step forward, thinking he had a visitor. I let the truck roll to a stop, door open. Ninja melted from the gloom and I hit the pavement, going at the guard like a man on a mission.

My shoulder slammed into his chest and drove him back against the gate post. He tried to shove me off, mean jaw snapping, but I ducked a wild hook, caught his wrist, and twisted. His breath left on a sound like a ripped boot. I drove an elbow up under his chin—short, sharp—and the man dropped like a sack.

I hauled the man behind the booth, shoved him down, and yanked the gate release. The motor groaned and the chain slackened. By then, Ninja had moved in and snagged the dead camera with a gloved hand and tossed it into the weeds like a bad souvenir.

We drove the truck through and shut the gate. The warehouse swallowed the headlights and we moved fast and low—our boots whispering on concrete.

The first man met us at the dock office doorway, mean and ready. He lunged, more bravado than skill. Ninja caught him with a short uppercut that rocked his head back and then wrapped a forearm across his throat, driving him to his knees. I came in and drove my shoulder into his sternum, then a planted palm against the back of his head popped him forward onto the concrete. He went out with a soft thud. Ninja patted him down, found a brass knuckle, pocketed it.

Two more were in the monitoring room, hard faces lit by monitor glow. One swung for the ribs—stupid, overconfident—and I met him with a counter elbow that cracked into his jaw like a branch. He staggered, turned, and tried to scramble for a radio; Ninja dropped on him with a leg sweep and wrapped his head in a choke until his hands went limp. The other turned to run, and I booted him in the calf so hard his knee folded like someone had cut the cable. He pitched into a pallet rack and lay still. No shooting. All muscle and timing.

A man with a clipboard froze halfway down the catwalk. He stared, then made the mistake of reaching for a phone. I closed the distance in two steps, grabbed his arm, and twisted so his shoulder dislocated with a wet little pop. He howled and crawled to the far wall, clutching the socket.

Two more came rushing from the back office, thinking numbers would save them. I dropped low, planted my shoulder into the first guy's midsection and used his momentum to throw him into the second. They collided like puppets and hit the floor in a heap.

Ninja ran a knee across one's throat—not to asphyxiate, just to stun—and then slammed a rear-naked choke until his arms went slack. The other had tried to scramble for a bat; I grabbed his wrist, twisted, and popped it clean—no bones out, just a field of pain that made him stop breathing right. He sagged against the crates, eyes rolling.

We moved like surgeons. Each strike was one part necessary and precise: an eye gouge avoided, a throat strike measured, a knee that didn't break but made a man forget how to stand. No blood fountains, no waking nightmares—just broken balance, teeth loosened, consciousness lost.

By the time we reached the glassed-in office at the back, seven men were down—groaning, sprawled, tied, or blinking like stunned fish. The warehouse smelled like hot concrete and knocked-out pride.

Gideon Crane was the last man standing and he looked like his math didn't add up. Pale, too-tight shirt, tie loosened, breath shallow. Sweat made his hair clump against his forehead. He brandished a small pistol with hands that trembled. Just a scared man.

We stepped in, guns raised. I leveled mine at his chest, to shut down any fantasy of heroics—and kept my voice flat. "You don't want to do that, Gideon. Throw it."

Ninja chimed in, half amused. "If we wanted to hurt you, you'd already be on the ground. Also, you've got hand tremors. Maybe switch careers—less adrenaline, more spreadsheets."

Crane's fingers shook. His eyes flicked between us—sizing, calculating, realizing the math wasn't in his favor. The muzzle of his gun went down.

He sagged against the wall, eyes huge and wet, his Adam's apple working like a trapped fish. "What—what do you want?" he stammered.

I watched him for a beat, the quiet measuring scale between threat and bargain. I needed Crane to move his mouth and his hands the way I told him, not because I had ripped them off, but because willing men make cleaner witnesses. I could have forced cooperation—made him sing with a bone-cracking timetable—but the easier—and safer—play was to make him volunteer. That meant selling him a thread of hope.

"I'll tell you what I can offer," I said, my voice level. "Even though I don't have to offer you shit. Look around." I let my eyes sweep the men lying around. If he had any doubt about who held the teeth in this room, the warehouse answered for me.

"And if you think you're in a bad situation now, you've got no idea of what's coming for you. Just get it into your head that your sweet deal with Harlan is over."

He opened his mouth to act innocent. "Save the bullshit," I snapped. "That consignment at Dover tonight? It isn't going to land in your warehouse. DEA is on the pad, and once they rip open the false compartments there's no saving this play. Harlan's clout won't stop a federal seizure. That part's done."

Crane again tried to open his mouth, like he was about to feign innocence again.

I put a finger to his sternum, calm and precise. "Shut up and listen," I said. "Harlan took fifty million up front from New York and Philly. He's promised product he doesn't have. When there's no product in their hands, they'll want blood."

Ninja leaned against the doorframe, casual as a man at a cookout. "And guess who's first on the mob's list to get skinned alive when the money disappears?" He cocked his head, grinning in that stupid way of his. "Hint: it's the guy whose trucks signed the paperwork."

Crane's gulp was audible. His eyes darted to Ninja, to me, back to the ruined men on the floor. "So I'm—"

"Screwed," I finished for him. "The way you get screwed depends on timing. DEA could pick you up and put you in a cell, which is one kind of ugly. Or the mob finds out first, and that's a different kind of ugly altogether. Either way, Harlan's going to vanish the second he feels heat—bank accounts, safe houses, people paid to disappear him. He'll leave you holding the bag."

He looked at Ninja, then at me, like he was weighing whether to jump off a cliff or be pushed. "Jesus," he whispered. "I know I'm fucked. So what—what can you offer me?"

I let the offer sit like a coin on the table. "I can offer you a chance to stay alive," I said. "I can offer you the only thing Harlan will never give you: leverage. Help me make sure the mob's wrath gets focused on Harlan and not on every driver and dockhand who fucked up. You help me make Harlan look like the traitor he is, and maybe you don't end up being the first throat they cut."

"And just to help you make up your mind, this offer's got a ten-second expiry," Ninja said, voice low and cold. "You do it willingly, or we start breaking your bones one at a time. I like starting with the pinkie and working up." The menace in his voice wasn't a joke.

Crane's hands shook. He looked past me as if he were searching for the door that had just closed. "OK," he said finally, voice thin but steady. "I'm in. Tell me what to do."

I pulled Reaper's phone out of my jacket, turned it on, and sent a text to Harlan: *"Routed eighty kilos from Baltimore to Crane's yard. Heading there now. Battery dying. Will call when I get a charger."*

Short. Plausible. The kind of throwaway text a man on the run would send. It put the location in Harlan's head without spelling out the trap.

The phone buzzed seconds later. Harlan's number lit the screen. I expected that. He had fallen for my previous texts, but would want to crosscheck this time around.

I let it ring once, twice—then hit answer. For a heartbeat Harlan's voice came through, clipped and furious. "Is the stash at Crane's warehouse?"

I let the line live for a beat so he would think it was Reaper about to bark details. Then I killed it like a battery dying mid-sentence—no hiss, no fake static, just a clean cut. Worked every time.

"You're going to get a call," I told Crane. "When he rings you, say exactly what I told him—confirm the delivery. Don't improvise."

Crane's face was a map of nausea, but he nodded. "Right. I'll be ready."

And then the sequence I had planned unfurled. Harlan called Crane. Crane's face went white and then steady, the lie sliding into place. I heard Crane's voice, shaky but rehearsed: "Yes—delivery confirmed. Eighty kilos. At Ironbridge yard."

That confirmation was the final stitch. Harlan had a location now. A place to go if he managed to pull rank at Dover and get out of there somehow. I had covered the contingency: Dover could collapse into chaos and still feed him the illusion of a fallback.

I pocketed the phone and let the plan settle. Harlan had taken the bait, and I had given him a road map straight into the trap. I was ready.

Time to make the final move.

CHAPTER 47

Dover Air Force Base at 0200 hours felt like a city that worked while the rest of the world slept—rows of lights marching across concrete, the smell of jet fuel hanging low and constant, and the distant thrum of HVAC and idling gensets. Hangars yawned like giant mouths against the moon, their doors half-lit, and the tarmac was a cold, black ocean that reflected point-lights like a starfield. Everything moved on schedules here.

Then the C-17 came in—big, hulking, steady. You could feel it before you heard it, a deep vibration in the chest, like a freight train in the sky. The plane's approach lights glowed white through the haze, wings banking once before it lined up with the runway. The landing gear kissed asphalt with a long, drawn-out screech, then the roar of reverse thrusters drowned everything else.

The giant bird rolled to a stop, its ramp lowering with a hydraulic groan, mist swirling around the floodlights. Inside: pallets, crates, shadows of loadmasters moving with purpose. Business as usual—except this cargo wasn't just another shipment.

Nate stood beside me, hands in pockets, his breath visible in the cold. A few yards off, DEA agents crouched behind a fuel rig, radios whispering static. Their black SUVs sat lights-out along the perimeter road—silent predators waiting for a signal. This was their show. Nate and I were ghosts, observers on loan. I didn't like just watching, but sometimes the best way to burn a man down was to let him build his own pyre.

Two Ironbridge Logistics haulers rumbled in through the north gate—big, box-style trucks with reinforced side panels, heavy-duty suspension, and faded white paint with the Ironbridge logo stenciled on the doors. The kind of trucks built to move serious weight. They pulled up near the C-17, diesel engines idling low, and the drivers didn't even step out—they just waited for the signal. Then a dark military SUV rolled up behind them, headlights slicing the fog.

Colonel Victor Harlan stepped out with that calm, practiced smile of a man used to doors opening for him: starched uniform, pressed coat, polished shoes that didn't belong on a tarmac. He had that rigid military posture, the kind that said *untouchable.*

The C-17's cargo bay was a hive. Loadmasters moved like ants, guiding pallets onto rollers, cinching straps, calling weight figures into headsets. The door cycled down and the ramp became a working floor—pallets on rollers, pallet nets yanked free, the clack of metal and timber. I watched the first crate slide out: a wooden box stamped with crude markings and military stencil—*weapons crates*, heavy and cold with the promise of destruction. Dozens of them rolled past.

Harlan didn't waste time. His eyes scanned the plane, the crew, and finally the two trucks—then he strode forward with an air of command that made the loadmasters straighten automatically.

"Move pallets three through six to those trucks," Harlan ordered, voice crisp. "Keep the rest sealed until I give further direction."

The airmen hesitated for a second—maybe it was the tone, maybe the presence of Ironbridge logos on those civilian trucks—but rank carried weight. They obeyed, guiding pallet jacks under crates marked with serials that didn't match anything on the flight manifest. Guys in Ironbridge vests hustled, checking manifests, nodding, shoving pallet jacks under the specified loads.

For a second I watched Harlan's confidence—he expected the night to bend to his authority. He expected his men and his paperwork to make reality behave.

Then, out of the dark, headlights flared.

DEA trucks rolled in—three of them—gravel crunching under tires. Doors opened in sync. Agents moved fast but deliberate, spreading out in a half-moon around the ramp. No shouting, no posturing. Just that professional chill that made men like Harlan lose color in their face. The lead agent, a tall woman in a dark jacket with a DEA patch barely visible, held up her badge and a folded paper.

She spoke up, voice firm, steady: "We're executing a federal warrant for seizure and inspection of this cargo."

Harlan froze mid-command. Then he tried to recover, stepping forward with authority that's used to get things done. "You have no jurisdiction on a military installation. You're interfering with an active transfer under U.S. Air Mobility Command."

The agent didn't blink. "Warrant's jointly signed by Justice and the Pentagon, sir."

She unfolded the document, let the floodlight hit the seal. "You'll find the authorizations are solid. Please step aside."

The look on his face was something between disbelief and panic. He opened his mouth to argue again, then thought better of it. Behind him, the Ironbridge drivers were sweating bullets, eyes flicking between the DEA and their colonel. The agents began cutting open the straps, tagging crates, and moving in their inspection teams.

From where I stood in the shadows, it was like watching a domino fall in slow motion.

Nate gave a small, satisfied grunt. “Guess your bait worked.”

“Yeah,” I said quietly. “Now let’s see how far he runs before the hook sets.”

The DEA’s evidence team got to work fast—clinical, quiet, efficient. Flashlights cut through the fog and floodlights, sweeping over the pallets that had just come off the C-17. A K-9 handler moved in first, a lean Belgian Malinois sniffing along the crates. The dog’s nose froze, tail stiffened, then it sat—classic alert. The handler gave a short signal. That was all the cue the agents needed.

They brought in the inspection team—visual check first, then vacuum probes to test for air gaps inside the steel. It didn’t take long. You could tell from the way the tech’s head tilted—something didn’t line up. One agent called for a pry bar. Another pulled a hand drill. When the first false panel came off, I could smell it before I even saw it—that bitter, chemical tang of raw heroin cutting through the diesel and tarmac stink. The agent peeled back a layer of insulation and exposed brick after brick of wrapped brown packages stacked neat and tight inside the crate’s wall.

A low whistle came from one of the agents. Another just muttered, “Jesus Christ.”
Evidence photos started snapping. Sample bags

came out. The whole thing turned from suspicion to felony in about ten seconds flat.

Harlan stood off to the side, watching the scene unfold. His face changed in slow motion—from that smug bureaucratic calm to the hollow look of a man realizing the ground had just fallen out from under him. For a heartbeat, he looked human—shocked, pale, and utterly lost. Then the officer mask came back on.

He straightened his coat, smoothed his hair, and raised his voice. "This is outrageous," he barked. "Those aren't Army manifests. Those crates belong to Ironbridge Logistics." He pointed at the contractors, who were already sweating like pigs in a slaughterhouse. "Detain them. Now."

The soldiers hesitated, unsure, but Harlan's voice carried rank, and rank moved mountains. The contractors were grabbed, hands behind their heads, confusion thick in the air.

"I'll get to the bottom of this myself," Harlan said, voice full of righteous anger. "No one smuggles contraband under my command. I'll have their entire company gutted."

I almost smiled. The man could improvise; I would give him that. He was playing the only card he had—shifting blame to the civilians, controlling the story. Classic damage control. He thought if he shouted loud enough, maybe the DEA would buy it.

But I had already played my move hours before this dance started. With the shipment now sitting in DEA hands, Harlan had nowhere to hide. He had lost his product, his cover, and soon, his allies. The only thing left for him now was to run—and I was counting on it.

Harlan's voice dropped low as he barked orders to his aide. "Get the vehicle ready. Now." He started walking toward his SUV, trying to look composed but not fooling anyone. Even from a distance, I could see the nerves bleeding through. His shoulders were too tight, his stride too fast. He was trying to outrun the panic.

That's when I saw the small flash of movement near the SUV's front bumper—Ninja, my ghost in the dark, doing what he did best. He slid out from under the vehicle, light on his feet, face unreadable under a black ballcap. That SUV wasn't going anywhere.

I wanted Harlan out of the airbase before taking him out. But it couldn't be with his security detail next to him. I didn't want any uniform catching stray fire for the sins of a corrupt officer.

Harlan snapped at the soldiers, "Move it, damn it! I want that vehicle running now!" Then he stormed off toward a nearby administration office, disappearing through a side door.

That was the cue.

Ninja didn't miss a beat. He shrugged on a DEA field jacket he had snagged earlier—tag still half hanging from the collar—and moved toward a truck parked by the hangar. He climbed in, started it up, and rolled toward the admin building.

That was the cue for me to slide into my pickup, with Crane in tow. He had just witnessed firsthand how Harlan didn't think twice before throwing his men under the bus to save his skin.

I watched through binoculars as Ninja stepped inside the office and found Harlan pacing by the window, phone in hand.

"Colonel," Ninja said, cool and polite, "there's been a little mix-up on the tarmac. My bosses need you back out there for clarification. Something about the manifests."

Harlan hesitated. "Now?"

"Yeah, sir. Sooner the better."

Harlan muttered something under his breath—probably a curse—and followed Ninja back outside. They reached the truck, and Ninja scratched his neck, acting casual. "If you don't mind, sir, I just need to take a leak real quick. Long night."

Harlan gave an absent nod. Ninja stepped off, heading toward the corner of the building. The driver's door hung open. Keys dangled in the ignition, engine idling low.

The Colonel looked around once—one heartbeat, two—and then instinct took over. He climbed in, slammed the door, and gunned it out of there.

From the office window, Ninja leaned his shoulder against the frame, grinning like a cat that had just watched a mouse jump into a trap.

I exhaled, slow and steady. Everything was falling right into place.

I pulled my truck up to the curb. Ninja hopped out of the doorway and landed in the passenger seat with the easy arrogance of a man who knew he had just stolen the show.

"Worked like a charm, boss," he said, flashing that grin. "World-class tactical planning, by the way. You gonna autograph my playbook later?"

"Yeah, sure," I replied, starting the engine.

I didn't have to guess where Harlan was headed—he would run straight for the one place that still felt like a last chance: the Ironbridge warehouse where the rest of his stash was supposed to be stored.

Even if he changed course, I didn't have to worry about losing him—Ninja had slipped a tracker on the truck. Harlan could drive all the way to Mexico, and I would still be waiting at the gate when he pulled in.

Truth was, I could have ended Harlan the second he cleared the airbase gate. One pull of the trigger, neat and clean. But that wasn't the point. I didn't just want him dead—I wanted him to *feel* it coming. To know he was being hunted. To see it coming and still not be able to stop it.

"You notice how fast your buddy Harlan threw your boys to the wolves?" Ninja smirked at Crane. "Didn't waste a damn second. Soon as the DEA cracked that crate, he was all—'Arrest those contractors! They went rogue!' Real leadership material, huh?"

Crane muttered a curse under his breath and rubbed his temple. "Son of a bitch sold me out the first chance he got."

I knew Harlan would call Crane the moment he got close, to make sure the coast was clear. That's why Crane was sitting right here, wedged between Ninja and me. I needed him close—to control the narrative, to keep Harlan walking blind straight into the cage.

Harlan would run to Crane's warehouse looking for safety, for his remaining stash, for control. But all he would find waiting was me.

Time to close the trap shut.

CHAPTER 48

The night stretched out in front of us—flat, black, and quiet, the kind of quiet that comes before things go to hell. The headlights carved twin blades through the dark as we rolled through the backroads outside Dover.

Crane had shown me the shortcut earlier—an old trucking route running behind the industrial park, past a half-dead lumber yard and a row of warehouses that looked like they had been forgotten by time. The asphalt was cracked, weeds growing through like veins, and the only light came from a busted streetlamp stuttering in the fog. It was perfect.

Harlan would need longer to get there. The man wasn't built for dirt or darkness—he liked running his empire from clean offices and air-conditioned SUVs. Guys like him didn't get their shoes dirty unless they had to. He had been to the warehouse maybe twice, both times in daylight and probably with someone else driving. So I knew he would be creeping through the maze of warehouses, trying to remember which one was his.

I cut off from the main road and rolled the truck to a stop just shy of the Ironbridge lot. The warehouse squatted ahead in the dark, a low, wide shape of corrugated steel, half its floodlights dead, the rest dim and sputtering. It looked like the kind of place where bad things came to rest.

I glanced at the tracker. Harlan's signal was two miles out and closing slow.

As if on cue, Crane's phone buzzed. The sound was sharp in the still night. He fumbled it out of his jacket and glanced at the screen—*Harlan*.

Crane looked at me. This time, no fear in his eyes, just the kind of cold hate that grows when you realize the man you served was never on your side. I nodded. He took the call.

Crane's voice was calm, almost casual. "Yeah, everything's here. Got the stash safe, no eyes on us."

I could hear Harlan's muffled voice through the phone, fast and nervous.

Crane asked, "Everything go smooth at the base?"

Harlan lied, his tone just a shade too tight. "All clear. Routine inspection. No problems."

I smiled to myself. That kind of lie always carried the stench of panic.

Time to move.

I gave Ninja a nod. He didn't need a briefing; he already knew the plan. He would hang back with Crane, stay in the shadows, and wait for the next phase. Crane had done his part—he had already passed the word to his mob contacts that the stash was gone, busted by the DEA, and that Harlan was trying to bolt with whatever was left. He had even dropped the warehouse location for good measure. The mob's enforcers were en route, ready to collect their debt.

I stepped out into the night. My boots crunched gravel as I made my way toward the warehouse. The air was heavy, quiet, the kind of silence that comes right before thunder.

Inside, the place was dark and empty. Crane had cleared his men out after our earlier not-so-friendly visit. The only sounds were the creak of the rafters and the faint hum of a generator somewhere in the back. I moved past the crates stacked against the walls—empty now, or at least empty of anything worth dying for—and took up position behind a forklift near the center of the floor.

I checked the tracker again. The blue dot blinked once, then veered off the main road, cutting toward the compound.

Then it stopped.

Harlan was here. I took a slow breath and let it out.

The first sound of his arrival was the horn—one short, arrogant blast that echoed through the empty lot like a challenge. Even at two in the morning, the man still thought his rank carried weight, that somebody somewhere would snap to attention when he barked.

Nobody did.

The Ironbridge yard stayed dead silent. The sodium lights flickered overhead, throwing long, fractured shadows across the corrugated steel. No guards. No trucks idling. Just the sound of Harlan's engine ticking as it cooled.

I watched from inside, still and patient, the Ka-Bar's handle pressed tight against my wrist, the flat of the blade running parallel to my forearm. That leather-wrapped handle was warmer than the rest of my hand. It was Ryan's knife. He had carried it into more things than I cared to remember. Tonight, it would be the instrument of Harlan's reckoning.

The driver's door opened with a heavy metallic groan. Harlan climbed out, slamming it shut like he wanted to remind the world he was in charge. He took a few steps toward the warehouse, boots crunching gravel, and stopped cold at the threshold. Something in the quiet got to him. Instinct, maybe. Or guilt—it has a smell if you know it well enough.

He reached for his sidearm, drew it low and ready. A SIG Sauer M18. Standard military issue, even for a man who had spent his career behind desks, pretending to be a soldier.

He stepped inside, scanning the shadows, eyes darting like a rat in a maze. His posture was stiff—he was trying to project control, but the edges of fear were already there.

"Crane?" he barked, voice echoing off the steel walls. Nothing.

He pulled out his phone and started calling. I could see the glow of the screen light up his face—tight jaw, tension in the eyes. He tried Crane once. Then again. Both went unanswered.

He was halfway through figuring out his next move when his phone lit up with another name. *Reaper.*

I had turned on Reaper's phone and placed the call myself, so Harlan would hear life where there was none. You want a man to run toward a voice, give him hope.

Harlan exhaled, the relief almost audible, and holstered his weapon before answering. "Where the hell are you, Sergeant? What's your—"

I didn't say a word. I just let the silence hang for a beat and then killed the call.

He froze, frowning, then called back.

This time, I let the phone buzz in my hand.

He heard it—the faint vibration echoing from behind the forklift. His head snapped toward the sound. He moved slow, one hand drifting back toward the gun on instinct.

"Reaper?" he called out, voice tightening. "What kind of game is this?"

Every step he took brought him closer to me. That was the geometry of the trap: make him move into the kill zone.

Then I stepped out of the shadows. "You're trying to raise a dead man, Colonel."

Harlan spun, and the look on his face was priceless—shock first, then dread as the pieces slid into place.

But still, he thought he had a play, as he tried to reassert authority. "Captain Blaze. What's the meaning of this insubordination?"

"Let's cut the crap, Colonel. It's the end of the road," I said quietly.

He didn't see any point in keeping up the act. He gave it up, his eyes darting to the phone in my hand, then back to me. "Reaper's dead?"

I tilted my head. "Take a guess."

"What about Shade?"

I didn't answer. Didn't need to. The way I looked at him was enough. His Adam's apple bobbed once.

Then he tried the moral high ground. "You think you're different from them?" he spat. "You're not. You're all killers. No difference."

I took a step closer. "You're wrong, Harlan. I kill for a just cause. You killed for profit. That's the difference between a soldier with a code and a rat in uniform."

He squared his shoulders, trying to reclaim authority he no longer had. "You forget who you're talking to, Captain. Those men were civilians. I'm a Colonel in the United States Air Force. You *will* stand down—"

He started moving back as he talked—small steps calibrated to widen the gap between us. Ten feet now. His hand hovered near the holster, trying to act casual.

I knew exactly what he was doing—buying space. Trying to get far enough so that he could draw clean, get his sights up and squeeze before I reached him. Combat pros can do it in about a second. For a desk warrior like Harlan, that would take at least two seconds, maybe even three. In his head, he was trying to improve his odds.

But he had no idea what kind of math he was working against.

There's a 21-foot rule in knife fights, that's like gospel among fighters and law enforcement. Inside that distance, a trained blade fighter could close before a holstered gun cleared leather and fired. I had trained for scenarios like this—close, brutal, surgical. At ten feet? That was suicide range—for Harlan.

I saw the moment he made his decision. His right hand twitched.

"Don't," I said softly. "You're not built for this. You're a desk jockey with a badge, not a warrior. Don't make me prove it."

He went for it anyway. The second his fingers brushed the grip, I was already moving.

One explosive step, then another. My body low, silent, pure momentum. The Ka-Bar came up like a flash of black lightning. I didn't aim for meat or chest. I aimed for leverage—control points. Disable, not kill him.

Before he could even clear the holster, the blade tore through the soft inside of his elbow joint—precise, clinical. Ligament, tendon, the fibers that open a hand—torn. The sound was wet and final, like a rope being cut. His gun skittered out of his hand and clanged against the concrete. He screamed, grabbing his arm as blood ran down his sleeve.

I didn't stop. My goal wasn't theatrical—wasn't to spill more blood than necessary. I wanted his options removed. I pivoted on my right foot and brought the blade across the front of his knee in one clean, controlled arc aimed at the tendons that stabilize the joint. The Ka-Bar bit through fabric and flesh. The knee folded like a snapped hinge. He went down hard, face first onto the concrete, the air leaving him in a single broken, gasping breath.

I stood over him with my chest still, the knife slick in my hand. He clawed at the air, eyes big and wet, trying to understand the arithmetic of damage he had just been taught. I felt no triumph, only a cold, iron satisfaction—the sort you get when a plan works and you have paid for it in patience.

Ryan's Ka-Bar felt heavier than it used to. It wasn't just metal; it was history, and tonight history had hands. I didn't sheath it. I let him look at it, let the reality settle that the instrument of his undoing had belonged to the brother he had taken from me.

He lay there, one arm useless, one leg a dead weight. The man who had ordered fine soldiers to die for profit couldn't manage the small act of crawling to safety. He was a broken figure on the concrete, and the math had been fair and final.

"I told you not to draw," I said, voice even.

The Ka-Bar dripped between my fingers and I remembered Ryan's laugh, the way he used to sharpen the blade and called it habit. Tonight that habit paid off.

CHAPTER 49

Ninja's voice crackled through the earpiece, low and steady: "Cowboy, we got movement. Blacked-out SUV, lights off, creeping in from the east."

"Copy," I replied.

The confirmation was the last piece I needed. Everything else was math and timing.

I already knew who was inside the SUV—the mob's cleanup crew. The kind of guys who didn't bother with masks because everyone who saw their faces ended up face-down in a drainage ditch anyway.

My plan was simple and ugly and it relied on predictable human reactions. Guys who come to finish a job like this aren't thinkers in the moment—they see trouble, they lash out. Make them angrier, and they will spray the place trying to vent instead of carefully pulling a clean, controlled hit. Make them think the man inside fired first, and they will forget any nuance; they will empty everything they have to make sure their enemy is dead. That was the leverage I wanted—the kind that doesn't leave witnesses who can contradict the story.

I grabbed the M4 assault rifle I had taken from Reaper's stash off the table and checked the mag—thirty rounds of bad news. Chambered one, safety off, and moved toward the front window. My boots were silent on the dusty concrete, every breath measured. Outside, the SUV rolled in slow, like a predator scenting wounded prey.

I slotted the M4 to my shoulder, fingers checking the texture of the handguard without thinking. I wasn't trying to shoot anyone's face off; I was trying to scare the hunting dogs and make them furious. Precision doesn't help when you want chaos. Suppressive fire that tears up a vehicle and breaks a formation turns trained killers into angry savages. And angry savages shoot first and think later. That's exactly what would make Harlan's fate certain.

From the window I watched the SUV ghost in—low, sound-checked, crawling like a shadow. The men in it thought they had the element. They thought they would arrive, see the target, and finish the job while the scatter and noise of the warehouse masked them. They had come with a purpose: make sure Harlan didn't leave the building alive. That suited me fine. I just didn't want Harlan managing to cut some kind of a deal.

The SUV's tires crunched over the gravel. The engine idled down. That was my cue.

I took a breath and composed the angle. Bracing the butt against my shoulder, I dug the toe of my boot into the window sill. I tuned my breathing to cadence like I had done in other lives. Then I let the first controlled burst go—three-rounds, then another, then sweep—and the muzzle climbed and walked across the hood. Glass spidered. Steel shrieked. Tires went soft under a rain of controlled punishment. I watched sparks scatter in the dark. The muzzle flashes turned the inside of the warehouse into a strobe of death.

When the bolt locked back, I was already moving. Dropped the mag, left it where it fell. My ears rang, lungs filled with the bitter tang of burnt powder. I sprinted to the back, vaulted over a stack of crates, and dove through a half-open window into the night.

The cold air hit like a slap.

I rolled once, came up crouched, and melted into the dark. Behind me, the SUV's doors blew open and the night erupted.

Automatic fire tore through the quiet. They weren't aiming anymore; they were venting pure rage. The warehouse took the punishment meant for me. Concrete cracked, metal screamed, and glass rained down like shrapnel.

They weren't trying to pick off silhouettes. They were painting the interior with lead, trying to make sure nothing inside could move. Their fire wasn't surgical; it was purge. That meant hits everywhere—on crates, on the concrete, on anything breathing.

There was a pause—brief and pregnant—then two shotgun blasts that slashed the air like the final punctuation of an execution. They were the enforcers' death-check: make sure the target was down. I had seen this pattern before; mob hits were messy, loud, and hateful. They finished with instruments that didn't allow for second chances.

That was the final *friendly fire* from Harlan's mob friends.

I didn't look back.

I just walked—slow, steady—down the side road that curved away from the warehouse. The air smelled of gunpowder and wet asphalt. Up ahead, a lone truck waited by the shoulder. Ninja leaned against the hood, arms crossed, a ghost of a grin under the sodium glow. He watched me close the distance and held his mouth shut until I was nearly beside him.

"You going to tell me that was surgical, boss?" he asked finally, voice dry. "Or are we inventing new definitions for the word tonight?" His humor was thin, but it was there—my barometer for sanity.

I let a crooked smile out. "You think it got a little loud?"

"Yeah, boss, that's the thought I had in my mind. But we like loud, don't we?" And then, with a serious expression, he asked: "You get your closure, Cowboy?"

"Close enough to sleep," I replied.

He nodded, and that was all that needed saying. The man standing in front of me wasn't blood by birth, but he was the closest thing I had left. The kind that stayed when the world fell apart.

Ninja pushed off the hood and stepped forward, gave me a quick, hard bro hug—the kind that says *we made it out again, somehow,* then climbed into the truck. I followed, slammed the door, and the engine growled to life.

We rolled out, tires humming over cracked asphalt. As we pulled away I watched the warehouse recede—shadows and lights and the thin bleeds of synced sirens starting to echo in the distance. The dark rolled over the place like a hand covering a wound.

Ryan's face flashed in my head—my big brother, Marine to the core, the kind of man who believed in honor and country and all the things the world had long stopped paying attention to. The Ka-Bar that had been his was sheathed at my belt, still warm from the fight earlier. Tonight it had earned its keep.

Ryan was never coming back. I had accepted that a long time ago. But the men who had sold him out were gone now, and that counted for something.

Some debts can't be settled with words. They can only be paid in blood.

And tonight—I had made the final payment. Tonight the ledger closed.

EPILOGUE

The sun was slipping behind the cottonwoods, throwing long shadows over the back pasture. I sat with Mom on the old wooden bench behind the ranch house—the same bench where Ryan and I used to whittle sticks and pretend they were rifles. Dad's and Ryan's headstones stood a short walk away. I felt them both there.

Mom studied those stones the way some folks read scripture. Her breaths were thin but calm. Cancer was eating away at her, but she looked... settled. Like she had finally gotten answers she had been chasing for years.

"You seem calmer, Axel," she said suddenly.

It surprised me a little, like she had plucked the thought right out of my skull.

"I finally got some things put right," I replied.

That was putting it mildly. I had hunted the last of Ryan's killers. Harlan was dead—same "mob-style" exit I had arranged for Shade and Reaper. Three men who murdered my brother to protect their heroin pipeline from Afghanistan. Now everybody knew the truth—every last dirty detail.

But exposing the truth was another battle entirely. Madison had blown the doors off the whole thing, torching the conspiracy in print: the heroin stuffed into military flights, the dirty officers running cover for Harlan's empire, and the lie that smeared Ryan's death as friendly fire. She didn't hold back. Didn't flinch. Ryan finally got the honor he deserved—the honor he had earned the day he ran toward the fight instead of away from it.

Madison wrote the truth like she owed him personally. It grew bigger than I ever expected. And it pissed off half the Pentagon.

I knew it would. Hell, part of me wanted it to. Those brass suits wanted the whole mess buried in the deepest hole they could find. And sure enough, the rumors started—whispers that maybe I had nudged Madison, maybe I had pushed the story, maybe the hits on Shade, Reaper, and Harlan weren't mob work after all.

Lieutenant Colonel Flynn, my CO, stood behind me like a granite wall. Never blinked. Never wavered. That man had more backbone than any ten officers I had ever met. But I could see the pressure building around him, storm clouds stacking on the horizon.

And that was exactly why I had to walk away.

I wasn't going to let my CO pay for my choices. Better I leave the Army than let those jackals take a run at him. So I walked. It was time. I had gone too far down the road anyway. Some roads didn't bend back into daylight. And yeah, I would miss the brotherhood— any soldier who says otherwise is lying. But we all know the deal: one day, you hang up the uniform. But the brothers I was leaving behind in Delta? Those bonds didn't break. Not in this lifetime.

Mom gently squeezed my wrist. "Your brother would've been proud of you," she said.

A tightness hit my chest, sharp as any knife. "He was our star. Made us proud. I just did what needed to be done."

"That's all any man can do, Axel." She looked toward Ryan's grave, eyes steady. "Your dad used to say, 'Justice ain't fast, but when it shows up, it walks tall'."

I smiled at that. Dad always talked like an old western sheriff, even when he was just fixing fence posts in ninety-degree heat.

We sat there listening to the cottonwoods. Crickets tuning up for the night. The air cooling against the heat still trapped in the dirt. Simple things—things I had forgotten mattered.

"You ready to breathe again?" Mom asked quietly. "A man can't live forever in the dark, Axel. Even cowboys ride home sometime."

I let out a long, honest breath. "Yeah," I said. "I think I am."

Mom rested her head on my shoulder. "Good. My boy's back. I can rest now."

The wind rustled the cottonwoods like the world was sighing in agreement.

I wrapped my arm around her gently. "Yeah, Mom," I said softly. "I'm back."

Peace and heartache hit me at the same time—like two tides pulling in different directions. I had rid myself of most of my ghosts, but the quiet dread of losing her sat heavy in my chest.

I had gotten justice for Ryan.

But some battles you can't win.

You just stand beside the people you love... and walk them as far as the road will go.

– THE END –

BOOKS IN THE AXEL BLAZE SERIES

BLAZE RETURNS (Book One)

US Marshal Carter has gone missing in Little Butte, Nevada. The Dawsons own the town. A Mexican cartel is moving in. A gang war is coming to town. Blaze returns for one last assignment to find Carter before all hell breaks loose.

LETHAL FORCE (Book Two)

When Blaze takes out a Mexican cartel's operations in Nevada, the cartel sends hitmen after him and everyone he cares about. Bad move. What the cartel doesn't realize is, it has messed with a Lethal Force.

HARD TARGET (Book Three)

When Blaze stops at an isolated gas station, he Prevents an execution about to go down. Blaze's intervention gets a pack of mercenaries after him.

MEAN STREETS (Book Four)

Midnight in New York City. A car stops at an intersection. A girl in the back gives Blaze a distress signal. The chase that begins in Manhattan takes Blaze on a treacherous chase through the city that never sleeps.

UNCHAINED FURY (Book Five)

There is a contract out on Blaze and his old team. Floated by the Cady brothers—ruthless arms dealers who will stop at nothing to get revenge. In this no holds barred game, there's nothing to hold back Blaze's fury.

NO ESCAPE (Book Six)

Chaos erupts in Bison Creek, Wyoming. Two slain officers. Blood-soaked ex-Marine Logan on the scene. A sinister link between a cult and a pharma company. One man will move heaven and earth to get the truth—Blaze.

FEAR CITY (Book Seven)

Blaze heads to Boston after a shadowy group of investors—rich, powerful, and ready to bulldoze anything in their way. Blaze is up against these ruthless players who would sooner bury the truth than face it. They play dirty. But so does Blaze.

DEAD CALM (Book Eight)

The book goes into Blaze's past as a US Army Ranger. Blaze promises to rescue a dying friend's kids from the Taliban. The hunt takes him from Afghanistan to a trafficking network run by the Bulgarian mafia.

NO MERCY (Book Nine)

CIA agents in the Middle East are turning up dead. Blaze must save trapped agents and stop a rogue analyst from blowing their covers. With the Italian mafia and terror outfits in the picture, Blaze has only one rule: No Mercy.

WARPATH (Book Ten)

Blaze and his Delta team head to Mexico to dismantle a powerful drug cartel. But when the cartel brings the fight to US soil and targets Americans, Blaze makes it personal and goes on the warpath.

CROSSFIRE (Book Eleven)

Americans are caught in the inferno As Yemen goes up in flames. Blaze and his team are sent to extract an Al-Qaeda informant, who is the key to saving lives. Facing betrayals and deadly odds, Blaze won't just hold the line—he'll obliterate the enemy.

DEVIL'S HOUR (Book Thirteen – March '26)

Blaze comes to Georgia for closure—and walks into hell. A missing girl, bodies marked with twisted symbols, and a ritual called "Devil's Hour". A Savannah dynasty built on terror and trafficking. Blaze goes to war—because the devil chose the wrong hour to rise.

Printed in Dunstable, United Kingdom

74190258R00184